Firefly of Immortality II

Firefly of Immortality II

THE GUARDIANS OF LIGHT SERIES

BOOK FIVE

Kasey Hill

Azoth Khem Publishing
Huntsville, AL
May 2025

AZOTH KHEM

Azoth Khem Publishing
29931 Copperpenny Drive NW
Harvest, AL 35749
www.azothkhem.com

Ordering Information:
Quantity sales and exclusive discounts are available on quantity
purchases by corporations, associations, and others. For details,
contact the publisher at the address above. For orders by U.S.
trade bookstores and wholesalers, please contact
Azoth Khem Publishing: Tel: (256) 221-5498 or visit
www.azothkhem.com

Printed in the United States of America

Check out these other series by Kasey Hill

The Guardians of Light Series
Firefly of Immortality
The Shining Ones
Firefly: The Half-Blood Angel
The Valley of the Shadow of Death: Nephilim Rising

Dark Woods Series
Devil's Claw

The Whispering Spirits Series
The Haunting at Foxwood Village
Dark Coven

Coming Soon to The Guardians of Light Series
Firefly of Immortality II
Black Wings of Death
Firefly of Immortality: Anniel Unveiled
Alpha and Omega
Firefly of the Apocalypse

Coming Soon to The Guardians of Light Series Universe

The Guardians of Light: Darkness Falls Series
Bloodlines: Into the Shadows

For my Luxina, the starchild

Note from the Author

It has been a while since I have released a book in this series, and you will see why as you read through this installment. I know I promised this book and book six many times for the past few years, but health problems kept me away from writing. However, that didn't stop me from planning what to write next in this ever-growing series. A lot of research and development went into creating the remaining portion of this series. It took time and effort to get the words right to curate the perfect climax and ending for you. As always, I encourage you to read any and all prologues and epilogues the books have because they contain key details that shouldn't be missed!

If you have made it this far in the Guardians of Light and have enjoyed this series as much as I have enjoyed writing it, please leave a review! Reviews are what keep me going as an author! And I appreciate each and every review that is left, even if it is just a star rating!

Thank you for your fandom! And keep your eyes peeled for the next installment! Book six won't be far behind this one for release, and it will be jam-packed with even more action and adventure.

Much love to you all!

XOXO
Kasey Hill

Firefly of Immortality II

Prologue

I SAT IN silence as those around me bickered and argued. I had traveled alone to Stygia to hold council with the Watchers. Half of them didn't want to engage with Alpha and half of them wanted to wage the war that had been long overdue. I sighed heavily as I squeezed the bridge of my nose in annoyance. I hadn't a clue as to why they weren't as furious with Alpha as I had been for the past millions of years. My emotions began to run rampant, and I could feel the burn bubbling to the surface. I had repressed my anger and resentment for far too long, and it was ready to rear its ugly head.

"Why is it so hard to decide?" I yelled out, erupting into flames.

Silence fell over the quarreling room as all eyes rested on me. The flames receded as I composed myself. I looked at each face that sat in the room. The scars of war were painted on their skin. Runes of power etched their arms and faces. Their eyes… they told a story that no one could hear.

"You were all abandoned by Alpha. You were left to rot, and for what? Doing your duty?

Listening and doing what Alpha told you to do? You were all cast aside because he created something he himself could not destroy. You others," I stated, looking out toward the Nephilim in the room, "you were created from angels, and he turned his back on you, calling you abominations! He loves no one but himself. He must be brought down to the level he deserves."

Glances were exchanged amongst themselves with quiet murmuring.

"Incaendiel is right," Sophia insisted, standing from her seat. "We were made into Children of the Night. Alpha is growing his numbers by the day, and soon, we will be battling replicas of ourselves that are evil, twisted, and manipulated into thinking we are the bad guys. That is what Alpha does; he manipulates others to bend to his will, and if you don't, he will make you one way or another. Look at Incaendiel's poor daughter, Luxina. She stood against Alpha, and he nearly killed her with those injections. We need to stop his tyranny. We need to stop being afraid of the father who disallowed our entrance back into heaven. It is time to stand and fight. When the Seelie courts pledge their allegiance, we shall, too. Both Watcher and Nephilim."

The room nodded as the murmuring grew to a loud hum and turned into boisterous chatter. I nodded to Sophia and smiled. I needed this. Alpha had taken so much away from me. Sophie had been the last straw. My heart sank as I thought of our last words before the Glade imploded. I balled my fists in fury and heartache. I would avenge whatever happened to her.

A loud siren began to echo throughout the war room, and everyone scrambled to their feet.

"What's going on?" I called out to Sophia over the noise.

"Intruders," she yelled back. "Quick, we need to get the kids to safety!"

She began to run down a narrow hall that opened into an atrium. She disappeared down a corridor as I rounded the corner behind her. Hands snatched me from behind, and before I could even react, I felt all my power drain from my body as someone wrapped around my wrists the one and only thing that could subdue all angels, something made from unicorn hair.

Chapter One

IT HAD BEEN so long since I had seen daylight that I had forgotten what the sun looked like as a sliver of light seemed to find its way into the dungeon I had been locked away in. Time was a moot point, and there was no telling how long I had been left to rot in this cell. This place couldn't have been the place Alpha had been hiding this entire time. That would have been too easy, plus the Watchers would have immediately executed a strike in retaliation for the bloodshed left behind when Alpha captured me. All I have been able to think of is whether my babies were able to make it out safely. I know Sophia would never let anything happen to either of them. She knows more than the rest of us about what they are. She told me how we all are the key to saving the world as we know it, before Alpha completely ruins it all with his new breed of angels.

It is so odd to think of me having more than one child when it has been just Luxina and me solely for the last eight years. I saw the look on Xavier's face. He isn't too fond of me, but from my understanding, he isn't too fond of anyone except for Mother Lilith. She was the one who raised him while Sophie was off traipsing the galaxy for her son, Damian. Just the thought of that little red-headed boy sent both sorrow and hatred through my bones. He was the reason Luxina was taken. However, he was also raised by Alpha without any choice. And the experiments Alpha has performed on him... the poor kid.

As if by cue, the door to this dreary place popped open, and in he strode. You couldn't mistake his fiery curls on his head nor the astonishing blue eyes that shone like the stars. He was his mother made over. He didn't have a single feature of Lucifer about him, except maybe his attitude. I got a closer look at his face. His eyes were sunken in with dark circles under them. He was bone thin, as well. Were they feeding him? Torturing him? I saw a red mark that trailed down his neck and under his shirt that looked fresh and was still bleeding a bit. He lingered at the door as if he were contemplating what he was doing. He straightened, and his demeanor changed. I waited for others to follow, but none did. He was alone, but that didn't erase the cocky smirk from his face as he shut the door behind him, walked over to me, and pulled a chair up sitting down and staring. I stared back, studying his face, trying to read his mind. He was a blank slate. I wonder what Alpha wants him to do to me.

"Nothing," he stated with a poker face.

I know a look of confusion had to spread across my face because he sat back in the chair, placing his arms behind his head as he teetered the chair off its front legs, watching me as if pleased with himself.

"I know. It's confusing. And no, Alpha has no idea," he replied with a confident grin.

My brows shot up, and I tilted my head a bit. "You can read minds?" I asked in disbelief.

"Yes, but I haven't always been able to. I'm sure it is something that has to do with the experiments that Alpha does on me," he replied with a shrug. "It may have been the connection with my siblings that triggered it. I will never know. All I know is that one day, I could hear the thoughts of every person who stood in the room with me. Some may think it's a curse, some a blessing. I find it to be a useful asset in times of war."

"Your mother and I could read each other's minds. It might have something to do with that," I offered. I still didn't understand how Sophie and I could talk to one another silently.

"She is not my mother," he responded heatedly, his eyes dead set on me, roiling beneath the surface with an icy fire.

6

I watched as he composed his anger and returned his gaze to me. His face once again registered a cool, calm, collected look.

My brows knitted together with uncertainty. "Why do you say that, Damian? Why do you speak of Sophie in such ill regard?" I asked, not understanding why he held so much contempt for her.

He looked away as a moment of sadness washed over his face before he could replace it with the cold, emotionless expression he likes to sport.

"She may have created me with my father, but neither of them will ever be my parents. They will never understand me. They will never understand the endured torture I have been put through while being with Alpha." He looked at me earnestly, and I empathetically nodded my head.

"You know, Luxina and you have that temper thing going for yourselves. She gets angered and explodes into fire so easily. I can't imagine who she gets that from," I added with a chuckle escaping.

"From my understanding, she gets it from you," he remarked with a smirk.

I watched him intently. "What does *he* want with me, Damian?" I asked, gazing deep into his eyes.

His face was solemn. "The same thing he wanted with me. The same thing he wanted with Sophie, and the same thing he wanted with my brother and sister," he answered. "He wants to build an army of new angels."

"I thought he no longer had the power to create? He can't just go around injecting people, hoping the injections take. And I certainly hope he doesn't think we can procreate a new race for him."

"He isn't going to do any of that," Damian confessed with a sincere, concerned look.

"What are his plans?" I pressed, leaning forward as far as the chains would let me.

Damian looked around the room and leaned forward to me, the chair legs settling softly on the floor. "Once our blood accepts these injections, he plans to use Lilith at his side to create a special race from our newly formed blood. The creations won't be mindless anymore because he has Lilith at his side now. However, they thought the original werewolves and vampires were horrible in the beginning, but these new creatures, these new angels he wants to make… they will destroy everything." He stared at me with bewilderment and fear.

I mulled over what he was telling me. "Why are you helping him?" I probed. "Why do you fear this plan but still help him?"

"I have no choice," he replied, straightening up and returning to his position in the chair he had been in. The nonchalant, not caring attitude washed back over him.

My eyes bored into his. "We all have a choice, Damian," I refuted, shaking my head. "There has to be a reason you are helping him."

A mischievous look replaced his poker face. "Who says I am truly helping him?" he teased with a sly grin.

I scrunched my face in puzzlement. "You helped him take Luxina and Xavier," I stammered.

He narrowed his eyes at me. "Incorrect. Lucifer was the one who orchestrated both of those incidents, not I," he countered. "I don't want them anywhere near Alpha."

A snicker escaped my lips, and before I could stop myself, I quipped, "Afraid he would choose them over you and you would be the outcast once more?" a bit too sarcastic. I expected him to fill with rage, but he did not.

"Yes," he murmured very quietly and simply. "And they don't deserve that as a punishment."

It took me a moment to process what he meant by his last sentence. I studied him closer underneath the poor lighting. There were tiny scars all over his face. The sunken eyes I had noticed were more than just sunken, but were hollow and lifeless. The spunk and spirit he had the day he took Luxina had been replaced with bruised and broken. The fresh blood I noticed was now pooling more and had spread further on his shirt, while other spots on his torso began to bleed through. While I couldn't let him know, I truly ached for the treatment he had been dealt.

"You care for them, don't you?" I queried, squinting at him.

"Why wouldn't I? They are what I am missing in life. They are my blood," he remarked, squinting back at me. "I keep everyone at arm's length. I don't wish to get close to anyone. It's been my thing since I was a youngster. Alpha never showed me what love is. He never showered me with affection. He just wanted me to create this stupid army of his. However, I have seen the way Luxina looks at me. She looks at me with love and empathy, and sorrow. She doesn't see me as a monster. At least, she didn't until the attack of the Watchers. I have no idea what her thoughts are of me at this moment. She could hate me for all I care. All that matters is that she and Xavier stay safe and as far away from Alpha as I can keep them."

A warmer look overtook my face. "So, when you took her from me, all of those things you said. Your cold demeanor… that wasn't you?" I asked.

He shook his head. "The injections Alpha gives me make me vulnerable to mind control. I have to do whatever I am told. Lucifer struck a deal with

Alpha to deliver both Xavier and Luxina to him in exchange for me. Alpha took the deal, but he won't hold up his end of the bargain even if he still had them in his grasp. Alpha needs us."

"Mother created us. She can create more of us. Why does he need us specifically?" I questioned.

"Because the Unseelie Queen will no longer help him, nor will she aid Lilith in creating more of the Shining Ones," Damian replied, shifting in his seat. "She is the key to it all…"

"How?" I began when the door busted open.

Lucifer walked in, grinning ear to ear. "Ah, son, starting early are we?" he inquired, walking over to Damian. "Did Alpha give the orders to start on him?"

"Yes and no," Damian answered, settling his chair back on the ground and standing up. "We were just having a small chat. I needed to know where my siblings might be hiding and who but their father would know that answer. However, you interrupted."

A voice echoed in my head. *I will return to speak with you again. I have a lot to fill you in on before things get so out of hand that they cannot be controlled. There will be another visitor, and after they leave, I will be back to free you.* I looked at Damian, who was staring at me intently. I nodded with my eyes.

"Well, does he know where they are? Do we need to force it out of him?" Lucifer prodded, grinning madly.

"He doesn't know," Damian responded, walking to the door.

"And you believe him?" Lucifer shouted.

Damian spun on his heels and grabbed Lucifer, pinning him against the wall by the shirt collar. "Do you question my authority?" Damian demanded, glowering at Lucifer. "He doesn't know."

I could see the fear settling on Lucifer's face and nearly grinned. That boy does hate him, and who could blame him? He was dealt a crappy hand by this whole thing.

"That is not how you talk to me! I am your superior, and I am your father! You will respect me!" Lucifer bellowed.

"Respect is earned, and you do not have a single respectable bone in your pathetic existence," Damian retorted, pointing his finger in Lucifer's face.

"Is that why you're in here? Buttering up to Incaendiel in hopes he would adopt you as his?" Lucifer demanded, glaring over at me.

"At least he proves to be a better father than you ever have," Damian seethed. "Now, leave the room and do not bother the prisoner. Alpha wants him to remain untouched and unharmed. Those are orders!"

And with that, Damian left the room. Lucifer scowled in my direction and followed, shutting the door behind him. Once again, I was left in the dark, dank room with everything whirling around in my head. Could that be it? Could Damian be looking at me as a father figure? I processed everything we had spoken about. I believed him. His fear of what Alpha was planning was real. I believed him when he said he was being forced into doing what Alpha wanted. He wanted to be free. If I ever escaped this hellhole, I was going to be the one to free him, too. I owed it to Sophie. I owed it to her memory. I owed it to her soul. She had spent so long searching for him to get him back. I had to save him just for her. She wasn't here to do it herself...

One thing that Damian had said bothered me the most. He spoke as if he had seen the chaos and destruction of the future if Alpha were to succeed in making this new race of angels. He had the ability to read minds; could he see the future as well? Did all of the children have this gift? When did it start? I know Luxina would have mentioned hearing people's thoughts if she could, but I had just met Xavier before I was seized. I didn't even get a moment to speak with him, really. Is he like Damian? Did he have special gifts as well? Does Damian dream like the twins do? These were all questions I needed answers to, and I couldn't even go to search for

13

them. I was trapped here. I knew if I pulled hard enough on the chains that they would break free from the wall, but what good would that do? I would still have to fight my way free. If they captured me once, they could do it again. My only choice was to sit here and wait for Alpha to appear and share his grand plans with me. Damian gave me a taste of what the plans are, and I needed more than that. I needed to see who my visitor would be.

With the sight of Damian, I couldn't help but be consumed with thoughts of Sophie. Grief overtook me as I sat there thinking of the only person I had and would ever love. I had spent millennia trying to convince her mortal mind and heart to love me once more. As fast as I had gotten her back, I had lost her. I agree with Luxina that it wasn't fair of me to let her go. Lucifer wasn't supposed to hurt her either. When I had seen her locked away in that tower, so helpless, so vulnerable, every empathetic fiber for Lucifer snapped within me. After he orchestrated the kidnapping of Luxina, my blood boiled in regard to him.

The last few moments I had with Sophie were... the most painful ones I had ever experienced. Wanting to wrap her in my arms and float off into eternity was thwarted for I had more pressing issues at hand than my own selfish love interests. Our children needed to be saved.

What bothered me the most, though, was when Luxina broke free of the nightmares inflicted by the injections Alpha gave to her, speaking of her mother. Her mother blaming her as she burned in the fire. Was it possible that Sophie's soul spoke beyond the potter's field of angels? Our last words together, she was enraged, thinking I only wanted to keep Luxina safe and not Xavier as well. As if I would let my own son be harmed in any way. I had no clue I had a son until Lucifer informed me right before he took Luxina.

The Watchers told me that Luxina spoke of burning in a lake of fire in her moments of lucid talking. Was it possible that Sophie was also in that lake? Could Sophie have genuinely reached out to Luxina? Was Alpha punishing Sophie for Luxina escaping with Xavier? Dozens of thoughts flooded my mind, and I couldn't even escape them. The one that lingered the heaviest, though, was who my visitor would be.

Chapter Two

I SAT UP groggily with my vision zoning in and out from light and then to black. Little flecks of light darted around in the black, and I sucked a gulp of air into my lungs. As my eyes came into focus, I surveyed my surroundings. I had no idea where I was or how I got here. I touched the back of my head and winced in pain, withdrawing my hand that had blood smeared on it. What happened? I tried to focus my thoughts on one single moment, but everything was a blur. The last coherent thing I remembered was chatting with Damian and Lucifer busting in. I tried to concentrate on what we had been talking about, but my mind was foggy.

My eyes still circled the area where I lay. I looked down to see exactly where I sat to see if there were any clues as to how I got here, what I was doing here, or even why my head was bashed in. A soft bed of peat moss with pink and purple flowers growing all around it lay beneath me. My eyes moved out a bit further than where I sat, unfocusing and focusing from my head trauma, and I noticed that there was a circle of stones around the bed of moss. *Circle of stones…. Circle of stones… I know there is….* I tried to think hard and remember what a circle of stones in the forest meant. The harder I tried to think, the worse my head hurt.

"I can fix that up for you, love," a voice cooed in the wind ever so softly.

I whipped my head around, trying to see who it was. My eyes began to unfocus and blur again, with the blackness threatening to take over.

"Do you know how you got here?"

The voice was a female voice, melodic and soothing. I tried focusing again, looking around. My eyes landed on what looked like a small woman. I squinted to try to ease the blurriness of my double vision.

"I can't remember anything," I replied as I tried to stand.

Nausea and dizziness overtook me, and I sank back into the ring of moss. *Ring of moss… circle of stones… fairy circle…*

"Are things coming into focus now?" she asked, stepping closer, but still maintaining her distance.

"You're a fairy," I blurted out.

She giggled. "Aye, that I am. But do you know which fairy?" she mused, chiding.

"If I knew what fairy, I would have said your name," I retorted, irritated and a bit snarky.

"I'm not just some measly sprite or brownie, now. I'm a real faery with some real power in my punch. I'm fey, part of the Seelie court," she offered.

Seelie court… it can't be…

"You wouldn't happen to be the Queen herself, would you?" I inquired, attempting to stand to my feet once more.

"You're a quick one, Incaendiel," she cooed. "Aye, it is I, Queen Titania."

"How do you know my name?" I asked, walking over to her with wobbly legs and a loud thump on my head.

"I know all about you. You're a Shining One, just like your children are. Sweet lad and lass, you have there," she sighed and smiled.

"You've met Xavier and Luxina?" I stammered with mixed emotions.

"Of course, I have," she replied with a giggle. "Come with me, and I will tell you all about it."

She extended her hand to me, but I hesitated for a moment about taking it. The fey have never provoked the celestial realm, never caused any trouble with angels or fallen angels, but they could be nefarious, whether they were Seelie or not. I weighed my options. I could stay here, wherever here was, and try to find some way to go where I needed to go, even though I couldn't remember where that was supposed to be. Or I could go with her, and she might be able to fill me in on what exactly was going on.

I took her hand, and she smiled as she walked me through a meadow. Birch trees wrapped around us as we walked, and either my vision was still weird from the hit to my head, or there was something strange about how our surroundings looked. They look almost... warped.

"That is the portal you see," Titania responded as if she knew what I was thinking. "Birch tree groves are direct portal paths to the Seelie court."

The more we walked, the more our surroundings transformed into a beautiful world. Angels had never ventured into the Otherworld before. We were forbidden. It was a grand sight. Meadows and mountains as far as the eye could see, with skies that twinkled varying shades of light blues, pinks, and purples in a similar fashion to the aurora borealis. Creatures that humans had long since forgotten bounded around the area. A giant cyclops stomped around the mountains in the distance. A harpy flitted around like a hummingbird. A sphinx soared overhead of us, letting loose a deafening roar.

"The world had grown too dangerous for these beasts to survive and not be killed off," Titania stated as if she were reading my mind.

As if on cue, a solid white unicorn galloped in front of us, and I stopped dead in my tracks in the middle of the field.

"Do not fear it, love," Titania chuckled.

"Unicorn hair renders us powerless," I replied, keeping my distance.

The unicorn walked closer to me, and just as I was about to step back from it, it kneeled before me.

"As I thought," Titania squealed. "Hurry, love. Come with me. There is much work to be done."

"What does that mean?" I asked as she tugged me along, away from the unicorn.

As we walked, more and more of the mythological creatures that Alpha had told us had gone extinct after the flood of Noah began to appear. A pegasus flew high through the clouds in the sky, playing with a gryphon. Another deafening roar erupted in the sky as a red dragon breathing fire raced through the sky, holding gold in its claws. A squall followed as a red bird soared above the treetops, landing on one of the birch trees. A feather loosened from its body and floated down to me. I picked it up from the ground to inspect it. Another loud squall followed as it flew to the ground below and burst into flames.

"A phoenix," I breathed in awe. "They still exist." I tucked the feather away that it had left me with.

"You have much to learn, Firefly," Titania giggled.

"Firefly?" I asked, turning to her. "How do you know my nickname?"

"Because I was one of the ones that helped create you, deary," Titania replied with another childish giggle.

As she walked me through the meadow and away from all of the majestic beasts of lore, a castle appeared before us. A mote circled the castle as if it were plucked from the tales of King Arthur. We walked across a drawbridge as the Queen's knights stood guard.

"Good evening, Raul," Queen Titania stated, smiling as we walked through the gates.

Raul bowed to her. "Good evening, ma'lady," he responded.

"Tell me, Incaendiel," Titania began as we continued into the castle. "What do you remember about your time being held captive by Alpha?" she asked.

"To be honest, not much," I replied as I touched the back of my head. "I am fairly certain I was struck and lost my memory. I remember speaking with Damian while I was chained up, and that's about it."

"Ah, young Damian," Queen Titania sighed with a smile. "He is on his own journey as of right now through the Unseelie courts. Such a sweet boy, to my understanding. Very misunderstood because of Alpha's abuse."

"I wouldn't know. The few times I spoke to him are hazy, but he was also one of the people who grabbed Luxina. For his sake, I hope Alpha was controlling him," I replied.

We walked into a grand hall that had a large fountain in the middle. The water sparkled as if it had magic of its own. Queen Titania walked over to it and ran her hand through the water.

"This water is special water," she stated as she played with the falling water streams. "Would you like your memories back?" she asked, peering up at me.

"I would," I answered hesitantly. "How does it do that?"

"You will see," she said and motioned for me to climb into the water.

I walked over to the fountain and began to climb in.

"I'm afraid it will be painful," she warned. "You must fully submerge."

I nodded, finished stepping in, and lay down in the water. As soon as my head was submerged, a searing pain tore through my body. The water began to turn black around me as it leached whatever was in my body out. I screamed in pain, but it came out in gurgles beneath the surface of the water.

"I did warn you," I heard her reply in garbled words.

Memories began to pour in.

***

I was chained to the wall of the dungeon I had been locked away in after Alpha had kidnapped me. Even though there wasn't any way to gauge time in that room, it wasn't long after my capture when the door opened. Alpha walked through the door, and the room lit up. He looked younger than I last remembered him to be.

He pointed up to the bright lightbulb. "Funny how that happens whenever I grace a dark room," he chuckled. "Hello, my son."

I stared daggers at him and tried to stand, but the chains weren't long enough. "Where am I? Where is my daughter? Where is Sophie?" I demanded.

He took a seat across from me, and I lunged, the chains keeping me from reaching him.

A devious grin spread across his face. "Such spirit," he laughed. "I can't imagine where you get it from. Must be me."

I ignored his attempts at father-son bonding. "Answer my questions," I demanded again.

He pursed his lips. "You are in a dungeon in a hidden place away from the rest of your cohorts," he replied. "As for your daughter, I haven't a clue where she is. I was hoping you could answer that question."

I looked down my nose at him. "Even if I knew where she was, I would never tell you," I hissed in contempt.

He was quiet for a moment, studying my face with tight lips. "Why do you hate me so much, Incaendiel?" he asked, shaking his head. "What have I ever done to you that caused so much contempt to rile you in this manner?"

I scowled and sneered at him, "You know what you have done.

He raised an eyebrow as a defensive and innocent look spread across his face. "I have done nothing. It was your choice to fall with the others," he replied. "A moment of free will for you all. I allowed you to choose to stay with me or to fall with your mother. You chose your mother. If anyone should be angry, it should be me that you chose your mother over your father."

"You didn't give her much of a choice, did you? You asked one of us to fall, and when you grew angry, she took our place," I retorted.

A devilish grin lit up his face as if he knew something I didn't. "She has all of you wrapped around her finger, doesn't she?" he asked inquisitively. "She's not the saint you believe her to be, you know?"

I snorted. "I have to disagree," I replied. "Everything out of your mouth is a lie and always has been. You promised never to abandon us, and that's exactly what you did. You abandoned us once we fell."

"Did I? Or is that what she told you?" Alpha asked, cocking an eyebrow. "You see, son. Your mother and I had a marital spat in the Garden. She was the one who declared war, not I."

I glared at him. "Lies!" I snarled.

His brows shot up. "Are they? Then why would she be here with me?" he mused, leaning forward.

Anger tore through me. "You kidnapped her, too?!" I demanded, trying to break free of the chains.

Alpha laughed and leaned back in his chair. "That's what she wants you all to think. She is here out of her own free will. She chose to come back to my side."

I rolled my eyes in annoyance and disgust. "And why would she choose that?" I asked.

He smiled. "So, we can rule together again, of course," he replied. "And to make sure you don't steal our throne of power."

"Yeah, ok," I laughed.

As if on cue, the door opened, and in walked Mother. She walked over to me, knelt before me on the floor, and put her hand gently on my face.

I stared into her eyes. I hadn't seen her since the fallen had returned to the Summit. Just as he looked, she appeared a bit younger in age.

"Mother?" I breathed.

Her eyes were warm and inviting. "My son," she replied with a smile.

She stood from her kneeling position in front of me and walked to where Alpha was sitting. She stood by his side, placing her hand on his shoulder.

"So, it's true," I gasped, followed up with a glare.

Her eye twitched nervously. "Yes," she replied, swallowing hard. "Your father and I have made amends."

Rage tore through me as I watched the two of them smile like some sort of hand-crafted puppets. I lunged again, and the chains in the wall gave some.

I had had enough of the small talk banter of deception. "Where are my kids?" I demanded.

The door opened, and to my surprise, Asmodeus, as well as a few others, rushed in to secure my chains. Asmodeus held me from the front with his back to Alpha and Lilith. His eyes tried to tell me something, but I had no idea what he was trying to convey to me.

"This might hurt, son," Alpha stated as a needle jabbed into my neck.

Everything went dark. When I finally came to, I was alone once more in the room. How long had I been out? The door opened, and Asmodeus walked in, carrying some water and food.

"You are a sight for sore eyes," I chuckled as he set the tray down in front of me.

"Brother," he smiled as he wrapped his arms around me and looked around nervously. "I haven't much time before they come in to give you another injection. The next injection is THE injection. Alpha will know everything at all times once you receive this injection. It is his mind control one. He can make you say and do things you normally wouldn't do or say."

"Help me, then," I urged.

He withdrew his embrace. "For now, this is the plan. Just go with it. These injections will manipulate your mind, and he will make you think things that aren't real. You will have to decipher what is real and what isn't real." He grabbed the back of my head, put his forehead to mine, and looked deep into my eyes. "Stay strong. Do not bow to him, Brother."

I nodded. Just as he said, as if on cue, in walked another person holding a needle.

"Do not fight it, Incaendiel."

"Mammon?" I asked. "Is that you, Brother?"

"I'm sorry," was all he said as he slid the needle into my neck.

Everything went dark again.

When I regained consciousness, this time, I was no longer in the dungeon. I awoke sitting in a field where a tree stood. A weeping willow. Strange, I thought. Luxina told me about a place like this once before.

Someone stepped out from behind the tree, and I squinted in the glinting sun to see who it was.

"My firefly," the voice sweetly called.

"Sophie?" I asked, scrambling to my feet.

I ran to the tree, and as I grew closer, her face came into view. It was indeed Sophie. I reached her and embraced her, bringing her face into mine and kissing her deeply. I took a step back to look her over for signs of torture or abuse.

"I thought I had lost you," I murmured, pulling her into me and wrapping her in my arms.

"You did," she replied.

When she pulled back, I saw that her eyes were black pools of nothingness.

"What's wrong with your eyes?" I demanded.

She stepped closer to me and leaned into my ear. "Give in to Alpha, and we can be together again," she whispered seductively.

"What are you talking about?" I asked, pulling away from her. "He wants to hurt our kids."

She shook her head innocently. "He doesn't want to hurt them. He loves them just as you and I do," she replied with a loving smile. "He has taken such great care of Damian in my absence."

"He turned him into a monster, Sophie!" I hissed. "He is a devil spawn."

Her loving face mutated into rage as she erupted into flames. "Don't talk about my son in that manner!"

Her fiery hand held onto the tree we stood beside, and the fire trailed upward, burning away the bark and leaves. Ashes and glowing embers fell around us like soft snow. Soon, the field was set ablaze, and we stood among the fire face to face.

"Don't you love me anymore?" she pleaded with her eyes.

"This isn't you," I hissed, grabbing her by the arms and shaking her.

She began to laugh crudely. "This is the real me, Incaendiel. The free me."

The field melted away, and I was back in the dungeon room, still chained to the wall. It was all fake. It wasn't real.

"He will use her against you," a soft voice spoke.

My eyes searched the room to look for the source.

"Mother," I sneered as my eyes landed on her silhouette in the corner.

"Resist him, Incaendiel. He must not control you both," she replied quietly.

"Why are you helping him?" I demanded. "Why are you allowing this to happen?"

"If I don't, he will destroy me along with you," she stated. "And I like existing." She paused for a moment. "And I can't bear the thought of losing you."

I glared at her.

"When Damian comes in here, do not tell him anything important. Do not let him tell you anything important. Alpha will be using you to spy on him," she urged.

"Why is everyone worried about that kid?" I asked.

"When you see him, you will understand," she replied.

She walked to the door and stopped for a moment. "I'm sorry, Incaendiel."

As she left the room, Mammon walked in with another syringe.

"It won't work," I told him.

"I know," he replied as he plunged it into my neck. "That's what we are counting on."

As soon as the dose was delivered, I yanked on the chains hard and pulled them from the wall. Mammon backed into the corner as I stepped past him and walked from the room. I began to wander hall to hall, trying to find my way out of the maze I had become trapped in.

"Incaendiel!" I heard shouted.

I turned to see Sophie smiling. Her smile faded, and a look of urgency replaced it.

"Quick, we must go!" she yelled, holding her hand out to me.

I ran to her and took her hand. She pulled me through the halls like she knew every twist and turn. She stopped in front of a door and pushed it. It opened, and the sun from outside filtered in through the door.

"We're free," she breathed, walking through the open doorway.

I followed her, smiling. "How did you do that?" I asked. "Isn't this place heavily guarded?"

"Alpha trusts me," she replied. "No one batted an eyelash when I went to see you."

Something tugged at the edge of my brain, but I couldn't quite grasp what I was trying to remember.

"I love you, Incaendiel," Sophie whispered as she leaned in for a kiss. "I have always loved you. I will always love you."

Our lips met, and the kiss deepened.

"Where are the kids?" she asked in between lip locks.

"I don't know," I replied.

"Yes, you do," she insisted. "Just tell me so we can go get them."

I pulled away from her. "I don't know where they are."

"Tell me!" she demanded.

"I don't know!" I hissed.

It was then that I realized what this was. It wasn't an escape. It was another fantasy.

"You're not real," I said flatly.

"I am real," she replied with a sinister smile. "I'm just not the being you thought I was."

Her eyes flickered black.

"Alpha is controlling you, isn't he?" I asked.

"Is he?" she asked, toying with me. "Or has this been me the whole time?"

"Sophie," I began.

"My name is not Sophie," she cackled. "Oh dear, Incaendiel. And you believe me to be the one manipulated by Alpha and toyed with. You don't even remember my real name. How long has Mother and Father been screwing with your head, my love?"

"What are you talking about?" I asked, completely confused.

"One word will unlock everything. One name will bring everything back to you," she sweetly replied. "But it's not time for it."

The mirage faded, and once again, I found myself in the dungeon, still chained to the wall. The door opened again. I was expecting Lilith, Alpha, or another stupid fantasy about Sophie to traipse in or even Mammon *with another syringe. Instead, it was Luxina and Xavier.*

"Daddy!" she exclaimed as she ran over to me.

She immediately started working on getting the shackles off my arms.

"What are you doing here?" I hissed. "It's not safe for you to be here at all! This is what Alpha wants."

"I had to find you!" she protested. "I couldn't bear it if Alpha hurt you or killed you. So we came up with a plan to rescue you."

"Are you two alone?" I asked as the chains dropped from my wrists and I rubbed them.

"No, Praeziel is waiting for us outside the compound," Xavier replied as he helped me to my feet. "We need to get out of here as quickly as we can."

"You two get out now!" I ordered. "I have a few things I need to do first."

Luxina stopped and turned on her heel. "No, you're coming with us!" Luxina ordered. "Rescue mission for **you**! No one else!"

"We can't leave without a couple of people!" I protested.

"Sophie?" Luxina asked, crossing her arms.

"Yes, her, among a few others," I replied.

"No one else matters!" Luxina argued. "Now, let's go!" She tugged me by the arm again, but I didn't move.

"We have to at least help Damian," I urged.

"Why?" Xavier smirked. "He's where he belongs."

"No, he isn't," I hissed. "He is most likely being controlled and tortured by Alpha."

"Good," Xavier chuckled. "He gets what he deserves."

"We need to go now!" Luxina ordered.

Just as the words left her mouth, the Forsaken filled the room, grabbing Luxina and Xavier. Hands were on me as I fought them off as they dragged the twins from the room.

"No!" I bellowed.

I could feel the heat and anger bubbling beneath the surface, but I couldn't use my powers even though there wasn't anything on me to prevent them. Alpha walked into the room with a curt smile.

"I knew it would be just a matter of time before they came to rescue you," he said, leaning against the wall.

Rage filled me, and those holding me were thrown into the air as I ran over to Alpha. My fire burst forth on my arm as I rammed it into his chest. His eyes filled with shock as I held his heart in my hand. I squeezed it, feeling its every beat pulsate in my hand before I ripped it from his body, and he slowly collapsed to the floor. I stood in shock at what I had done.

"I did it," I murmured. "I… killed him."

"Or did you?" a voice asked from the door.

I immediately recognized the voice and looked to see Alpha standing in the doorway. My hand began to shake, and I turned my attention to the body lying crumpled on the floor.

"No, no, no, no, no, no," I repeated over and over as my voice began to crack. "Sophie..."

I knelt beside the body of Sophie, who lay in a pool of her own blood. Her eyes were lifeless, and blood trickled from the corner of her mouth.

"I told you to leave with us, Daddy," Luxina said as she walked into the room and touched my shoulder. "It's your fault she's dead."

"I didn't know," I cried as I picked her body up from the floor and rocked back and forth with her in my arms.

"I can bring her back," Alpha offered me.

Tears streamed as I stroked her fiery red locks from her face.

"I am the almighty, powerful God," he continued.

I gently kissed her forehead as I felt what little part of my heart that had held onto her slowly begin to die.

"All you have to do is join me," Alpha said as he bent down beside me. "Join me, my son."

"If you truly loved your children, you would bring her back either way," I hissed through gritted teeth.

Alpha smiled. "You are right."

He waved his hand over her, and a bright light glowed beneath his hand. Sophie gasped for air as she came back to life. I pulled her quickly into my chest and heaved in relief as she wrapped her arms around my neck.

"I do love my children, Incaendiel," Alpha said. "I still love you, my son."

"We could be one big happy family here, Daddy," Luxina offered, smiling at me. "He's not going to hurt us anymore."

I looked at Luxina, and her smile seemed to touch her eyes. I looked at Alpha, whose face was full of compassion, something I hadn't seen in millennia. Xavier stood behind Luxina, smiling as well. My eyes trailed to the door where Damian stood, leaning against the door frame. His face was not a smile, and even though he didn't speak, I could read what they said without needing to hear him.

"Join me, my son," Alpha repeated. "You will have everything you ever wanted."

Damian shook his head quietly with pleading eyes. Luxina's smile seemed to grow wider, and I noticed her teeth. She had a mouthful of razor-sharp fangs. Xavier did as well. I heard a clicking noise emitting from Sophie as I held her close. I slowly pulled away from her to see her smile full of the same teeth as the others.

"Join me!" Alpha insisted again.

"No," I murmured. "This isn't real."

Sophie lunged at my neck, and I snapped awake in a sweat in the dark dungeon room, still shackled to the wall. A lone person sat in a chair across from me. I squinted in the dark to see who it was.

"You will be the reason she dies. You know that, right?" the voice asked.

I sat quietly and didn't respond.

"You will be the reason they all die. Do you really want that, son?"

I glared at Alpha. "Why are you doing this?" I demanded. "Why give us free will if you want us to submit to your will in the end?"

"I didn't lie to you," Alpha responded as he stood from his chair. "I do love all of my children, including you, Incaendiel. You and Sophie were always my favorites."

I rolled my eyes. "You have a funny way of showing it," I grumbled.

"Your mother dragged you all into our marital spat," Alpha contested. "It was never my intention to use any of you for personal gain or as pawns in our ego trip."

"You abandoned us," I huffed. "You said you would always love us and would always be there for us, and you abandoned us."

Alpha swallowed hard. "I know. And I am sorry for that. But there was more to it than any of you know."

"Like what?" I asked.

"Omega... Lilith," he began, "Lilith kept you all from me. When we had our argument in the Garden, and I selfishly talked to Adam about our marital issues, she started a war. She told you everything you wanted to hear. That I no longer loved you and had abandoned you. She hid you all away in the glade and kept you all from me. I didn't abandon you, so to speak. She kept you all away from me and put in your heads that I didn't love you and fostered a deep hatred of me. Did you know she spent time with the rest of your brothers and sisters who remained behind with me?"

"What?" I asked. "What do you mean?"

"When she wasn't in the Glade in her throne room, she was meeting with the others to spend time with them. She kept her relationship with them and kept you all from me so that you would hate me, and in turn, you all would help her overthrow me for the throne in heaven. And she succeeded, didn't she?" he asked. "As soon as your brothers and sisters made it back to heaven, I had to flee, and she claimed my throne. You're not just a pawn in my game. You are a pawn in her game as well for her power grab."

I remained quiet as I mulled over everything he was telling me.

"I never understood why you all were so angry at me until that day... the day you died and came back to life. Who do you think brought you back to life?" he asked.

I glanced up at him questioningly.

"I brought you back," he answered for me. "I couldn't lose my son over the petty fights."

"You sent them there to kill me," I protested.

"I did no such thing, and Dean was punished for what he did to you," Alpha replied.

"What do you want from me?" I asked. "What do you get out of all of this?"

"I get my family back," Alpha answered.

"Why? So, you can torture us as you do, Damian?" I asked heatedly.

"Damian has done unspeakable things for which he gets punished. He has everyone convinced that I make him do the things he does. He does those things willingly, Incaendiel. He manipulates everyone into feeling sorry for him. He is evil, a little monster who I have to keep in check or else he would run, causing everyone heartache and pain. He thrives on pain," Alpha replied.

I leaned forward and looked Alpha in the eyes. "I. Don't. Believe. You."

"I see he has you fooled, too, and you haven't even sat down to talk with him yet," Alpha sighed. "He will use his power of deception to fool all of you. He will kill Xavier, you know? And he will convince Luxina that he is on her side just to use her powers for his own gain. He is a master manipulator and will make you all believe he is on your side when in truth, he is on his own side to take the throne from all of us. You will see."

"Yeah, I guess I will," I replied.

***

I came up from the pool for air, coughing up all the water I had swallowed. I looked at Queen Titania, still sitting there with her hand in the water, waving it back and forth.

"You're not done," she said sweetly.

"How much more can there be?" I asked.

"More than you can imagine. You were trapped there for a long time. You want to remember everything, right?" she asked as she pushed my head back under.

***

"At least he proves to be a better father than you ever have," Damian seethed. "Now, leave the room and do not bother the prisoner. Alpha wants him to remain untouched and unharmed. Those are orders!"

And with that, Damian left the room. Lucifer scowled in my direction and followed, shutting the door behind him. Once again, I was left in the dark, dank room. It had been months of fake fantasies of Sophie trying to persuade me to their side when Damian had come in to talk to me. I didn't know if he had been real or not at first. It wasn't until the voice conversation and Lucifer busting in that I really did realize it was real. And then, she walked through the door.

"Incaendiel?" Sophie gasped as the door opened, and she stepped through. "Is it… is it really you?"

I laughed, "And here I thought it was all real. But the boy was fake, too. It's proven now that you're here."

Sophie ran over to me. "Incaendiel, it's real. This is real." She stroked my face. "How long have you been here?"

"You should know. You're just him pretending again," I replied snidely.

"What are you talking about?" she asked as confusion spread across her brows. "Who is 'him'?"

"Alpha. You're Alpha, guised as Sophie, trying to get me to bow to him. Trying to get me to tell him things. Well, I'm not. So, you can just disappear. Fade away."

She grabbed my face with both of her hands. "It is me!"

She leaned in to kiss me, and I pulled away. I leaned in, glaring at her. "You're. Not. Real."

She grabbed my face in her hands and pulled me in. Our lips touched, and I could feel the power radiate between us as I always had. There was no questioning or deniability. It was the real her.

"Sophie?" I breathed in disbelief.

"Yes," she cried.

"Quick. Unchain me," I ordered, shaking the chains and looking around.

She stood up, and her face saddened. "I can't."

My brows knitted together. "Why can't you?" I asked.

"I'm not even supposed to be here. He didn't even tell me you were here. I cannot disobey him," she replied, quietly sitting down on her knees.

I rattled the chains again. "Sophie, untie me!" I demanded.

She shook her head. "He will hurt Damian. Every time I disobey, he hurts him."

"I know he hurts him. I saw him earlier. I didn't know why, though," I replied.

"Alpha tells him it's because he's not obeying, but it's my fault," she cried, placing her face into her hands, ashamed.

"Alpha is manipulating you both. We need to get both of you out of here," I growled.

"Sophie!" Asmodeus hissed, walking through the door. "You know you can't be here. You weren't even supposed to know he is here."

Her eyes burned with intensity as she stood up. "You knew all along and didn't tell me?!" she cried. "I should set you ablaze, Brother."

Fire started creeping up through her skin.

"He couldn't tell you either for the same reasons," I replied. "Right, Brother?"

He nodded nervously, and her flames sputtered out. "We have to move soon. I don't know what Alpha has in store for Damian, but he has the gladiator ring set up again for him. He hasn't allowed any of us to see what he has been creating. We have to get him out before Alpha kills him. Alpha knows he is not obedient to him anymore and wants to dispose of him," Asmodeus urged as he paced the room.

"When?" I asked.

"Tomorrow morning."

I quickly ran it all through my head. "Come back then. Release me, then. I will get him out of here," I replied.

"I don't know if that will be in time or not," Asmodeus refuted. He sat down and ran his hands through his hair. "That boy is hanging on by a thread. You saw him," he said, motioning to me.

I nodded. "How long has his torture been going on?" I asked. I inquired, remembering the scars that painted his body.

"Long before he ever helped take Luxina from you," Asmodeus replied. "Alpha went to Queen Mab for her pure Seelie blood to use on him. He thrashed in agony for so long whenever he would receive the injections. When he helped the twins escape from here to Stygia, his punishment was the dungeon, where he was beaten. I tried to get him to run and escape, but he wanted to protect the twins from Alpha. So he remained his lap dog."

"He sacrificed himself to keep Xavier and Luxina away from Alpha?" Sophie asked.

Asmodeus nodded. "When he failed in securing them from Stygia, Alpha sent him back to the dungeon where he was tortured relentlessly. You saw him, Sophie. They nearly killed him," Asmodeus responded.

"I only saw him briefly. He wouldn't allow me in to talk to him, really," Sophie stated.

"The last beating, they broke his ribs, and it punctured his lung," Asmodeus growled, inhaling a deep breath. "I had to leave him hanging overnight just so he could breathe. I have been rallying up the others to support Damian. When the time comes, we will fight to set him free."

I nodded. "I will help. He doesn't deserve that kind of treatment. No one does," I replied.

"That will anger Alpha if you take Damian from him," Sophie snapped. "He will kill us all!"

"No one cares what will anger Alpha anymore," Asmodeus spat. "Of all people, you should be the one who bets for Damian's safety above everyone else. Isn't that why you're here?"

"I have to go," Sophie replied flatly, walking toward the door.

My face fell. "You're seriously going to stay here with Alpha and not leave with us?" I asked. "With me?"

She stopped. I could see she grappled with things in her mind. I had no idea what Alpha had done to her, but he was controlling her in some fashion.

"I love you, Incaendiel. I always have and I always will," she replied, turning to face me. "Where are the kids?"

"Fuck off," I seethed and squeezed my eyes shut. "It's all in my head again. This is all in my head again. It's not real. Nothing is real," I repeated over and over.

"Incaendiel?" Asmodeus asked, breaking my mantra.

I opened my eyes to see him still sitting there. I looked at the door, and Sophie had left.

"Is this real?" I asked, tears of frustration dripping from my eyes. "Because I don't know what is real and what isn't whenever she is around."

"That's how he is trying to break you," Asmodeus sighed. "Of course, that would be his strategy." Asmodeus put his hand on my shoulder. "It's real,

Brother. We've got to get you out of here, along with Damian. I made a promise to Damian to help you escape even though the little turd didn't know I was already devising a way to get you out. But we have to figure out how to save him. That ring will kill him tomorrow. The things Alpha has made for him to fight..."

"Morning? Right?" I asked, wiping my face on the sleeve of my shirt.

"Morning," he nodded and walked out of the room.

***

Once again, I popped out of the water, gasping for air. Queen Titania sat on the edge of the fountain, still waving her hand around in the water.

"There can't be more!" I pleaded.

"Oh, child, but there is," she replied, pushing me back under water.

Chapter Three

AS MY HEAD went back under water, more of the memories I had lost came racing forward again.

***

I couldn't tell how long after Asmodeus left when another visitor came to see me.

"Hello, Mother," I huffed.

"Incaendiel," she smiled. "We have much to discuss, you and I."

"What could there possibly be for us to discuss?" I asked. "You are in league with Alpha. You are helping him torture that poor boy. You are helping him hold me captive so he can get his hands on the other two. Did I miss anything? Please, enlighten me."

"I know you must think horrible things about me," she replied softly as she walked in front of me. "I can't blame you for it either. But you must know I have done everything I have to protect you and Sophie."

"Protect us?" I sneered. "How is this protecting us?"

"Alpha would have destroyed you and could have destroyed you easily when you were first created. You two are far more powerful now than he could have ever imagined. I gave you the time to grow and to flourish."

"Is that what you call it?" I asked. I leaned forward and spat at her. "We are nothing but pawns in your game."

She was taken aback for a moment and then recomposed herself, taking a seat across from me. "There are things you must know that I don't have a lot of time to tell you. So just listen," she said. "First and foremost, there is a war far greater than what you have fought that is coming."

"Let me guess, the biblical apocalypse Father had the humans write about?" I asked, laughing.

Her face remained calm, but her eyes showed fear. "Yes, son. That is exactly the war. There is a reason why the Hebrews didn't believe Lucifer was the messiah or son of God. He isn't the messiah. Do you remember the young girl that you were overseeing right before the war broke out?" she asked.

"Yes," I replied. "Eva."

"She is quite special, Incaendiel. She needs to be found and protected at all costs. She is your prophet. She is your messiah," she replied. "She is the key to everything."

"She isn't a prophet," I retorted. "I would know if she was a prophet."

"You have to have your powers activated by Starfire," she reaffirmed. "Those powers activate every single starseed you have ever had charge over. The humans you helped create. You must protect her, understand?"

"Is that all?" I asked curtly.

"When they release you here shortly, you make sure you save Damian before Alpha has him killed," she said. "You cannot leave without him!"

I eyed her suspiciously. "What do you care?" I asked. "What's in it for you?"

"He is my grandchild," she replied. "He doesn't deserve what is happening to him. No one deserves what is happening to him."

I nodded. "I agree with that."

"After you get him to safety, find your brothers and then get to Lightshade where Starfire is," Lilith said quickly while glancing at the door.

"Which brothers?" I asked. "I have a lot of those."

"Gabriel and Raziel." She glanced nervously at the door again. "They have more knowledge for you to help defeat Alpha. I am sorry. I must go now."

She quickly stood from her seat and ushered toward the door.

"Wait," I commanded.

She stopped and turned around.

"What's in this for you?" I asked once more.

She smiled sweetly. "Nothing is in it for me." She turned on her heel and walked nimbly out the door.

"Yeah, sure," I muttered.

Within minutes after she left, there was a deafening rumble that shook the entire building. Not long after the rumble stopped, Asmodeus showed up, running as quickly as he could through the door.

"We have to hurry," he yelled as he clambered to my chains. "Alpha sent for him earlier than expected. It's time. He is already in the ring." He plopped a bag down beside me.

"What's in the bag?" I asked as he fumbled around with the chains.

"Weapons," he replied as he clumsily dropped the key.

"Get me out of these damn chains," I seethed.

"I'm trying! Don't yell at me!" he hissed.

Asmodeus unlocked the clasps as fast as he could, and I stood to my feet and stretched. Every muscle in my body ached from the movement. I hadn't been able to stand the entire time I was here.

"Where is the ring?" I asked as I picked the bag up from the floor, and we began to run from the room.

"Follow me," he replied as we raced through the halls. "There's a whole fleet of us ready to fight on yours and his behalf. We were up all night making these plans."

"I will get him out first and then come back for Sophie," I said as we ran up numerous flights of stairs.

"She is a lost cause, Incaendiel!" Asmodeus urged. "She didn't even try to stop the gladiator fight."

"She probably thinks Damian is strong enough to withstand it," I replied. "He has my vote. That kid has spunk."

A loud gong echoed through the building.

"What was that?" I asked, looking around.

His eyes widened. "Faster!" Asmodeus urged.

We rounded the hall that led to the entrance of the ring. Asmodeus went to lift the gate with the drawstring mechanism. "They cut the rope!" he screamed, grabbing the pieces sliced in half in his hands.

I dropped the bag and peered through the gate and saw Damian backing away up to it as a horde of monstrous beasts filled the arena, all heading toward him. His back was against the gate when I reached for the bottom of it and, with all my strength, pulled it up and held it with one hand as I grabbed him with the other and pulled him through, letting it crash back down into place.

"Now, did you really think we were going to let you die in there?" I asked as he stared up at me, bewildered.

I picked the bag up, then dragged Damian away from the gate and out of the arena entrance, winding through the tunnels.

"But, how?" he began stammering.

"Less talking and more running!" I shouted.

I pulled him along the dark corridors as the sounds of the hungry creatures echoed through the hall.

"We have about three minutes before that gate is lifted and those things come after us," I said as I jerked him from hall to hall.

"How are you free?" he asked, still confused.

"Asmodeus is an old friend of mine. He has been filling me in on you for a few weeks. He told me about this, about what Alpha was going to do and how you refused to leave without setting me free," I replied. "Kid, what part of no one cares about themselves as much as they care about you three do you just not get?"

I pulled him down long corridors that he didn't seem to recognize as his eyes scanned his surroundings.

"Where are you taking me?" he asked, looking around.

"To freedom," I answered.

I ran at full speed and busted through the wall ahead of me. As the dust settled, I looked around. It was a beautiful meadow with a forest just on the other side.

"Alpha is going to be hot on your trail," I stated as I handed him a bag full of weapons. "You need to lead him on a wild goose hunt before you meet up with Xavier and Luxina. He's going to be sending everything he has your way, including those things he made to tear you apart. You have to be fast and remain strong."

"Aren't you coming with me?" he asked, taking the bag from me.

I shook my head. "I have someone else myself to save before I leave here," I replied.

Sophie, he thought.

"Yes, Sophie," I replied, reading his mind. "Now, go! That's an order! I can take care of myself. There's an uprising. Alpha will have to flee. The Forsaken *weren't too happy when they found out about this plan of his with you. You have friends in low places, kid."*

"Make sure Asmodeus stays safe," he urged.

I placed my hands on his shoulders. "You have my word," I replied. "Now, go!" I pushed him off.

He was gone in the blink of an eye. A searing pain shot through me, and I turned around to see Beelzebub shove a needle into my neck. "Have fun escaping now, Brother," he snickered.

With one quick swipe, I took his head off with my hand. Whatever he injected me with burned through every nerve ending in my body, and I toppled to the ground.

"I have to find Sophie," I murmured.

I stood to my feet but was dizzy. Everything seemed to spin around me. I held the walls and shambled through the building. "Sophie!" I called out. "Sophie!"

Asmodeus ran up to me. "Why are you still here?" he demanded.

"Sophie," I breathed, hardly able to stand while holding my neck.

"What the hell happened?" he queried.

He pulled my hand away from my neck and looked concerned.

"Who did this?" he asked.

"Beelzebub," I replied breathlessly. "I killed him."

"Forget, Sophie. We have to get you out of here and that poison out of your system before it kills you," he said, wrapping my arm around his neck to help me walk.

"Sophie!" I called out.

"I'm right here, Incaendiel," she replied.

I looked for the face to match the voice, but my vision was going in and out.

"Come with me, Sophie," I said. "Damian is safe. You can leave now."

"Oh, Incaendiel," she laughed. "But I like it here."

Hands were on me, and I began to fight them off one by one. I couldn't see anything at this point, and the few glimpses of blurred faces I did see were revolting creatures or black-eyed monsters. Sophie stood off to the side, just smiling and laughing with her black eyes. She waved and walked away from me.

"Sophie!" I yelled.

It seemed like the hands multiplied, and I fought each and every one of them away. I began to run as fast as I could. "Asmodeus, where are you?" I called out.

Where had he gone? Was he mauled by those things, too? I reached the hole in the wall I had made and took to the sky. My wings barely wanted to work, and I was feeling fainter and fainter the more I moved. Those things were chasing me. With what energy I could muster, I sent a blast of fire out through the sky, striking them down. I didn't make it far before I was struck by something in the back of the head and careened to the ground.

***

I came to the top of the water, gasping for air.

Instead of sitting in her usual position, Queen Titania was standing beside the fountain. "Well, now that you are up to speed on everything, let's get you into some dry clothes," she stated with a smile.

I stood from the water and felt that my energy had been restored, and I was no longer dizzy.

"Did that pull all the poison from my system?" I asked.

"It indeed did," she replied. "This fountain is fed by the Lake of Purity. Not only did the injections distort everything you had seen, but they also caused you to lose your memory of what had happened."

One of the Queen's chambermaids appeared. "Please see to it that Incaendiel is given some new clothes and a fresh bed to rest," she ordered.

"Yes, ma'lady," the chambermaid responded with a curtsy.

"Incaendiel, this is Anika. She will take good care of you until the morning," she stated with a smile. "Then, we have much to discuss."

"Thank you for your kindness," I replied with a bow.

She giggled and scampered off.

"Follow me, sir," Anika said as she began to lead me through corridors.

I watched Anika admire her unique features as we walked.

"You're taller than the Queen," I declared, breaking the silence.

"I am a halfling," Anika responded.

"I didn't think halflings were allowed to live in the Seelie Court since they aren't purebloods?" I asked.

"They are when they are the daughter of Queen Titania," she replied with a crooked grin.

"I see," I said, also with a smile.

"Here we are," she affirmed as she opened a door for me.

She led me into the room and bustled to the closet, pulling out an outfit for me.

"We have had many guests in the Seelie court before, and some of them left behind their belongings," she explained as she laid the outfit on the bed for me. "This should fit you fine."

"Thank you," I replied with a bow.

She snapped her fingers, and a cart pushed by another servant appeared in the room with cheese, fruit, meats, and all kinds of goodies.

"Don't worry," she began before I could ask. "All of it is safe to eat. Nothing will trap you here. Unlike the Unseelie court, Queen Titania doesn't believe in harming free will."

I nodded. "Thank you."

"I will be here in the morning to wake you for your meeting," she replied with a curtsy, closing the door behind her.

I quickly changed from my drenched clothes into the dry ones. I sat on the bed with all of the memories from Alpha's dungeon swirling around in my head. A knock came on the door, and I stood and walked over to open it.

"Gabriel!" I exclaimed.

"The Queen told me you were here," he replied, walking in. "We have wondered where you have been all this time. It's been a year since you left to go and see the Watchers. We all thought you had been murdered by Alpha."

"Tortured more like it," I replied. "What news do you have from the others?" I asked, taking a seat at the small table in my room.

"I haven't been with the others since your departure," he replied, taking a seat across from me. I motioned toward the cart of food for him to get some, but he held up his hand and passed. "It's not safe for me to be out and about with Alpha any and everywhere. I came back to hide out in the Otherworld. I have been here since Alpha tried to destroy me. Queen Titania helped heal me, and this has become my home since then."

"We all wondered if you had made it or not. We were surprised when you showed up at the Glade after it had been destroyed. Did you at least tell the others where you were going?" I asked, munching on some bread and cheese. "So, they didn't worry about us both?"

"I told Metatron and Samael. I am sure Samael told Azazel," he replied quietly. "I don't trust anyone else. I am afraid, and those two swore they wouldn't tell anyone about my location. I'm sure it has already gotten back to Alpha that I am alive and well."

"Everything seems to get back to Alpha about everything. He is always two steps ahead of us," I stated, popping some strange fruit in my mouth. "The all-knowing almighty God," I joked sarcastically.

"The Queen said you got your memories back after taking a dive in the fountain," Gabriel chuckled while playing with a grape.

I groaned. "That water is the devil in disguise," I breathed.

"What memories had you lost?" he asked.

"All of them, pretty much," I replied, taking a sip of water. "I could only remember my brief talk with Sophie's son, Damian, and remembered how much he hated Lucifer when Lucifer came into the room."

"What did Alpha do to you?" he asked, shifting uncomfortably in his seat.

"He injected me with some sort of mind control substance and then made fake fantasies about me being free and being with Sophie," I replied. "He did it so often, I couldn't tell the difference between the mirages and reality. I am sure it would have become more brutal had I not escaped."

Thinking back on everything from the dungeon, realization hit when I remembered who I was talking to. "Lilith came to see me when I was in there. She told me to find you and Raziel. That you had information for me to use to defeat Alpha."

Gabriel nodded. "We do. But we all need to be together before it's divulged because it is a lot."

"She told me I had a prophet?" I asked, a bit perplexed.

"You do. The girl you are in charge of is your prophet," Gabriel replied. "She will activate when you activate."

"What does that even mean?" I huffed, walking over to the bed and flopping back in it. "Everyone keeps saying that like I am supposed to know what it means."

"You haven't had any visions yourself?" he asked, baffled.

I shook my head. "No, I haven't. Everything I have witnessed firsthand," I replied.

"Do you want one?" he asked, cocking an eyebrow. "Do you want *the one*?"

"You can share your visions?" I asked, sitting back up.

He nodded and held out his hand. "Touch your forehead against my hand."

I did as I was told and leaned forward.

I didn't know exactly what I was seeing, but somehow, I knew it was the end of creation. I watched as Alpha rode through the sky in the chariot he had created in the beginning for himself. He hardly ever used it except for special occasions. It was being pulled along by the horses he had created from varying universes, where he had extracted dirt to mold them. A red one, a black one, a white one, and a pale gray one. In the scriptures of humans, these were known as the horses of the apocalypse. War, famine, pestilence, and death. Below him in the valley, hordes of creatures crept, slithered, crawled, and bounded in one massive black wave toward the angel fleet that was stationed on the corresponding side of the valley. Fire and brimstone rained from the sky, exploding as they hit the ground below. Those standing in the wake of destruction were burned to a crisp, leaving an ashen body, or were struck down into pillars of salt that blew away in the wind.

The advancing mass of creatures had draugrs, werewolves, vampires, demons, both greater and lower, and whatever other mutts Alpha had created in his laboratory using stolen Seelie blood. I watched, waiting for Lilith or Lucifer to appear at his side, but neither of the two was there. Sophie was nowhere to be seen as well. However, I stood at the forefront of the army of angels who all stood waiting for my command to charge against the stampede hurtling toward them.

Alpha rode by on his chariot, smiling at me as the ground began to quake beneath me.

I scanned the area and saw Damian, Luxina, and Xavier waist-deep in a tarry, black pit, all struggling to break free from it. The ground broke free beneath me, and I jumped, landing on the ground before me as the rest of the angels fell to their burning deaths. I returned my attention to the kids as they sank deeper into the pit, struggling against the tar. Alpha arrived at the pit with a laugh.

"Join me and be free," he yelled, laughing maniacally.

"Never!" I heard Damian seethe.

"Then die, young Shining Ones." Alpha stared at them emotionlessly. His eyes were like bottomless pits, cavernous and oblique. It was a look I had never witnessed before in his cold, dead-set eyes. He had completely gone off the deep end and most likely had planned something even more terrifying than the nature of the apocalypse. I heard the sound of a gong and a loud crack in the air. I watched in frozen horror as molten lava came racing toward them across the valley, burning all the creatures he had made. From behind them, water crashed through the valley. The universe seemed to implode on itself as bits and pieces of planets and asteroids rained down around them, along with the fire and brimstone. Every star in the sky seemed to supernova and explode all at once, and just as he had sparked the universe into existence, he began to dismantle it.

New beings swarmed the air. They had the wings of angels and grotesquely disfigured faces of animals. No doubt, these were more of Alpha's experiments that he had let loose on Damian in the arena. When they opened their eyes, they shone like the sun. He had done it. He had created his muddled shining ones that were half demon, half shining ones. Above these creatures floated a single angel with black wings I had never seen before. He smiled maniacally and raised his hand. As if he commanded them alongside Alpha, they rushed through the air, heading for me.

"If I can't have what rightfully belongs to me, no one will," Alpha bellowed. "I will just start over and do it the right way." It was then that the lava and waters reached Luxina, Xavier, and Damian in the pit just as they reached for each other's hands.

"No!" I screamed as everything crashed in on the kids and the flying monsters enveloped me.

"What the hell was that?" I cried out as I jumped back from his hand, bewildered.

"That, my brother, is the end of everything," he replied solemnly.

I panted, still feeling the adrenaline from the entire vision. "What do we do?" I asked. "How do we stop him?"

"Now that is the million-dollar question," he remarked, leaning back in his chair.

A riotous commotion erupted outside the castle walls. Gabriel and I shuffled over to the window and saw hundreds of fey pouring in from the meadow.

"Are those Unseelies?" I asked in disbelief.

Gabriel nodded. "What the hell is going on?" he asked, wide-eyed and confused.

We left the room and made our way down to the grand hall, where he led me to the throne room of Queen Titania and King Oberon.

"Ma'lady," Gabriel enunciated, taking a knee. I followed suit and bowed as well. "What is happening?" he inquired.

She fixed her eyes on both of us. "The Otherworld is under attack," she explained. "Those creatures Alpha created followed young Damian to the Unseelie Court. Queen Mab sent all of the Unseelies here for protection."

Oh, no. He's in trouble. "I have to go help Damian," I replied, turning on my heel to leave.

"No!" she pleaded. "Those beasts can come here, too. They have Seelie blood in them. Pure Seelie blood. They will kill us all without your protection."

I was torn. I didn't know what to do. *Do I stay here and protect those who helped me, or do I go help Damian?*

"You stay here and protect us," Queen Mab insisted, walking into the throne room.

I turned to face her. "Where is Damian?" I asked her.

"I sent him into the Nightmares and Shadows realm," she answered nonchalantly.

I was filled with frustration and anger. "Are you insane?" I barked. "That place is the most dangerous place you could have sent him!"

"He will be fine," Queen Mab smiled, eyeing me with interest. "I gave him weapons and a map to navigate through there."

I paced back and forth. "He's just a kid!" I fumed. "And that kid... that kid is important," I rasped. "More important than any of you know."

"I see Gabriel shared his vision with you," Queen Mab mused, glancing in his direction. "Yes, we all know how important he is, as well as Luxina and Xavier. He is on his way to find them."

"Then you know why he needs to be protected at all costs!" I shouted.

"You saw him fight," Queen Mab remarked. "He can take care of himself. He is just like you," she smirked.

"He is only half Shining One," I retorted.

She waved her hand dismissively. "Half or whole. He is still powerful," she replied with a gleam in her eye.

"They are right, Incaendiel," Gabriel interjected, placing his hand on my shoulder. "We need to protect them. Damian will be fine."

"Are you sure?" I asked, piercing his eyes with mine for an answer.

"The vision I had has not changed. So, the future has not altered. This was supposed to happen like this," he assured me.

"Now that we are over the whole do I stay or do I go, do you mind going and killing the beasts?" Queen Mab asked, pointing her finger through the gates of the castle. "I would very much like not to die today."

I agreed silently and made my way out of the castle. I walked to the meadow and stood in the center, listening for any sounds. The wind blew, and every creature I had seen coming into the Seelie Court was hidden away from sight. There wasn't a single sound to be made, and it was eerily quiet. I readied myself, waiting for the beasts to burst through the portals at any moment. A stench filled the air, and I grabbed my face to keep from vomiting. It was rancid and putrid as if rotting meat had sat in the summer's heat for a week straight. A shadow overtook me, and drops of liquid hit the ground around me, sizzling like acid. I turned around, and behind me stood some sort of beast that looked like a beefed-up werewolf. A low growl began to emit from its throat as it bared its teeth at me.

Fire erupted through my body, and I prepared to fight barehanded with the beast. A sword came barreling through the air. I jumped and caught it just as the beast lunged. My hand touched the hilt of the blade, and my powers became one with it as it lit up like a torch. I swiped the sword in a downward motion as my body came down to the ground and cut the beast's head off with one clean stroke.

I examined the sword I had been tossed, and my eyes went wide. It wasn't an ordinary sword at all.

"I figured you could use an extra oomph to your power," Gabriel explained as he readied his own sword, preparing to fight by my side.

"It's *the* flaming sword," I breathed. "I thought Uriel possessed it."

"I stole it," Gabriel laughed, cocking his head to the side and shrugging. "Why do you think Alpha was so pissed at me."

A herd of creatures broke through the brush as if waiting to pounce. Gabriel and I stood side by side, fighting them off, slicing through them one by one.

"There are too many of them," Gabriel yelled as his blade moved back and forth.

"I know," I shouted. "You need to get out of here."

Gabriel shook his head. "I'm not leaving you to fight them alone," he refuted.

"Go!" I commanded. "I got this!"

Gabriel scowled but listened. He disappeared as quickly as he had appeared. The rage built within me as I slashed each monster that attacked. I stopped, and with a deafening howl of my own, I unleashed all of the built-up energy outward, leveling the trees and burning the creatures into ashen embers with one large fireball. As the smoke cleared, I collapsed to the ground as I looked at the devastation I had caused.

"Oh no," I murmured as I looked around the meadow.

Everything was burned to a crisp and destroyed.

"Thank you," Queen Titania said, walking to my side.

"I'm sorry," I cried, looking all around me shamefully. "I... I didn't mean to ruin your meadow."

She smiled. "It is quite all right."

"What about all the creatures?" I inquired, with tears forming. "They were the last of their kind, and I destroyed them."

She touched my hand. "They are safe, Incaendiel. They returned to the Garden."

"The Garden?" I asked, puzzled. "But how?"

"Xavier traded the Garden back to us. It was a part of our universe given to Alpha and crafted to his liking as a gift for letting us reside peacefully in his universe. We sent everyone there as you fought with great bravery against the creatures," she replied. "We helped create you. We know how powerful you are. We knew what we were asking when we asked you to fight against the beasts."

"I can fix it," I offered, looking around and placing my hand down on the ground.

"That's quite all right for now. It will heal in its own time," she chuckled, patting me on the back. "For the time being, we will reside in the Garden until it is safe here in this universe."

I was silent for a moment. "How do I stop him?" I asked, lost. "I am just me."

"Incaendiel, you are a powerful being. You have to believe in yourself. That has always been your problem. You don't have faith in what you can do, and you have always feared your power because it brings destruction with it," Queen Titania replied. "And *they* conditioned you to fear your power. You have to accept yourself. Accept the darkness inside you. Accept the power inside you. You are it, and it is you."

I looked around at what I had done in the meadow. The area was already starting to restore itself with new life.

"Incaendiel!" Gabriel called out. He ran to my side and stopped in his tracks. "Woah," he gasped in surprise. "I have been gone for far too long. When did your power grow to this?" he asked.

"After we fell," I replied quietly.

"Well, I must be on my way," Queen Titania interrupted, making her way back to where the castle had stood. "I can't have Queen Mab convincing everyone she is in charge now, can I?" she giggled and then looked at me. "We believe in you, Incaendiel. Just believe in yourself."

She walked back across the field and disappeared into nothing.

"So now what?" Gabriel asked, facing me.

"The vision is the same, right?" I asked. "Damian is still safe?" I had to be sure.

"Yes," he replied, bobbing his head.

"Then it's time to return to the Summit," I stated. "We have to convince what's left of our brothers and sisters to join me in the fight against Alpha before he destroys us all."

"Will they listen to you?" he wondered, his eyes clouding over with doubt.

"I don't know," I replied. "But I have to try."

Chapter Four

I ARRIVED AT the Summit with Gabriel at my side when Metatron met us at the portal.

"Incaendiel!" he shouted and gave me a hug, picking me up from the ground. "We thought you were dead."

"I would have rather been dead than deal with what I have dealt with," I replied, pulling back from the embrace after he put me back on my feet.

"Alpha captured you at Stygia, didn't he?" he asked.

I agreed silently. "I need to convene a council with everyone. There's a lot that needs to be said, and things have to be brought to light that you would never have imagined."

"Ok," Metatron affirmed, with a slap on my shoulder. "I will gather everyone in the throne room."

I rubbed the spot Metatron had smacked as he walked away, and a loud voice, as if on an intergalactic intercom, erupted through the heavens. "All angels are to report to the throne room for an important meeting immediately."

"I see he still likes to act in charge," Gabriel mused, smirking.

I laughed. "Now, as for you, you need to hang back out of sight and out of my mind until it's time for you to make an entrance. We don't know how well your reception will be with everyone together. Alpha told us all he had dealt with you, and you would never return. Many of our brothers and sisters here didn't fall and have accepted everyone back, but we still don't know who is really loyal to Alpha still."

Gabriel nodded. "Got it," he said as he threw the hood up on his robe, shrouding his face.

"Nice disguise," I chuckled.

I made my way to the throne room at the end of everyone as they filed in and stood waiting. I walked to the front of the room where Alpha's throne stood empty and gazed upon it. I could recall a time when I would gaze upon Alpha sitting on the throne with love and affection. In the beginning, he wasn't all that bad. He was a doting father, as one would expect. He looked fondly at Sophie and me, and Mother quite often told us that we were their favorites. I smirked, thinking how he must hate us even more now as we grew into our powers. He still wanted to control us. He couldn't have a power out in the universe that could challenge his own, and we were the closest it could come. If we had allies, we would be all-powerful. I turned around and looked out at the crowd.

I once again stood before my brothers and sisters to convene another critical meeting. This place was like an estranged relationship to me, even though I had spent my formidable years here prior to the fall. It felt wrong and right, all at once. It was my home once before, but it no longer called to my soul. I didn't have a home anymore. The Glade had been destroyed. I was a real Wanderer now. I lived among the humans for so many years that, at times, I forgot I wasn't one of them, especially once I had started raising Luxina among them.

The roar of voices speaking and arguing among one another about why they were called here echoed and reverberated hard off the walls of the room. The tension and stress that had inflamed my mind and soul already wore heavy on my heart. I stared at each of their faces in solemn musings. Azazel and Samael stood at the front of them all as they had since the day they had all fallen from the Summit. Others joined them, such as Raphael and Michael, as well as Metatron and a whole fleet of those ready to go to battle. My words would be the make it or break it point of the fight to be held between Alpha and me.

"I come before you, once again, my brothers, in hopes you would hear my pleas," I began.

70

The room fell silent as they waited for me to continue on. "Alpha has yet to be tamed or reprimanded for any of his actions against us all. His betrayal cuts deep into our wounds that we have let fester for millennia. He abandoned us and then used us as chess pieces in his game of war with Mother. He has upped the stakes in the game. He commands an army of monstrosities that I have personally witnessed myself as I watched young Damian battle against them one after another."

A hushed murmur fell over the crowd.

"These monsters are different than anything I have seen. They are worse than the hellhounds. They are worse than the Forsaken. And they are worse than the Draugrs," I commented. "These monsters are the heralds of Alpha's apocalypse against his own children of light. We must fight them to preserve not only ourselves but also the future of mankind. Quite possibly even the cosmos. For when he is finished with us, he will let them loose upon earth and everywhere else, and it will end in fire and brimstone as he has told the prophets of Revelations."

"There's also the possibility that he does not intend to bring the mortal souls back to Lailah for the Giving Tree in the Summit. He is most likely going to feed the souls to the monsters and give them the everlasting life promised to his devout mortal followers. When he is done with this world and this universe, he will move on to others that he has yet laid waste to and claim them for himself as well. If Lailah has no souls to replenish the Giving Tree, then all life would cease to exist, period," a voice called from within the crowd.

"That is correct," I replied, then motioned with my hand. "Step forward, please, and reveal thyself."

An angel emerged from the crowd in a cloak and came to the forefront where Samael stood, removing his hood.

"Raziel?" I asked, squinting my eyes. "Is that you?"

"It is, Brother," Raziel replied. "And do I have a secret for you."

Azazel snorted, crossing her arms. "Secret? We all know it was you and Gadreel who plotted against Father in the Garden. Mother already told us."

"That is true. Gadreel and I both were accused of the deception of Eve, which in truth is not the real reason we were punished," Raziel replied, looking at Azazel, then back to me. "But I did something even worse than that of Gadreel, who by the way, is still locked in the damned tower as well. Have any of you ever thought to release him?"

"Once we hear what you two did, we will release him," I assured him. "Tell me, Raziel, what is it that you did?"

"Michael knows, don't you, brother?" Raziel asked, turning toward Michael.

Michael pursed his lips. "He gave Adam and Eve his book."

My eyes widened. "*The* book?" I asked.

"It doesn't matter," Michael scoffed. "Raphael and I snatched it from them and tossed it into the sea."

Raziel's face erupted in a snickering grin. "Or did you, Brother?"

Michael's brows knitted together in frustration and confusion. "Out with your point!" Michael demanded. "Or we will throw you in the tower with Gadreel."

"Let him speak," I said to Michael.

"Tell me, Incaendiel, where is your beloved?" Raziel asked, looking around the room.

"She is with Alpha," I replied, gritting my teeth. "It is one of the reasons I stand before you all. I wish to rescue her."

A riotous commotion fell over everyone. There was yelling and shouting against the very idea of risking their exposure to Alpha so he could lure them away.

"As you should," Raziel chimed with wide eyes.

All eyes turned to Raziel.

"What gives you the right to dictate what we shall and shan't do?" Metatron asked, bucking his chest up.

"Sophie has my book," Raziel proclaimed.

"What?" I asked, confused.

"Think long and hard about the last twenty-five mortal years or so," Raziel replied. "What was your charge?"

"Watching over Sophie until she came of age again," I answered, shaking my head, confused.

"And?" Raziel asked, cocking his head and leaning in for more.

"And what?" I replied, pinching the bridge of my nose in frustration.

Raziel sighed, rubbing his forehead with his fingertips. "Your beloved was born into a special family. An old bloodline of hunters. You may remember them as the Magen and then the Order of the Shield. Then, there were the Knights Templar, and finally, what we call them today, the Diakonian Order. Hunters for Alpha."

"What does that have to do with Sophie's family? She was adopted after her birth mother died during labor?" I implored.

"Because her adopted grandmother and her adopted mother were also members of the Diakonian Order," Raziel replied. "Her birth mother was part of the same order."

"I'm not following!" I shouted, exasperated with the back-and-forth banter. "Out with it!"

74

"The Bible, Incaendiel, where is her grandmother's Bible?" Raziel asked.

"I'm not sure," I replied, with a shrug. "Most likely with Sophie's mortal mother. Why?"

"Do I have to spell it out for you? Are you that daft you can't put the puzzle pieces together? Do you not remember who the sons that comprised the Magen were descendants of?" Raziel asked, flailing his hands in irritation. "What mark do they bear as a birthmark, a symbol of their heritage?"

"The Mark of Cain," I replied, becoming impatient.

"And who was Cain?" Raziel implored.

"The son of… Adam and Eve," I sighed, as the realization of what he was getting at finally clicked for me.

"And when God banished Cain to the land of Nod, Eve took pity on her son and handed him the book of all mysteries of life. My book. The tell-all book. The book with the real story of our creation and our fall. And throughout the years, I have added to it and righted the story of Cain. Cain was a pawn of Alpha's, just as his descendants are. It was Lucifer who slew Abel. So, Cain was imbued with the Mark and sent off into the desert. And each generation of his offspring, whom I ensured survived the Great Flood, passed the book down to their sons and daughters until it ended with Sophie. The family is destined to help put an end to Alpha since he corrupted their bloodline to begin with. Unlike Sophie, who was born as Abel, Lucifer only possessed Cain when he murdered Sophie. Cain witnessed it all and was unable to stop it from happening."

"Sophie's grandmother's Bible is the Sefer Raziel Ha Malakh?" I asked, unable to believe it.

"It is much more than that, my brother. 'Tis much more than that," Raziel grinned madly. "We must rescue Sophie and search out that book. It has secrets in it that none know of and secrets that need to be brought to light. Now, do you mind releasing our brother from his prison like we agreed upon?"

I nodded and turned to face Metatron. "Metatron, go free our brother, Gadreel."

Metatron agreed silently and left the room to retrieve Gadreel from the tower.

"It's funny that you are here," I remarked to Raziel. "Mother told me to find you and a few of our other missing brothers."

"She did?" Raziel asked, raising an eyebrow.

"Yes, she said you all would have knowledge that I would need," Incaendiel replied. "And I do believe she was right."

Raziel's face darkened. "There is a reason I have been missing since Gadreel's capture, Brother."

"Yeah, you didn't want to be locked away with Gadreel," Azazel chimed in.

"No, Sister. It's because I know truths about Alpha and Lilith that no one else knows about," Raziel retorted, worry spreading across his face. "It is why we must find my book. It contains everything. There were pages that were unreadable by the hunter family Sophie had been born into. I couldn't chance Lilith's top fleet finding the book and trying to destroy it, thinking it was all a lie. The text is encrypted, and it looks to read as nonsense."

"What does it have in it?" I asked. "I don't remember seeing pages like that."

"It has *everything* in it, Brother. Every single thing Alpha has ever done. Every single thing Lilith has ever done. The real truth about the Apocalypse to come. There are only two beings in existence that can read it. I am one of them," Raziel answered, shifting his weight to his other foot.

"Who is the other?" I demanded.

"You already know who," he replied.

I began to think back to the conversation I had with Lilith. She mentioned a girl...

"Eva?" I inquired.

"Yes," Raziel responded. "And we have to protect her at all costs once she becomes activated."

"We will get to all of that in due time, Brother. I promise. We have another bigger problem as well," I stated, looking at those in the room as they waited for me to continue. *How can I tell them this without them rebelling against me?*

"Out with it, Incaendiel," Samael commanded. "We have things to do."

"Mother. Lilith. Omega. Whatever you want to call her," I began and stopped.

"What about Mother?" Raphael urged, murmuring following his statement from others in the room.

I hesitated for a moment, unsure if they would believe me. "She is in league with Alpha now," I breathed.

"Lies!" one called out.

"Not true!" another reiterated.

"She would never do that!" a third yelled.

The voices began to clamor in the air, and the deafening roar of anger tore through the room.

"Quiet!" Metatron yelled as he returned with Gadreel in tail. "Let Incaendiel speak. He has never lied to us before. He wouldn't start now."

"How do we know?" one demanded.

"It could all be a lie!" another yelled.

"I said quiet!" Metatron bellowed in his god voice.

The room shook, and the angels immediately hushed.

"Continue, Incaendiel," Metatron stated softly.

"Thank you, Brother," I began, clearing my throat and pushing back the conditioned feeling of fear at the sound of his voice. "When I had been captured by Alpha, Mother came to talk to me there."

The room remained silent as I looked from face to face in disbelief.

"She told me she was by his side for self-preservation, but I don't believe that either," I continued. "Not only did she allow young Damian to be tortured by Alpha and thrown to the wolves to be destroyed, she also allowed him to torture me with some sort of mind control substance he had been using on the children. There were a few other things Alpha told me about her, but now is not the time to go into those."

"For all we know, you could be under his control right now," Zadkiel refuted, stepping forward. "How can we even trust you?"

"Everything was leached from my system when I went to the Seelie Court and stepped into the Fountain that pulls from the Lake of Purity," I assured.

"But *how* do we know you speak the truth?" Zadkiel reiterated, crossing his arms. "Just because you say so? Who else here doubts Incaendiel and believes him to be the adversary Alpha asked us to be all those years ago? Who believes him to be the Great Deceiver? The Silver-

Tongued Devil?" Zadkiel asked, waving me off with his hands.

"Alpha warned us about this," someone spoke out.

"He did!" another affirmed.

The crowd began murmuring once again, and I knew I was losing them.

"You bunch turn on one another so quickly," a voice said.

I smiled and breathed out in relief. "Gabriel, Brother. Glad you could make an appearance."

"Gabriel?" others repeated over and over. "He was supposed to have been destroyed by Alpha."

"Alpha tried," Gabriel stated, removing his hood from his face. "But he did not succeed."

"You revolted against Alpha!" someone yelled out. "You are just as deceitful as Incaendiel."

"So did Metatron. So did Michael. So did many of you!" Gabriel yelled, turning in a circle to face them all. "You all fell to help them return to their rightful place in the Summit. Every single one of you who reside in this room revolted against Alpha. It may not have been in the beginning when a lot of them did and fell with Lilith, but you are just as guilty for seeing through the façade Alpha had put up."

Gabriel made eye contact with me and nodded his head. "I have been in the Otherworld for many years, hiding among the fey. The Seelie Court has been quite accommodating for us angels. I was there when Incaendiel swam in the fountain. He no longer has anything in his system that could put you in harm's way with Alpha. He speaks the truth."

"Continue on, Incaendiel," Metatron spoke, putting a silence to all of the chatter with his hand.

"I need your help, Brothers and Sisters," I began again. "I need to keep the children safe, and I need to rescue Sophie from Alpha. If we do not, then Alpha and Lilith will destroy us all. I have only come to you once before, and it was to save my daughter for selfish reasons. But it is more now. More is threatened than just a simple child being taken. These children are special, as most of you have attested to with Xavier here in the Summit. They are different than what we were. They have special abilities that angels do not possess. They are the future. They are the ones who can destroy Alpha."

"Says who?" Zadkiel huffed, with his arms crossed.

"Sophia," I replied.

"Lucifer's old concubine?" Zadkiel snorted, rolling his eyes. "Isn't she also the mother of the Nephilim? Another traitor against Alpha with an axe to grind with him."

"Oh, but she is much more than just a simple angel," Gabriel laughed, harboring his own secrets. "We have hidden truths that none of you know about. We have more knowledge than even Raziel's book contains."

"Like what?" Zadkiel demanded, turning toward Gabriel.

"Like, for starters, we're not angels," a voice said, breaking through the crowd.

"Sophia!" Gabriel exclaimed, running toward her and embracing her. "You are a sight for sore eyes."

"What do you mean you're not angels?" I asked, turning toward her.

"We have a secret that Alpha has kept from you all for years," Sophia began as she walked to the front of the room. "In the beginning, Alpha never told you about the Council of El. They are gods of old. The gods that came before him and the gods that told him you all were too powerful. We are part of those gods. It was true, as not only Gabriel and I had joined Alpha in disguise, but for far more reasons."

"Then who are you?" Zadkiel asked, drawing a sword. "Deceivers like Incaendiel?"

"No," Sophia smiled warmly. "Gabriel here is not an angel of Alpha. He is my luminary." Gabriel bowed before Sophia. "You all have been led to believe that Alpha was the all-power of the universe, but he is not. Alpha was created just as you all were created. He is a lowly god throwing a tantrum and revolting against the elder gods."

"Then who created Alpha?" Azazel queried, full of wonder.

"I did," Sophia replied, turning to Azazel.

"That means... you're a god too?" Samael asked as everything began to click together for him.

"Yes," Sophia replied, looking around at all of the angels. "I am the mother of Alpha. I hid my shame when I created him and toted him away to a universe of his own for him to believe he was an almighty god. I hid among you all to watch over him because a mother loves her child, no matter how evil they are. He began to learn of the other gods and sought their counsel. The rest is history."

"You're our grandmother?" Metatron asked.

"Yes, dear Metatron," Sophia smiled, placing her hand gently on Metatron's shoulder. "I am your grandmother. And what Incaendiel speaks is the truth. You all are in great danger."

"So, when Alpha is defeated, do you take his throne?" Michael asked.

"No," Sophia said flatly. "I have no desire to rule this universe."

"Then who will take over Alpha's throne?" Michael asked, raising an eyebrow. "One of us?"

"Yes, one of you will be the new Alpha," she replied, looking around at us all.

"Who?" Michael asked, straightening his stance. "One of the higher-ranking angels? Azazel? Samael? Metatron? Me?"

"I am afraid not," Sophia answered apologetically. "You are archangels, yes. But you do not possess godlike powers."

"Then who will replace him and mother?" Azazel asked, looking around the room at everyone who stood in there.

"Ntidus Assis," Sophia responded.

"What does that mean?" Michael asked, scrunching his face in confusion.

"The Shining Ones," Sophia replied.

"Who are the Shining Ones?" Metatron inquired.

Sophia looked at me. "A god was hidden among your ranks in secret. Well, not one god, but two. Twin flames," she replied. "With the feather of a phoenix to give them power over fire. The energy of a dying sun belonging to an old God is fading into the darkness. Power from the fey belonging to the Goddess Tiamat and the power of Alpha and Lilith combined created a pair of Shining Ones."

"Power over fire," murmured through the crowd.

"What?" I demanded, furrowing my brows.

"Yes, Incaendiel," Sophia answered. "You and Sophie are the Gods of the new generation and were expected to take over after Lilith and Alpha's powers began to fade."

"I don't believe it," Michael laughed, walking closer to Sophia. "Incaendiel is not a God. Hell, it took him the age of the world to even learn how to control his power over fire."

"Incaendiel has one more step to complete his transition into a god," Sophia continued, ignoring Michael. "The power of the fey came with an enchantment to hide his power from Alpha so Alpha would not grow jealous and destroy him. Alpha knows the children are Shining Ones, and that's why he wishes to have them all together so he can control them. He thinks they are the only ones. He still doesn't know about Sophie and Incaendiel. It is the one thing Lilith made sure to do right in this little game they play with one another."

"I believe it," Azazel stated, nodding her head. "When Incaendiel died, he willed himself back to life. And he also brought Sophie back to life when she died as well. Remember?" she asked, looking around at everyone. "Angels can't do that."

"It was Sophie and he alone who could raise the portal between the mortal world and the Summit for us to return. We also witnessed him raise it on his own," Metatron added. "Only Alpha had that power."

"I'm afraid Alpha does know about Sophie and me," I replied, a grave look washing over my face. "He skirted around it while I was held captive, but he knows. It's why he wanted all of us together to control."

"Then you all are in more danger than you realize," Sophia replied.

"Incaendiel is not a god!" Michael shouted, interrupting the conversation.

"Why does this anger you, Michael?" Gabriel asked, shaking his head and turning toward Michael to confront him.

"Because… because it's Incaendiel!" Michael laughed, pointing at me. "He can't even go long without him being overpowered by his own lack of self-control and burning something to the ground."

"Or it is because you are not in alliance with us as you say," Gadreel demanded, stepping forward.

"And here we go," Michael sneered, glaring at Gadreel. "It was a mistake letting you out of that tower."

"Only a mistake for you. Everyone believes I was locked away for helping Lilith deceive Eve, but that's not the true reason. Is it Michael?" Gadreel asked, walking closer to him. "What was the *real* reason, Brother? Why was I banished to the tower and not even have visitors?"

"Because you betrayed Father!" Michael hissed, stepping up to him nearly nose to nose.

Gadreel smiled in his face. "You and Lucifer make a wonderful pair. Most everyone forgets that you two are twins. Where is Lucifer, by the way?" Gadreel asked, looking around the room. "Still pretending to be an alliance to you all, or has he taken his place by Alpha's side publicly?"

I looked at Michael as his face contorted in anger. "I am not like Lucifer."

Gadreel's smile widened as his constant barrage began to work against Michael's ego. "So you're not Alpha's little spy? You don't know the secrets that Alpha has buried, waiting to come to light?" Gadreel asked.

"Lies," Michael hissed, reaching for his sword.

I played every single detail over in my head from the beginning to now. Michael's fall with Sophie's memories. Beelzebub taking on Michael's form to confuse Sophie when she was mortal. Michael eagerly coming forth to join us in searching for the kids. It was Michael who had sent us on a wild goose chase through Alabama. It was Michael who knew I wasn't the one who brought the Glade down. Michael was the one who knew we were going to Stygia, where the children were being guarded. It was Michael who wished to know if the Watchers were joining us in the alliance against Alpha.

"You have been reporting to Alpha about our every single move since you fell with those memories," I snarled, walking toward him. "You have been lying to us the entire time. You and Lucifer." Michael's eyes narrowed at me. "When Lucifer arrived, he was so buddy-buddy. I didn't want to trust him. He had been nothing but horrible to me the entire time we lived in the Summit. It was Lucifer who released Sophie's first memory to gain our trust. And then it was you who carried the rest with you when you fell. It was Lucifer who told us that you were being weird and distant from the others right before you fell. I challenged you about being a spy, and Lucifer intervened. Beelzebub disguised himself as you to throw us off your scent when Sophie had made it back to the Glade after being tortured by *you*. It was right under our noses the whole time, and we just couldn't piece it together."

"Do you also forget that if it hadn't been for my fall, none of the others would have joined?" Michael spat in contempt.

"We questioned whether you had a double that fell. But your charm after we found Beelzebub disguised as you…" I looked around at everyone who had fallen that day. I stopped at Metatron's face. "How can I trust any of you, now?" I asked, shaking my head.

Without missing a beat, Metatron walked before me and stared deeply into my eyes. "I will follow you anywhere, Brother," he said. He took a knee. "All hail the King of Kings!" he shouted.

One by one, angels dropped to their knees, all repeating the same phrase. I looked around at the masses of angels on bent knees. My eyes stopped on Samael and Azazel, who were still standing.

"I never wanted this," I said, walking toward them. "I have known you two from the beginning. You have been there for me through every single test I have gone through. You helped me get Sophie back. You didn't hesitate to help me find my children. You don't have to bow to me. You don't have to prove yourselves to me. The day Mother told you about my powers and how they were greater than yours, I did not want to take your place in charge. I still don't know if I really want to. You are the angel in command, Samael." I looked at Azazel. "And you are my second in command. You always will be."

Samael crossed his left arm over his chest, and Azazel followed suit. "Hail to the King," Samael replied and took a knee.

"Hail to the King," Azazel repeated, also taking a knee.

I scanned the room, and Michael and a third of the others who had spoken out against me or didn't trust me were the only ones left standing. Even Gabriel and Sophia had bowed down to me.

"I refuse to bow to you," Michael hissed, hand on the hilt of his sword. "You are not my god. You are not my leader." He drew his sword from its sheath and released his wings. "All hail Alpha!"

In the blink of an eye, he was gone.

"So, it was true," I murmured, a crushing wave of mistrust displacing my fighting spirit.

Everyone stood from their knees. I walked over to Sophia and asked, "What do we do now?"

"You go to Lightshade," she informed me. "There, you will meet Starfire, the Oracle. She has what you need to restore your full power."

"What about the kids?" I queried.

"They're safe. They're there with her performing the task needed to retrieve the ingredients to activate you," she replied.

I turned to look at the fleet of angels assembled before me. "Will you join us against Alpha?" I asked, scanning the room and every face that stood there. "Will you turn your back on your creator to follow me into the Valley of the Shadow of Death?"

"You know the answer to that, Brother," Samael replied with a nod and thrust his sword in the air, letting loose a battle cry, and the rest of the angels followed suit.

"Then it's off to Lightshade!" I shouted.

"Where is it?" Azazel asked.

I stopped for a moment. "I'm not sure how, but I know where it is," I replied.

Chapter Five

I WALKED THE Summit with Sophia by my side as everyone else prepared to make their way to Lightshade. Everything bounced around in my head and made my brain hurt.

"It's a lot to take in, isn't it?" she asked.

I nodded. "It is."

"Doing it all alone isn't easy, as well?" she asked, peering at me.

I sighed. "I tried to get her to come with me, but she has been so manipulated by Alpha that she can't tell right from wrong anymore."

"I understand," she replied with a shake of her head.

"You do?" I asked.

She smiled. "When I first fell in line with Alpha and Omega, pretending to be one of their angels, I met Lucifer. He was made without a mate, you know?"

"We all thought he was made with you," I replied, my eyes scanning the skies as a meteor flew overhead. "Obviously, he wasn't."

"No, he wasn't. Instead, he was made with Michael as twins," she replied. "I took pity on him. It wasn't fair that all of you were paired up, but he and Michael had to be the right and left hands of Alpha. In the beginning, he wasn't the gnarled piece of hardened coal he is now. He was different then. It wasn't hard loving him. He became so consumed with you and Sophie, so jealous of you two. It wasn't fair that you had special powers and also a twin flame. All he talked about was gaining power over you and separating you from Sophie. In the end, his jealousy won out over his love for me. So, I left. He never forgave me for leaving him either. I embarrassed him. When they attacked Stygia, he gave the command to Damian to kill me. He was so cold to me, as if I were the reason we had fallen apart. Sweet Damian," she smiled. "He didn't want to hurt me. He was stuck between a rock and a hard place there. So, he faked my death. Alpha knew he didn't kill me. I believe that was why he was tortured even more after capturing you."

"Yeah, that kid has been through hell," I replied. "He doesn't deserve all of that."

She glanced at me and looked me in the eyes. "You love him like he is yours, don't you?"

I smiled and nodded. "Yeah, I can't help to. Even when Sophie told me about the affair and about the baby, at first, I was angered and really hurt. But I would have loved him and raised him as my own had she stayed. Instead, I pushed her into Lucifer's arms to keep her safe."

"You loved him before you even met him," she laughed.

"I did," I chuckled. "And then he helped kidnap Luxina, and I was so angry with him. I felt like my own child had betrayed us, even though I had never met him before or spent any time with him."

"And now you know everything he did was out of self-preservation and manipulation by Alpha," she replied.

"I do," I said, nodding my head. "When I was in the Otherworld, he was going through the Nightmares and Shadows realm by himself. I had to choose between keeping the fey safe or making sure he stayed safe. I chose him."

"But?" she asked, pushing for more.

"But Gabriel told me he was safe, and the vision hadn't changed. So, what was happening had already happened in the vision. So, I knew he would make it out," I answered.

She smiled. "Gabriel is a mighty fine luminary."

"What exactly is a luminary?" I asked.

"An angel," she replied. "But not like Alpha's angels or even his archangels. I created eight angels of my own, with permission, of course. Alpha was not created with permission." She sighed heavily. "My actions are why he is so evil. I let him become this thing. Had I not hidden him away and just accepted what I had done, he would be different. He is arrogant. He doesn't even know he has a mother. He just thinks he came to be out of his own energy swirling around."

"Did you know about Michael?" I asked, glancing at her face. "That he was a spy for Alpha."

"I didn't. I had already left by the time you all had fallen. I don't think anyone but Gadreel knew the truth. It's why he most likely set up the deception of Eve."

"Is Alpha your only kid?" I asked, watching her face for a reaction. "Or do I have an aunt or uncle?"

She whirled and faced me, eyes wide, while glancing around, and whispered. "Yes, but you mustn't tell anyone!" she warned.

"Why?" I whispered back.

"Because it is not safe for her," she replied. "The first thing that Alpha did after Lilith fell was slay Tiamat. He started searching out all of the elder gods, and the ones who wouldn't help him, he killed. If he found her and then learned about himself and me, I would definitely be next on his list."

"How do you know he doesn't already know about you?" I asked. "You were ordered to be killed."

She pondered. "Even if he knew I was a god, he would have confronted me over being his creator."

"Where is she? What's her name?" I asked, bombarding her. "I can protect her."

She smiled. "She is hidden away, much like how Sophie was all those years. Her name is Zoe."

"I have so many questions for you," I began. "Who is your creator?"

"My father is Yahweh, and my mother is Barbelo," she replied.

"Where do they reside?" I asked.

"I have no idea where my father has gone to," she responded. "But my mother," she smiled, "my mother lives within us all. She is the energy of the universe. But, most importantly, I believe she was the energy used to create you and Sophie. When she grew tired of seeing everything going awry with Alpha, she decided to disperse herself. I believe that was when Lilith collected the energy to create you two."

"Why didn't Lilith just create us on her own the way Alpha was created by you?" I asked.

"Don't you know, Incaendiel?" Sophia replied. "Alpha is a jealous god. And neither of them could create without the other. His one selfless act of creating her was all the power he could muster on his own. He needed her energy to create more because she *was* his energy."

Thoughts of the vision that Gabriel shared with me tumbled through my head. Lilith was not in the vision at all.

"When he slew all of the other gods, did he take their power?" I pondered, running the premonition through my head.

"Yes, he has grown more and more powerful over the years. But they were old gods, so they weren't as powerful as they had been in the beginning. It was like feeding him crumbs," Sophia replied.

"Can Alpha reabsorb Lilith without destroying her so her power isn't dissipated like the others?" I inquired, stopping to think.

She stopped in her tracks. "Oh no," she whispered and faced me. "Indeed, he can."

"She wasn't in the apocalypse vision," I stated.

Sophia put her hand on her forehead and began to pace. "You need to go to Starfire, now!" she barked.

I nodded and jogged back to where the angels were waiting for me.

"Is everyone ready?" I asked.

"We are," Metatron answered, putting the final touches of his armor on.

I nodded. I started waving my hands around as if by nature.

"What is he doing?" Azazel whispered to Samael.

"I believe he is summoning a portal to Lightshade," Samael replied in awe.

The wind began to swirl, and it was like I was looking through a window. I saw Damian and Luxina standing in the middle of a field. I walked through, and the others followed. Meteors pounded against a force field that Starfire had up around her safe haven. Warlocks filtered their magic to the sky as havoc rained down against the dome of protection.

"Alpha," Damian sneered.

"You are quite right," Starfire replied, walking up beside them and watching the sky. "He is angry."

"I took what was his," Luxina replied, her eyes fluttering in Damian's direction. "This is my punishment."

She is safe, I sighed

"What can we do?" Damian asked, turning to Starfire.

She closed her eyes and smiled. "What you do best."

They both looked at her, confused.

"Shine."

I was about to step forward to help when Damian and Luxina looked at one another and took hands. The fiery glow of their souls erupted to the surface, and I shielded my eyes from the blinding light. Damian glowed his icy blue fire while Luxina blazed in red and orange embers, much like her mother and me. They lifted from the ground, holding tightly to each other's hands. Each lifted their free hand, and light exploded, shooting across the valley. Their bodies grew brighter, and soon, nothing but pure white light was visible to the naked eye. I watched in amazement as the powerful glow gathered at the top of the sky in the center of where the magic dome encased the valley. Its tendrils slowly crept across the dome, latching onto every bit of magic that swirled above and solidified it in its place. It sparkled and crackled as it wound over and out across the entire paradise. I could see they pushed hard with their light, and the descending meteors began to slow and hover in midair, suspended briefly before bursting into clouds of stardust.

Alpha's scowling face appeared in the sky, glaring at them.

"Parlor tricks," he hissed.

"We're coming for you, Alpha," Luxina replied. "You can try to run, you can try to hide, but we will find you, and you will fall like the ashes of Eden." *She is just like me,* I mused.

He laughed deeply. "Do you think you can take me alone? A handful of Nephilim and Warlocks? A meager fleet of angels. You will still fail in the end! My army grows by the day, and they are bloodthirsty." He smiled, rolling his head and cracking his neck. "Bow to me, and those you love will live in the end. Defy me, and well, nothing will be left to mourn. Not even you two."

Damian shot an icy fireball into the sky, and Alpha's face distorted and disappeared. The two of them descended to the ground below, and we all watched in awe. As their feet touched the ground, Praeziel walked up to them. He put his right arm across the center of his chest, then took a knee.

"I pledge my allegiance to you," he shouted. "I will follow you to the ends of the earth, no matter how soon or far off that may be."

I looked around at the growing number of people who stood in Lightshade. While Damian and Luxina had been protecting it, the Nephilim had begun to arrive. One by one, each Nephilim who had entered the valley gathered around us, pledging their loyalty to Damian and Luxina. The warlocks took a knee, yelling their allegiances into the air. I looked around in amazement as they, one by one, each announced to follow them to the end of days.

"We shall fight alongside you as well, young Shining Ones," a voice called out behind them.

I watched as the Seelie and Unseelie Courts walked through a portal and stood behind them. The Dark Queen Mab, Queen Titania, and King Oberon stood at the forefront of the gathered fey.

All three of them bowed to Damian and Luxina, and every single one of their followers followed as well. More and more people began to appear from various portals into Lightshade. The sun eclipsed to cast a shadowy glow across the valley.

"The vampires pledge our allegiance to the cause as well," replied a young man stepping forward. "For too long, Alpha has experimented with humans, turning us into nightwalkers with the vampiric blood of those in the abyss."

"The werewolves do as well," a young woman said, stepping into the front of the crowd. "Alpha has mistreated our kind for far too long. It is time he pays for the crimes he has committed against all."

I smiled as the support of every imaginable creature that had suffered from Alpha's reign of terror stood in allegiance with us all. Damian and Luxina had convinced them all by protecting Lightshade and showing just how powerful they were together. I looked from face to face as millions stood before us, pledging their lives to stop him.

"We will follow you wherever you go," I yelled above the crowd.

Luxina turned around, and her eyes lit up as she ran toward me.

"Daddy!" she shouted as she wrapped her arms around my neck.

I hugged her, tightening my grip around her shoulders, near tears. I breathed in deep, allowing the scent of her soul to fill my weary heart.

"I have been so worried about you," she cried, tears spilling onto my chest. "I was so afraid that Alpha still had you and was torturing you as punishment to me."

"You don't know how good it feels to see you and know you are safe," I replied, pulling back from the embrace. "I never imagined in all of the worlds that you would be so powerful."

"I get it from my father," she replied as she swiped away a falling tear.

She looked behind me to see thousands upon thousands of angels that were left in the Summit when Alpha abandoned his throne in the sky. I watched as she scanned the crowd, looking for one face in particular.

"She's not here," I breathed. "I will explain it all, but right now, we have business to attend to."

Damian walked over to join us, and I patted him on the back.

"It's nice to see you again, kid," I said, smiling. "I see you kept to your word."

"Not quite," he murmured.

I looked at him a bit confused. Luxina exchanged glances with him.

"Where's Xavier?" I asked, looking around in the crowd for his face.

"That's a long story," Luxina replied gravely. "But for now, just know he is safe, and he is home."

"Welcome, Incaendiel," Starfire said, pushing through the crowd to stand face to face with me. I towered over her like a giant. "We have much to talk about and to do."

"Yes, we do," I replied, nodding in agreement. "It's my understanding you have something for me?"

"I do," she replied. "Follow me inside. I was hoping Sophie would be with you, but that was another alternative move in the vast game of chess."

My eyes lowered. "Yes, I had hoped as well."

"Come now, don't doddle," she said and led me into her cottage. "I understand that you have gone through just as much as Damian has to get here."

"I have," I chuckled. "It's been an experience of a lifetime."

She smiled. "I see you got the votes from the angels. Our numbers have increased tremendously. It is looking promising for our battle against Alpha."

"Yes, some joined that I never expected to, and some declined," I replied sadly.

"I am sorry you had to learn about Michael the way you did," she said, patting my arm. "Just know he was on the ropes quite often about it all being a spy for Alpha. He battled over it quite often."

"How do you know that?" I asked.

"I know everything," she laughed. "He may come around in the end. We shall see. It made him bitter that he wasn't the chosen one to take over for Alpha. Mirror of his father, I suppose." She produced a bottle from her robe and held it up. "This is what you came for," she said, placing it on the table in front of her.

"What is it?" I inquired.

"It's a potion to break your enchantment and bring you to full power," she explained. "It does not taste good, and I am afraid it will hurt."

"Does anything involving fey magic not hurt?" I asked.

She chuckled. "Ah, the Lake of Purity. Well, if you must know, it's quite the same, but most likely a bit more intense. It will make you feel like you're dying."

"Well, I have done that before," I laughed.

"Oh," she laughed, swatting my arm. "I had forgotten about that. Tell me, do you remember anything about that?"

"What do you mean?" I asked.

"After you died, what do you remember before you came back to life?" she prodded.

I began to think. "I remember floating along in darkness. I was bound for Potter's Field. I heard

Sophie call out my name, and it was like her voice alone gave me the power to return," I explained.

"Do you remember anyone being with you?" she pushed.

I thought harder. A face appeared in my mind, but as fast as it had appeared, it disappeared. "Barely," I replied.

She smiled. "Azrael," she stated.

"Who?" I asked, confused.

"Potion first, then we talk," she urged.

I sighed heavily. "Bottoms up," I groaned as I uncorked the bottle and drank it down.

It was sweet with a bitter aftertaste. I stood and waited for whatever to happen. I looked at Starfire.

"Just wait," she replied.

Almost instantly, I was doubled over with pain twisting through me like I had drunk ground-up glass, and it was shredding my insides. My body automatically heaved as if it could rid itself of the potion, and I lay gagging on the floor. She was right. This was worse than the Lake of Purity. Fire ran through my veins with an icy heat. I screamed in agony as steam rose from my skin, as I burned from the inside out. I had spent my whole life engulfed in flames and never had felt what the fire should feel like until now. I couldn't control my fire, and it began to burn uncontrollably on my skin.

"You need to leave," I heaved between breaths. "I don't want to hurt you."

"You won't hurt me," she replied.

"Ahhh!" I roared as my fire grew in intensity and burned inwardly.

I looked around, and nothing inside was catching on fire as I blazed out of control. It felt like she was pouring fuel on my fire as the burn deepened. I watched fire ringlets race through my veins on my arms up to my head. My head felt like it was going to burst from all of the heat. And just as quickly as it started, it stopped. I slowly stood to my feet, and Starfire offered me a chair to sit with her at the table.

"How do you feel?" she asked.

"Like I was boiled alive," I muttered.

"Want some tea?" she offered. "It will help soothe your insides."

"Thank you," I smiled.

She poured me a cup, and I took a sip. Immediately, every leftover feeling of being burned subsided. "That's quite the tea."

"Home blend," she said, smiling.

"Ready to talk now?" I asked, continuing to sip on the tea.

"I am!" she exclaimed as she picked up her own cup to drink from.

"So, who is Azrael, and why have I never heard of him… or her?" I questioned.

"Azrael is older than Alpha. She is older than most of the gods. If I am not mistaken, she was one of the first to come into existence. She goes by many names in many cultures. She is like Santisma Muerte to the Mexican Catholics. Nergal to the Sumerians. Mot to the Phoenicians, Charon to the Greeks. Azrael is Death incarnate," Starfire explained. "She ferries the souls to Sheol for them to rest. She ferries the immortal ones to Potter's Field."

"All immortal ones?" I pressed, shifting in my seat.

"No, Gods do not go to Potter's Field," she explained. "When they die, their energy goes out into the universe and is centralized into new gods waiting to burst forth into existence."

"Where was she taking me then?" I wondered.

"She was *trying* to take you to Potter's Field," she chuckled. "But your energy was too much for her to handle because in your dead state, you were pure, new god energy."

"So, she slipped, and I was able to will myself back alive, right?" I mused.

"Yes and no," she replied. "You resurrected yourself, yes. But she didn't slip. You were just too powerful for her to contain."

"I see," I said, taking another sip from my cup. "And you know also about Sophia and Gabriel and all of that too."

"Oh, child. I have known everything for what seems like forever," she laughed while picking up her cup.

"Sophia told me her secret," I commented. "Do you know about that too?" I asked.

"I do," she answered, smiling and taking a sip of her drink. "I also know where she is as well. But I will let Sophia tell you those things."

"And Yahweh?" I questioned. "Where is he? I didn't get a chance to ask Sophia. I already know about Barbelo."

"Yahweh is hiding," Starfire replied, setting the cup back on its glass plate. "Once Alpha is defeated, he will come out and bestow upon you and the kids his power."

"Why hasn't he given it to Alpha?" I asked, staring down into her eyes.

"Because he knows how evil Alpha is," she answered. "He wouldn't use the power for good. The reason Barbelo relinquished her energy to the universe was to give it a chance to live on past Alpha through you."

"Is Alpha going to destroy Lilith? Reabsorb her?" I wondered.

Starfire's face dimmed. "Yes," she stated. "He will be in full power then."

"When?" I asked, looking down at the table.

"Soon," she replied. I stood from my seat to leave. "Not that soon. You have time to stop him."

"Do I?" I inquired.

"You have just rejoined Luxina. Don't you want to spend some time with her before leaving again?" she questioned.

"You are right," I answered with a smile.

"Finish your tea."

Chapter Six

I SAT WITH Metatron and Gabriel as we watched more Nephilim arrive and check in. Hundreds of celestials showed up by the day. Our numbers had nearly tripled since Damian and Luxina showed everyone what they were fighting alongside when they fought against Alpha. It was beginning to look more and more hopeful for us as power built on our side.

"Is this place even big enough for all of us?" Metatron quipped, looking around at his surroundings.

"This place is magical," a young warlock interjected. "It will accommodate itself to the numbers."

"What's your name, kid?" I asked.

"Reikal," he replied.

"Oh, you're the one who gave Luxina those fancy hand knives," Gabriel interrupted and then turned to me. "She has been showing everyone those knives."

"Yes, sir," he boasted proudly.

"I am Incaendiel," I said, holding my hand out to him. "I am Luxina's father."

"Nice to meet you," he replied. He examined the sword that hung from my side. "Is that the flaming sword?" he questioned.

I looked down. I had forgotten I even had it. "It is," I answered

"Wait, since when do you have that?" Metatron demanded. "We were told it was gone."

Gabriel raised his hand. "That's because I stole it."

"Where is Michael's spear?" Metatron inquired.

"I stole that, too," Gabriel laughed.

"Is there anything you didn't steal?" Metatron drawled.

Gabriel thought for a moment. He snapped his fingers. "I left my horn. I have to go get it."

Reikal giggled as Gabriel sprinted off. "I can add some additional magic to your sword if you would like?" he offered.

"Like, what kind of magic?" I asked.

"I can make it where it cannot be wielded by anyone except those loyal to the Shining Ones," he replied.

"Now that would be useful," I remarked and handed it over. "How long will it take?" I queried.

"Back in a flash," he responded, running off.

"I hope I didn't just get robbed," I chuckled.

110

A loud trumpet echoed in the air.

"Gabriel found his horn," Metatron sighed.

I stood and watched as millions of lights lit up the sky.

"I think something is wrong," I said, pointing to the sky.

"Those look like…" Metatron began.

"Falling angels," I finished.

"What's happening?" Azazel asked, running up to us with Samael right behind her.

"I don't know," I replied. "Take down the force field!" I demanded. "They'll be burned alive falling like that through it."

Almost immediately, the force field came down. All of the angels who had returned to the Summit came careening down like meteors, hitting the ground with a burning thud. I ran to the first one to fall. It was Gabriel. He was burned pretty badly.

"Starfire!" I yelled. "We need to help them!" I examined him over. He was clutching the trumpet in his hand. "What happened?"

"No sooner had I returned to the Summit and retrieved my horn than Alpha and Lilith showed up," he replied. "He kicked us all out. He's closed off the Summit."

I looked around as more angels thudded to the ground and others ran to their sides to help them.

"Where are the kids?" I asked Azazel.

"They're inside asleep. They're pretty worn out from the past few days," she responded.

"Don't wake them," I ordered. "Starfire?" I called out again.

"I'm right here," she replied, holding a jar of some sort of substance. "Smear this salve all over them. It will heal the burns."

"Can you make sure they don't hear this inside?" I urged.

"I already did. It's soundproofed to where they can't hear anything outside of the walls," she replied.

"Thank you," I breathed.

I reached into the jar and scooped out a handful of the salve. I took my other hand and used it to apply it all over Gabriel. He groaned as the salve absorbed into his skin.

"It burns like acid," he screeched.

"It will only burn for a little bit," Starfire assured him. "Then it will be cooling."

I could see the relief wash over him as the burning stopped and the cooling kicked in. I handed the jar to Azazel.

"Quick, run the jar to the next angel and explain how to use it and hand it off," I ordered.

"On it," she noted.

"Raphael!" I shouted.

"Right here, Incaendiel," Raphael replied, running up to me.

"Heal as many as you can," I commanded.

He nodded and ran off to the first angel adjacent to Gabriel. He started running his hands over them, slowly healing their wounds.

"Are there any fatalities?" I yelled.

I watched a few hands pop up in the air and ran to them. The first I came across was Zadkiel. "Oh, no," I murmured as I hit the ground on my knees.

"There's nothing you can do for him, Incaendiel," Metatron mumbled. "Find the ones you can help."

His body began to dematerialize, and I looked up to see Azrael standing there.

"You," I stated.

"Me," she answered.

"Who are you talking to?" Metatron asked.

"You can't see her?" I stammered.

"See who?"

"They can't see me," she affirmed. "I am only visible to gods and other reapers. I will allow myself to be visible to others only when I want to be."

"Why?" I pressed.

"Because reapers are a different type of celestial," she explained.

"There are more of you?" I pressed.

She nodded. "And we will join your side."

"Is he going to Potter's Field?" I mused.

She nodded. "He will have a noble burial."

"I can't bring him back?" I protested.

She stopped to think for a moment. "I don't know. I know you brought yourself back and your twin flame. Why don't you try?"

"What do I do?" I asked.

"I don't know," she replied. "Try putting your hands on his chest and willing him back like you did Sophie."

I did as instructed and closed my eyes. I felt a buzzing in my hands and opened my eyes. Bright light emanated from them and was pulsating into Zadkiel's body. Zadkiel bolted upright, gasping deeply.

"I was dead," he blurted.

"Yes, you were dead," I replied, astonished.

"You brought me back?" he asked.

"I did," I answered, wide-eyed, still bewildered.

"Thank you, Brother," he responded.

"How did you do that?" Metatron asked.

"I don't know," I murmured.

I looked up at Azrael. "Can I save them all?"

She smiled and nodded.

I raced to each hand that was held up in the air, signaling a dead angel, and repeated what I had done with Zadkiel. Each one of them sprang back alive. It felt like it took an eternity to get all of the angels healed up with Starfire's salve and me reviving the dead ones. By the time we had finished, I was exhausted. I stumbled to the cottage porch and sat down on the steps. Metatron took a seat next to me.

"Who were you talking to earlier that I couldn't see?" he pushed.

Samael and Azazel ran up to the porch as well, both looking tired.

"You ok?" Azazel asked. "You look like you need a nap."

I laughed. "Yeah, I could use one," I replied.

"Who was that woman you were talking to?" Samael questioned.

My brows knitted together. "You could see her?" I asked in return, confused.

"Yeah, we both did," Azazel answered, nodding.

I scratched my head. "That doesn't make any sense," I stated, shaking my head. "She said only other gods could see her."

"Who is she?" Samael prodded, propping a foot up on the step and leaning down on his leg.

"Her name is Azrael," I replied.

"Who is she, and why couldn't I see her, but they could?" Metatron asked.

"She's Death and the leader of the reaper angels," I responded. "You can't see her because you're not meant to see her. I have no idea why those two could see her." I motioned between Samael and Azazel.

"Reaper angels?" Metatron wondered.

I nodded. "They help ferry the dead souls of humans and celestials," I replied. "She told me they were joining our side."

"I always wondered who was in charge of the dead souls," Samael remarked. "Neither Mother nor Alpha had ever told us about reapers. I just thought Alpha was in charge of that."

"I did too," I replied. "But you and Azazel seeing her doesn't make any sense. You're not gods unless…"

"Unless what?" Azazel asked.

Right when I was about to answer, Raphael ran up to the porch with a look of worry.

"What's wrong, Rafe?" I probed.

"Michael is among the fallen," he stated, glancing over his shoulder toward the fallen scattered across the grass.

"Michael?" I asked.

He nodded.

"Is he alive?" I urged.

"Yes. Gabriel is healing him up right now," he replied. "He asked for you."

I swallowed hard. "What do I do, Sam?" I questioned, looking at him.

He thought long and hard before he answered. "I would hear him out," he responded.

"I'm getting too old for this crap," I muttered.

Samael laughed loudly. "Aren't we all, Brother. Aren't we all." I began to walk off when he shouted, "Wait." I turned around to look at him. "Aren't you like eighteen years old?" he asked, laughing.

"Shut up," I laughed back.

I walked over to where Michael sat on the ground. Azazel was still applying the salve to his back when I knelt in front of him.

"Michael," I stated.

He looked at me, and I could see the pain in his eyes. "Why me?" he asked.

"Why not?" I replied.

"I did everything he asked of me," he cried.

"We all did. He still abandoned us," I sighed. "He doesn't care about anyone but himself."

"I did horrible things for him," Michael whimpered. "Horrible things in the name of a father who just tossed all of his kids out of their home. We didn't have a choice like you all did."

"It's the same game. It's the same story. It's just a different point of view for you," I replied. "Alpha wants power. He can't have power when he is outnumbered. He thinks by making you all fall, your power is diminished."

"It is," Michael cried. "It's gone."

"Do you trust me, Brother?" I asked.

He was silent.

"Will you follow me as your leader?" I pressed.

He hung his head, crying into his hands. "I don't have a choice, do I?" he whispered.

"You have a choice with me," I replied. "I won't make you choose my side. I won't make you leave this safe haven either if you don't. I am not our father."

I started to stand up when he grabbed my arm. He looked me in the eyes and inhaled deeply. "Hail to the King."

I nodded as I took his other hand in mine and pulled him in for a hug. Lights swirled around him as all of his power was restored to him.

"You don't need his power with me," I whispered in his ear. "I have my own power apart from his."

I stood up and looked out at the crowd of angels who sat on the ground, bruised and broken.

"For those of you who have not joined my ranks, I offer it to you now. Join me in the fight against Alpha. Accept me. In return, you will be restored like Michael here. It's your choice to make. I will not force you to choose between Alpha and me. I will not make you leave this safe haven. I will not abandon you because of your choice. But if you choose to join our ranks against Alpha, you will share in my power. Alpha has taken your power. Alpha takes everything for himself. When you fell, the powers he bestowed upon you went back to him to make him more powerful. He is absorbing all the power he can find to try to defeat us. I am offering you restoration. He is offering nothing."

One by one, angels stood from the ground and shouted. "Hail to the King." One by one, they each shared in my power. I was exhausted by the time everyone was all fixed up and part of the ranks. I could hardly walk back to the cottage. I stumbled and nearly hit the ground when Michael caught me.

"Let me help you, Brother," he said.

"Thank you," I slurred. "I just need to sit down."

"No, what you need is some rest," he urged.

"I will take him," Sophia said, stepping forth almost out of nowhere. "We have much to discuss once he has his nap."

"When did you get here?" I queried, barely able to form the words from exhaustion.

"I've been here since right before Alpha kicked them all out," she responded.

She walked over, and I leaned against her as she helped me inside the cottage.

"Can you trust him here?" she asked, eyeing Michael suspiciously.

"I don't know," I replied. "It didn't look or sound like an act. I do believe Alpha kicked him out like the rest of them."

"I still don't trust him alone with you," she sneered. "For all we know, he could be trying to kill you and steal the power for himself."

"Have a little faith in him," Starfire interrupted as we shut the door behind us.

I gave her a half smile and a nod. She *did* know things we didn't. If she believed he was to be trusted, I trusted her.

"Which room can I take him to?" Sophia asked, motioning to me.

"A lot of them are empty upstairs," Starfire replied. "The ones that are occupied have a sign on them."

Sophia nodded. She helped me up the steps and into the first empty room we came across. She helped me over to the bed, and I flopped onto it.

"Oh my god," I breathed. "This bed feels like a cloud."

"Don't you mean 'oh my me?'" Sophia asked with a laugh.

"Ha, good one," I groaned. "What are you doing here, Sophia?"

"Well, when Alpha showed up at the Summit, I waited around as long as I could to see what his plans were," she replied. "I had no idea that he was going to kick everyone out to absorb their powers. We didn't think of that one."

"No, we didn't," I remarked. "I feel stupid for not thinking of it when I thought of it with Lilith."

"You're not stupid, Incaendiel," she cooed. "You're just overworked and underpaid."

I rolled to my side and looked at her sitting in the chair beside the bed. "Are you sure the humans didn't wear off on you, too? You sure do have a lot of their sayings preprogrammed."

"Ha, humor," she mocked. "Did you take your potion?" she asked.

I nodded. "It was agonizing, by the way."

"I didn't think it would feel too pretty," she replied. "Have the kids taken theirs too?" she asked.

"Yeah, they took theirs before I got here. You should have seen them in action against Alpha with their unlocked power. They looked so majestic."

"You should have seen you and how you looked bringing all of those angels back from the dead," she replied.

"What did I look like?" I murmured, half asleep.

"You looked like a god," she responded, stroking my hair. "I am so proud of you, Incaendiel. You're going to restore the reputation of this family."

"Is that what you care about most?" I demanded, staring at her. "How the other gods look at us?"

"No," she replied. "I care about righting a wrong I committed so long ago."

"You sound self-absorbed like Alpha," I muttered. "You know what I care about?" I asked, propping myself up on my elbow. "I care about the world and what happens to it. I care about the universe crumbling in on itself. And I care about those kids down the hall. That's what I care about. I don't care about restoring a reputation marred by you. I don't care about being the most powerful being in the universe. I care about others, not myself."

"And that is what makes you such a fine god," she remarked. "You are selfless and not selfish. I was selfish. I wanted to create something of my own so badly that I did so without getting permission from my father. I ended up creating this universe and then the ass of a god that runs it. Out of my selfish act came things we had never witnessed before from gods. Well, aside from Enlil, but he is just an asshole. Wrath, vengeance, jealousy, pride, envy, greed, so many personality traits that gods aren't supposed to possess, came from me. All because I wanted to do something I wasn't permitted to do yet."

"You were a kid, too, Sophia," I explained. "You didn't know any better."

"Did I? I went on a quest to find out and learn everything my father knew. In turn, violence, sorrow, disease, vice, madness, and even old age are what humans suffer at the hands of their god because he decided to throw a temper tantrum, learning he wasn't the only god of his universe. Then, the petty games he plays with Lilith make it even worse for humans. It's so horrible," she said, shaking her head.

I brushed my hand against her cheek. "You're not as bad as you think you are. It's not your fault you made a mistake. Everyone makes mistakes." I inspected her closely. I hadn't noticed how much Sophie resembled her before now.

She placed her hand on top of mine and smiled. "No one has been as kind to me as you have since I left Lucifer." She leaned in closer to my face, and I cleared my throat.

She blushed and immediately sat back up straight.

"So, you're the mother of the Nephilim," I stated, changing position in the bed a bit away from her. "Does that make them demigods?"

"In a way, yes," she replied, adjusting in her seat. "More like the myths of Nephilim being half angel. Since they were created through mortals and not clapped into being with a snap of my fingers, they're not quite godlike."

"Did you create them all?" I asked.

"No, I created the first one and then helped Samyaza and other Watchers to create more," she explained. "They all look to me as their mother since I created the first one."

"Who was the one you created?" I asked, propping my head up on my hand.

She smiled. "You have met him already," she replied. "Praeziel is my son."

"Another good kid," I remarked. "I know he worked diligently to keep the kids safe from harm."

"He did," she smiled and nodded. "But he lives such a sad life."

"Why?" I asked.

"He can never be with another Nephilim," she explained. "After Alpha learned about the Nephilim, he did something to their bloodlines. When they pair up, they turn mortal and die. So, he has spent the last several thousand years alone because he doesn't want to lose his powers."

"Why would Alpha do that?" I demanded.

"Alpha was angry with the Nephilim being created. It didn't help that Samyaza and the others decided to teach humankind things that Alpha wasn't ready for them to learn, along with teaching them to sin. Samyaza taught the humans arts and technologies. He showed them how to make weapons, cosmetics, and mirrors, and even taught them sorcery. One of the reasons that the city of Atlantis was run off was because they were such an advanced civilization compared to his creations. He wanted humans to advance at his pace. It was a stab at Alpha, really, for abandoning the Watchers. So, Alpha's punishment to them was to make their children die out," she elaborated.

"And you can't reverse what he did to them?" I asked. "I mean, you are a god."

"No, I can't," she replied with a half-smile. "The only one that I can guarantee is Praeziel because he was made from me, but I haven't told him because when he pairs up with another Nephilim and they grow mortal and die, it will crush him that he lost a grand love. He has already lost many loves throughout the years. Gwynevere, I believe, was his breaking point."

"Who was Gwynevere?" I questioned.

"She was part of the Unseelie court," Sophia shared. "She had been with Praeziel for the last three hundred years. She was with him and the kids as they looked for Starfire."

"What happened?"

"She was in league with Alpha," she asserted. "Luxina killed her."

"What?" I snapped, sitting upright in the bed. "She killed her?"

Sophia nodded. "She didn't have a choice, really. Gwynevere had spent the last year playing games with them and keeping them from getting to Starfire. Luxina was enraged during a fight and walked through one of the portals from the Otherworld and landed right where they needed to be. When Alpha took control of Damian's mind, he told her that Gwynevere was his spy. She only needed to ask Starfire one question. Gwynevere had told her that Starfire's location kept moving and bouncing around, so they had to hunt for the location. It was a lie, and that was the question she asked Starfire. She killed Gwynevere without a second thought. Praeziel was crushed that Gwynevere had betrayed them. He loved her dearly."

"She should have given her a second chance," I muttered. "She shouldn't have just killed her. So many people are allied with him out of fear, not out of want."

"Luxina did what she thought was best for everyone. She is still learning. She was with Gwynevere for a year, and at any given moment, Alpha could have taken her prisoner. She was scared. She was scared of going back there and being tortured more." Sophia reasoned. "Praeziel understands that she needed to be dispatched. It's just another lost love on his long list of loneliness."

"Every single misfortune, or grief, or tragic tale always comes back to Alpha being the source of the grievance," I grunted. "He needs to be stopped."

"Indeed, he does," Sophia sighed gravely.

I eyed her face. "You know something, don't you. What he's planning. You mentioned it earlier. What is it?" I urged.

"They have a young angel with them that looks like the children," she replied. "I don't know his name or who he is, but he is a new creation."

I thought back to the vision Gabriel shared with me of the apocalypse. The angel that seemed to control the horde of creatures looked to be around the same age as the kids.

"How new is he?" I asked.

"I'm not sure," she responded. "I don't even know what his name is. But he radiates wickedness."

"In the vision Gabriel had, there was a young angel in it. I bet it is him," I said, sitting up in the bed.

I ran my hand through my hair and then rubbed my eyes.

"Who else was there?" I pressed.

"Those of the angels who have been by Alpha's side since the war," she answered. "The Forsaken as well. Well, at least those who didn't choose Damian's side. I heard some of them talking about how they split with Asmodeus, with him leading the other faction. Apparently, some kind of conflict happened when Asmodeus helped Damian and you escape from Alpha. There is also a faction of the Watchers who joined with Alpha, led by Baraqiel."

"When did that happen?" I asked.

"When Stygia was attacked. Watchers chose sides then. Alpha gave them a choice to join, but those who didn't join would still be spared as a pardon for him abandoning them," she replied.

There was a knock on the door.

"You can come in," I answered as I straightened upright to look more energetic than I felt.

The door opened, and Raphael stepped through. He looked just as tired as I did.

"You better come down," he stated solemnly.

"What's going on?" I sighed.

"You will just have to come and see," he replied.

I stood up from the bed and followed him from the room, with Sophia right behind me. We made our way downstairs and outside of Starfire's cottage to a loud commotion outside. I stepped off the porch and saw Michael squaring up against another who had their back turned to me. Michael had his blade drawn, as did the other person.

"What's going on?" I shouted.

"Intruders," Michael hissed. "They claim to be friendly, but anyone who was in Alpha's ranks cannot be trusted."

"Mind your words, Brother," I barked. "You are one of Alpha's former loyalists. Let's hear them out."

"They're not even angels anymore," Michael sneered, still in fighting position.

"I said to back off!" I shouted.

My voice echoed through the valley much like Metatron's usually sounds. Michael immediately sheathed his sword.

"That's my power," Metatron whispered, leaning into my ear.

"I am trying to be serious here," I whispered back. "Who is it?" I demanded. "Who do you think you cannot trust?"

The visitor turned around.

"Asmodeus, Brother!" I sighed in relief. I walked over and gave him a welcoming hug. "I have been waiting for you to show up. I had feared the worst."

"We had followed Damian into the Nightmares and Shadows realm to help him after Alpha dispatched Zephar and others who were his loyalists. We narrowly escaped. Those monsters he made were there. We helped Damian escape at the last minute. He must have walked into the portal that would have brought him to the other kids because the creatures just disappeared as fast as they had appeared," Asmodeus recounted as he sheathed his sword.

"Are you here alone?" I asked, looking around for more of the others who left Alpha.

He nodded. "I thought it would be best that the others wait on the other side of the force field so they weren't attacked, thinking they were still in league with Alpha," he growled, glaring at Michael.

"How do you know he can be trusted?" Michael petitioned.

"He helped Damian and me escape from Alpha's lair at Chernobyl," I replied.

"No one spoke of this to me," Michael retorted. "None of the other Forsaken mentioned a rebellion."

"They were probably ordered not to," Asmodeus explained. "Alpha already thought he had lost you to Incaendiel's side. So he wouldn't have let anyone tell you about any new plans or what had happened."

"Metatron?" I asked, glancing back in his direction. "Will you lead our other brothers into Lightshade, please? They need a safe haven."

"Yes, sir," Metatron replied and marched off to the top of the hill to let them in.

"Sir," Asmodeus mouthed.

"I'm kind of a big deal now," I whispered, with a shrug.

"Where is Damian?" he asked, peering around the crowd for his face.

"Upstairs in the cottage, sleeping. He and Luxina had a huge showdown with Alpha, and it zapped them of all of their energy," I replied.

"Looks like it zapped you, too?" he remarked, looking me over.

"That's another story," I sighed. "One reason Michael is a bit touchy right now," I whispered into his ear.

"What happened?" Asmodeus murmured, glancing over at Michael, who had turned to walk away.

"Alpha kicked all of the angels out of the Summit," I responded. "They all fell and lost the powers he had given them."

Asmodeus's face turned from a look of amusement to a look of worry. "It's almost time then," he blurted.

"Time for what?" I asked, narrowing my eyes.

"He's locked himself away in the Summit," Asmodeus replied. "He had told us that when it got closer to the beginning of starting this universal destruction plan of his, he would take those who followed him to the Summit and kick all of the angels out."

Metatron came running back down the hill in a panic. "They're being attacked! They need our help!" he shouted.

I took off in a sprint to make it up the hill, running past Metatron with Asmodeus behind me. I stepped through the force field, and it was a blood bath on the other side. Those who were waiting had been attacked by the creatures Alpha made, as well as a horde of Forsaken. Brother fighting brother and then being ripped apart by malformed werewolf beasts.

Asmodeus went to run to help them, I grabbed his shoulder and pulled him back.

"Stand behind me," I ordered.

I extended both of my arms out by my side and then clapped them together as hard as I could. A shockwave of energy knocked everyone from their feet in front of me and sent them spiraling into the air. I raised my hands and sent blasts of fiery energy at the beasts that were trying to recover, and disintegrated them where they stood. The Forsaken tried to scramble to their feet and attack once again.

"Stop!" I bellowed.

My voice shook the ground beneath our feet, and they cowered into a squatting position.

"Those of you with Asmodeus, get inside," I ordered.

"Come on," Mammon shouted to those who were on our side as he and Asmodeus stood at the gates, making sure no one slipped in who wasn't supposed to.

"You two go as well," I demanded as the last one of them ran through.

"What about you?" Asmodeus asked.

I turned around and told him, "I got this."

He nodded and disappeared into the gate with Mammon right behind him. I turned my attention back to those who still cowered in front of me.

"You have a choice to make here," I began, looking each of them in the eyes. "You can stay with Alpha and let him continue to mistreat and abuse you, or you can join me."

"What makes you think we will join you so quickly?" one shouted, standing to her feet.

"Naamah, Sister," I replied. "It's nice to see you."

Abaddon scoffed. "You think you're special because you have powers. You're nothing more than a little bug that needs squashing," she seethed, twisting her sword in her hand.

"I am not the one who abandoned you, Sister," I refuted, putting my hands up defensively. "I am not Alpha, nor am I Lilith. I did not make you into what you are now."

"You didn't stop it either, now did you?" she huffed, readying her sword. "Besides, I like who I am now. Alpha accepts me for who I am now."

"Does he?" I prodded, shaking my head. "Or does he just treat you like his slaves? Warriors that can be expendable. That's how he treated those who went after Damian. They were expendable to him. And so are you, or you wouldn't be here. Instead, you would be nestled safely in the Summit with him while those beasts he created carried out his dirty deeds."

"We are important to him!" Naamah countered, drawing the bowstring of her bow.

"You are his pawns," I insisted. "The pieces sent out first into battle that are dispensable and not essential to his grand scheme in the end. But you don't have to be! You can join your brothers and sisters. You can join us! You can become whole again."

"How can we become whole again?" she sneered, glaring at me. "We are Forsakens for a reason. No one can restore our light. No one can untarnish our souls."

"I can," I replied, holding out my hand. "All you need to do is trust me and join me in this fight because, in the end, nothing will be left. Not even you. Alpha is going to destroy everything and reabsorb every bit of power and energy he exhausted in creating it to be an all-mighty god. That includes you. You won't survive the end. Why do you think he created those muddled creatures? They're not an expense of energy to him."

"I don't believe you," she spat. "Alpha has told us his plans. Those loyal to him will reap the benefits in the end."

"I can show you the end," I defended. "Do you really want to see how this all plays out for us all? Because in the end, you are not in the final battle. None of you are."

"Lies!" she shouted.

"Gabriel!" I commanded.

Gabriel appeared at my side. "What do you need?"

"Show them the end," I said, pointing over at them. "Show them their fates."

"I can't show them that anymore," Gabriel replied.

"Why not?" I asked in disbelief. "You showed *me*."

"Because it has changed," he answered. "I am not allowed to show anyone the new future now."

"Then show him the old one," I demanded.

"Those get erased when the future changes. That vision no longer exists," he responded. "But you should be able to share it with him."

"What use is an old vision?" Naamah laughed. "Afraid to show us how we win in the end?"

I became irritated and held up my hand. A blast of white light came out of it, and all of their eyes lit up like stars exploding. Somehow, even though I didn't know exactly what I was doing, I shared the vision Gabriel had given me. The light disappeared, and the bright light that had shone from their eyes was gone as well.

"How did I do that?" I whispered to Gabriel.

"You should know," Gabriel replied. "You're a god, remember?"

Naamah stood quietly as she processed what she saw in her head. "Alpha lied to us," she murmured, tears filling her eyes.

"Alpha lies to everyone," I reinforced, taking a few steps closer to her. "Alpha is the Great Deceiver he warned you all about. The question is, what do you plan to do about it?"

Before she could respond, fiery brimstone erupted from the sky and struck down like lightning on her. She was turned into a pillar of salt right before me. More shafts of brimstone began to rain down as each of the Forsaken who stood there began to flee before they were struck.

"Quickly, into Lightshade!" I urged, waving my arm for them to follow toward the open portal.

They ran as quickly as they could as Alpha tried to smite them. Gabriel followed in after them, and just as I was about to turn and close the gate, a voice called out.

"Incaendiel! Wait!"

I turned to see a straggler trying to dodge the beams of hellfire pelting down. The anger boiled deep within me as I looked from the straggler to the pillar of salt Naamah had been turned into. I roared in rage and clapped my hands together toward the sky, taking my wrath out on Alpha. A powerful beam erupted from me and shot into the sky. Lightning struck, and thunder clapped, and the sky went silent. The straggler ran up to me breathlessly.

"Thank you, Brother," she said, removing the hood from her head.

"Uriel?"

Chapter Seven

URIEL WALKED BY my side as we came down the hill to the center of Lightshade, where everyone awaited my return. Asmodeus stood guarding the Forsaken I had let into Lightshade that Alpha had sent while everyone else was being bandaged up.

"Uriel!" Metatron gasped and ran up to her, grabbing her by her shoulders. "Why are you here?"

"I had no choice but to flee the entrance of Purgatory," Uriel shared. "Alpha cleaned house, and I was next on his list."

"Purgatory?" I interjected. "What the hell is Purgatory?"

"After Lucifer walked as Jesus, Alpha created a system of punishment for not just humans but for celestials as well," Uriel explained. "Only certain ones of us knew about it and were not allowed to speak about it. What the humans speak about is real. He made hell, limbo, purgatory, the abyss, and all kinds of other traps."

"Where are Sandalphon and Jophiel?" Metatron asked, shaking her.

"They fled inside Purgatory," Uriel went on. "I didn't have time to search for them. Alpha tried to smite me." She unsheathed her wings, and they were a tattered mess. "I took to the Otherworld and bounced through portals before landing here to witness the showdown between Alpha and Incaendiel."

"Showdown?" Samael inquired, looking between Uriel and me. "What showdown?"

One of the Forsaken who was being guarded by Asmodeus spoke up. "Alpha tried to smite us after Incaendiel showed us all the vision he was given by Gabriel."

"Astaroth?" Michael asked, pushing through the crowd.

"Yes, it's me," Astaroth responded.

"I *know* he is in league with Alpha," Michael hissed.

"I am aware," I reassured, motioning with my hands for him to calm down. "I gave them safe haven. Alpha just tried to smite them. He turned Naamah into a pillar of salt just now."

"They don't deserve a safe haven," Michael sneered.

"What is *with* you?" I demanded, turning on my heels to face him. "Do you think you are the only one worthy of a second chance? Everyone has had their fair share of manipulations and punishments by Alpha and Lilith. Everyone deserves a second chance, not just you."

"Incaendiel saved us," Astaroth relayed.

"After they all got to safety, Incaendiel was about to close the force field to Lightshade when I found him," Uriel recounted. "Alpha was also trying to smite me still, as well, and I showed up at the wrong place at the wrong time. Incaendiel tossed his own smite at Alpha. I am fairly certain he struck him as well. The sky went silent afterward."

"You smote Alpha?" Samael asked, bewildered.

I nodded. "I was enraged at what he had done to everyone. Naamah didn't deserve to die like that. None of them did. Seeing her frozen as a pillar of salt and the beams of hellfire still raining down as Uriel tried to get to me, I just exploded."

"I don't know about the rest of our brothers and sisters who came here allied with Alpha, but I pledge my allegiance to you, Incaendiel," Astaroth declared with a bow. "Hail to the King."

"All Hail Incaendiel, King of Kings!" Asmodeus shouted.

The valley was filled with the voices of the Forsaken shouting my name and bowing to me. Bright lights began to swirl around them, and they were lifted from the ground.

"What's happening?" Asmodeus demanded, panicking.

"I don't know," I stuttered.

The lights swirled around them like magical fireflies in the night sky. One by one, the lights entered their body, and a bright shining white beam erupted from their chests. Their grayed skin turned to a lustrous shine. Those who no longer had their wings from when the darkness took over them sprouted a new pair from their shoulder blades. Their dark hair turned back into the lustrous blond hues that they once had. Their dark eyes were once more a silvery blue as they had been in the beginning.

"My grace, my light," Asmodeus murmured, looking his body over. "It has been restored!"

"He has done even what Alpha has refused to do through all of our loyalty!" Astaroth shouted. "We are angels again!"

"So, it's true," Uriel started. "I have been sitting on the sidelines listening to both sides of the fence. I heard that those who join you will share in your power. Alpha has been telling all of his loyalists that it's just a rumor. That you don't have the capability of restoring power to anyone."

"It's true," Eisleth shared, stepping forward. "Alpha keeps those of us in check by saying that he will restore us once we prove that we remain loyal to only him, and that Incaendiel will offer false promises to us to gain our trust when, in fact, it is he who is deceiving us."

"And we need to act quickly against him," a voice called out through the crowd.

"Azrael," I stated, walking toward her. "It's good to see you again."

"Who is she?" many began to shout.

"They can see you?" I wondered aloud, looking around at all the confused faces.

"Yes," she elaborated. "I am allowing them to see me right now. We have a big problem."

"Wha's wrong?" I asked.

"Where is Lailah?" she demanded, looking around at everyone.

"Is Lailah here?" I shouted among the others, looking for her myself. "Did she fall with the rest of you? Has anyone seen her?"

I looked around at all of the faces, and they shook their heads.

"She is not at the giving tree," Azrael asserted, worried.

"How do you know Lailah?" I asked.

"Among you are reaper angels that do not know that they are reaper angels," she clarified. "They just handle the tasks as ordered without knowing *why* they do what they do. I have gathered many helpers throughout the millennia. However, Alpha has hoarded his lot of angels who were supposed to have been allotted to me during their creation. Lailah, among others, is one of them."

"She has never spoken of you before," Metatron emphasized.

"That's because she doesn't remember me after she sees me," Azrael revealed. "Alpha doesn't want any of you knowing there is a force greater than he that controls death and life."

"Alpha doesn't want them to know things, period," Gabriel interjected with a huff.

"Is Lailah not in the Summit?" I asked.

"No, she is not," Azrael replied, her worry growing deeper. "I went to look for her when everyone was kicked out of the Summit and fell since she wasn't among any that I could see. Without Lailah, there aren't going to be any new births. I can't give her souls to recycle."

"Sandalphon and Jophiel are missing as well," Metatron added.

"Who else does Alpha have stashed away that is vital in the upkeep of the world?" Samael asked.

"He has my Watchers."

I whipped around to see Samyaza and Belial standing together.

"Alpha came to Stygia nearly a year ago when we were having the council meeting with Incaendiel," Samyaza began. "Nice to see you're still alive, by the way," he added, looking me up and down.

"Yeah, it's been a helluva year," I muttered.

"When he infiltrated our sacred place, he took those he saw as he marched through our tunnels captive," Samyaza continued. "Belial and I hardly escaped."

"Wait," I started. "That's not what Sophia told me. She said that Baraqiel led another faction that had split from the Watchers to join Alpha after he made promises."

"Lies," Belial hissed.

"She just told me!" I retorted.

"Sophia is under protective custody of the fey," Samyaza asserted. "She isn't even in the universe right now. After Alpha tried to slay her, and Damian spared her, she was taken where she couldn't be found."

"Then who the hell was in my bedroom?" I demanded and turned around to scan the crowd. "Has anyone seen Sophia?"

"Not since Asmodeus arrived," Azazel responded.

"Check and make sure the kids are still safe in their room," I ordered.

Azazel nodded and ran off into Starfire's cottage.

"This doesn't make sense," I murmured. My eyes narrowed. "Where is Michael?" I snapped.

"Right here," Michael answered, stepping forward.

I ran up to him, grabbed him by his shirt, and pushed him up against a tree. "She showed up right after you did, just like how Beelzebub showed up right after you did all those years ago. Tell me, *Brother,* and don't you dare lie to me. Did you have anything to do with this?"

Michael's eyes were saucers of fear. "I swear to you, Incaendiel. I had nothing to do with this. I do not know who is faking being Sophia."

It began to thunder and lightning. The clouds began to swirl, and rain began to pelt down. "Tell me the truth!" I bellowed.

Michael looked around at those gathered around. "Please, don't let him smite me!" he pleaded.

The wind blew ferociously as I stood my ground with Michael.

"Incaendiel!" a voice shouted, and I looked behind me.

The others were on the ground, holding on to anything the best that they could as the winds picked up, nearly carrying them away. Their eyes filled with fear as they looked at me.

"I swear to you, Brother!" Michael implored. "I have nothing to do with this!"

I released my grip on him, and the storm that had rolled in disappeared just as quickly as it had appeared.

"Where is Starfire?" I muttered, stalking off to her cottage.

I met Azazel on the steps. "The children are sound asleep in bed," she reported.

"Thank you," I sighed in relief.

I walked past her and into the cottage. "Starfire?" I called out.

She emerged from a room to my left that was filled with potion bottles and books, closing the door behind her.

"I know what you want," she replied, walking out into the middle of the room. "But first, you must calm down."

"I *am* calm," I snapped.

"Are you?" she asked, not moving from her place. "Take in a deep breath and exhale."

I was growing impatient by the minute.

"Incaendiel, you are more powerful than you were before," she explained. "You don't understand or know how to really control these new powers of yours. You need to calm down." She looked frightened.

I breathed in deeply and exhaled slowly, letting all of the anger out with my breath.

"Who was pretending to be Sophia?" I asked.

"You already know the answer," she replied.

"It can't be Beelzebub. I killed him," I retorted.

"No, you only thought you did," she replied. "That injection into your neck took immediate effect. It wasn't Beelzebub that gave it to you. And there wasn't anyone standing there for you to strike down. Alpha was the one who gave you the injection. Beelzebub knows a lot of things that others do not because he has been by Alpha's side for a really long time. Against his will, but by his side."

"Is Gabriel real? Are the others real?" I begged, fearing I had been hallucinating this whole time. "The ones that joined my side, are they to be trusted?"

She smiled. "The others are real. Everything else is real. Beelzebub didn't know how to come to you and ask for safe haven, considering your past. So, he took on the role of Sophia and told you things he knew from Alpha. Most of the things were true. Some were not because he was going solely by information told to him or what he heard by eavesdropping on Alpha," she replied.

I nodded and left the cabin. "Beelzebub!" I shouted. "Show yourself!"

In the middle of the crowd of angels, one of them began slowly moving forward.

"Sophia?" Samyaza called out. "It can't be?"

"It's not," I answered him.

As the crowd parted to allow Sophia through, her body dematerialized, and before me stood Beelzebub. He dropped to his knees.

"Please, Incaendiel," he implored. "I wish you no harm. I wish everybody no harm."

I took slow steps toward him. "Are you spying for Alpha?" I glowered. "And do not lie."

"I am not," he cried. "I am here for safety. I knew about the Forsaken and their plans to revolt against Alpha. I knew they were going to release you and Damian. I didn't tell Alpha, and he is looking to punish me."

"How can I trust you?" I asked.

"I bowed to you, Brother," he insisted, crawling toward me on his knees. "I accept you as my leader. I am one of you now."

I bent down to look him in the eyes, and his eyes fell to the ground. "Look at me!" I barked. His eyes came up to mine. "If you betray me, I will not have mercy on you. At all."

"Everything I have done has been Alpha's demand of me. And if I didn't do what he told me to do, he threatened to smite me," Beelzebub whimpered. "I am at your mercy, and I am at your feet. I am begging you to believe me because those things I told you, the things Sophia thinks Alpha doesn't know, he does."

"What is he talking about?" Belial demanded. "What things?"

"There was a lot. To highlight, Sophia is the mother of Alpha, but she also has another child named Zoe, whom she hides among the mortals like Alpha did with Sophie," I replied.

"Even we didn't know those things," Samyaza declared. "How do we know it's not another lie like was told about Baraqiel?" he asked.

"Because Alpha has been searching for her," Beelzebub elaborated. "It's why he has taken Lailah and why he took over the Summit. He is going through the list of conceptions and births to figure out which person on earth is Zoe."

"He is right," Azrael cut in. "If Zoe is recycled the same way human spirits are, then Lailah would know who she is. But even I cannot handle godly souls. They are too powerful for me to ferry." She nodded toward me.

"It's why Incaendiel could will himself back to life, right?" Azazel added. "And why Sophie didn't die either?"

"That's right," Azrael replied. "So, who has been ferrying Zoe's soul to Lailah?"

"I have," an old voice croaked.

I turned around and behind me stood a very old woman.

"Who are you?" I asked.

"I am Maveth," she responded. "The mother of Azrael."

Azrael bowed low in response to the voice. "Mother," she said. "Why are you here?"

"Because this is becoming far bigger than we discussed," Maveth answered. Maveth smiled at me and touched my cheek. "You look just like Yahweh."

"You know about the others?" I asked.

"Of course, I do," she laughed. "I am not an old woman in person for no reason. I am as old as time itself. I was the first to come into existence. I brought forth my daughter, Azrael. The universe cannot operate if life exists first. There would be no order. Death has to exist before life because it is what brings life. Each universe created by the varying gods springing to life eventually all flows back to me. However, I choose not to title myself as the primordial being or the big bang that set off the energy for everything to begin manifesting. So, few know how I came to exist. And with that shroud of knowledge, I am able to work in mysterious ways."

Maveth moved past me to where Beelzebub still cowered on the ground. "Your brother here, he speaks the truth. Alpha is looking for Zoe," she said as she bent down and lifted his face to her by his chin. "You are safe here. Incaendiel will not hurt you." She helped him to his feet and then turned back around to me. "You must find Zoe before he does."

"What if that's what Alpha wants?" I asked. "What if I lead him to her by mistake?"

"You have to trust yourself, dear boy," she laughed. "How can you be the ruler of this universe if you still cast doubt against yourself? Believe in yourself, child. I do," she replied, raising her eyebrow with a grin. "If it wasn't such a universal apocalyptic ordeal, we would all have a pool running on you all to see who would win. And I would bet on you."

"So, what do we do first?" I asked. "Who do we find first? There are so many of us that Alpha has taken against their will. How do we know whom to find that will lead us to victory?"

"Everyone is a grand chess piece in this game Alpha plays," she elaborated. "He has already squandered his pawns. You're on to the key chess pieces now until he finishes his monsters and whatever else he has planned to create. Everyone is important now. Even the ones you think aren't important are."

Maveth began to wander away from us. "Wait!" I shouted. "Where are you going?"

"Home," she replied. "You don't need my help right now. You just need to figure out your strategy." She smiled and turned into stardust.

"She's right," I declared, turning my attention to the crowd of angels behind me. "We need a game plan."

"So we have Sophie, Sandalphon, Jophiel, Lailah, the Watchers, and Zoe to save," Raphael chimed in. "We need a head count of who else there is that we are missing that are important."

"Lucifer," I added.

A riotous commotion broke out.

"Are you serious?" one yelled.

"He has betrayed us all over and over," another insisted.

"He cannot be trusted!" one hissed.

"Beelzebub?" I called out, and the crowd quietened.

"Yes, Brother?" Beelzebub replied.

"Where is Lucifer?" I inquired.

"No one knows," he replied. "Alpha did something with him after Damian had come to see you. I believe he was punished for disobeying orders."

"What orders?" I asked.

"He had been trying for a while to lure Damian away from Alpha," Beelzebub explained. "He had bartered with Alpha, giving him your kids in exchange, but Alpha refused to hold up his end of the bargain. So Lucifer tried to sweet-talk his way into changing Damian's mind. That kid loathes him. Damian only went along with Alpha's plans to make sure Luxina and Xavier stayed safe. He had no idea that Alpha would subject him to more injections to control him. And then the arena where he was nearly killed."

"I know all of that," I replied. "Is there anything else?"

"He tried to get Sophie to disobey orders as well," Beelzebub recounted. "But Alpha had a good grip on her. The last I saw of Lucifer, he entered Alpha's office and never came back out. Only Alpha knows where he is."

"Is he still loyal to Alpha?" I asked. "Or was it out of necessity to get Damian?"

"From my understanding, he was only hanging around and doing Alpha's bidding to get Damian," Beelzebub replied. "Alpha knew Lucifer would keep Damian away from anyone who would try to set him free because he wanted to take Damian away from everyone to keep him for himself."

"You said you had escaped from the Summit after he tossed everyone out," I resumed questioning. "Was that before or after he had gone to Purgatory?"

"It was before," Beelzebub clarified. "I didn't know about the attack on Uriel until she arrived, or about the attack on the Forsaken that was going to transpire."

"Uriel," I called out.

"Yes?" she responded, stepping forth.

"What is in Purgatory that Alpha could use? Why is he interested in it?" I asked.

"Human souls are the only thing I can think of, and then those like myself and the others who guard it and make sure no soul escapes without purification," she replied.

I started thinking hard. *Purgatory. Souls. Can Alpha eat souls? For power?*

"When the time comes, we go to Purgatory," I asserted aloud. "I have a feeling about it that I just can't shake. For now, we will stay here and train. We need numbers, and we need them to be able to fight. Once we are all on the same page, we begin the rescues."

Chapter Eight

"DO YOU EVER sleep?" Asmodeus asked, walking into the kitchen of Starfire's cottage.

"Hmph," I snorted while sitting at the table. "I will sleep when I am dead, apparently."

Asmodeus stared out the window, watching everyone training through the glass. I followed his eyes and saw he was staring at Damian.

"Have you even told him you're here yet?" I prodded.

Asmodeus looked down and laughed, shaking his head. "I don't know why I haven't told him," he replied, taking a seat next to me at the table. "I'm just glad to see he's alive and isn't stuck in that dungeon of Alpha's anymore."

I nodded. "Yeah, he didn't deserve any of that. Alpha is... he never did any of that to us, you know?"

"Right?" Asmodeus remarked. "Like, I mean, yeah, he abandoned us after the fall, and we all have some form of complex from that, but I never saw him actually torture us the way he did Damian. It was ruthless. He had no compassion for him. He had no love for him. It's like he hated

153

his existence but tolerated him so he could be his soldier or weapon."

"You said it there," I replied, pointing at him. "His weapon. He knew what Damian was. I think he knew what we all were, sometimes. It just doesn't make sense that someone as all-knowing as he is didn't know that there were people among his ranks who had power like we did. Lilith, thinking she hid some grand secret," I laughed.

"Do you remember much of anything the day you two escaped?" Asmodeus asked.

"Apparently, what I remember isn't true," I responded. "I remember seeing Damian off into safety and then getting stuck in the neck with a needle. When I turned around, it was Beelzebub. I killed him right then and there."

"Is that all?" Asmodeus pushed, perking up.

"I remember you ran up to help me after I was injected," I answered. "Did that happen?"

Asmodeus smiled. "That did happen. And then you went psycho."

"What do you mean?" I asked. "I thought we were attacked, and then I saw Sophie laughing with her black eyes."

"That didn't happen either," Asmodeus said. "I had carried you partway back inside when the other Forsaken joined us to help fight our way out. Sophie saw you and demanded to know what happened to you. When I was telling her what happened, you freaked, man. You started fighting us. I don't know what he jabbed into your neck, but you almost killed us all trying to fight us off."

"Maybe that's what Alpha was hoping for," I mused. "Kill off those of you who sided with me while I was thinking you were all monsters and attacking me. Two birds, one stone."

"Maybe," Asmodeus murmured while thinking. "What happened after you left?"

"I was flying through the air, and something struck me in the back of the head, or at least I think? I don't know anymore," I replied. "I careened to the ground and woke up in a faery glade. Queen Titania found me and led me to the Otherworld and had me bathe in the fountain to leach all of the injections from my body and restore my memories."

"Memories?" Asmodeus asked.

"Yeah, whatever hit me in the head gave me amnesia or something, paired with that last jab in my neck. I had forgotten about everything but the small talk I had with Damian before Lucifer had busted in," I explained. "I had forgotten all about the torture and the injections. Seeing Sophie. Seeing you and Mammon. Talking with Alpha and Lilith. Everything except that one talk with Damian. I don't know why, but my brain held onto that one."

"That's so crazy," Asmodeus sighed.

"How did you all escape after I went insane?" I asked with a chuckle.

"We had to fight our way out through monsters and other Forsaken who had chosen to side with Alpha," he replied. "It was a blood bath. A lot of good men died for the cause."

"I'm sorry. I should have been there to help," I declared.

"It's not your fault," Asmodeus insisted, patting my arm.

"Where did you go?" I asked.

"First, we went to the Watchers when we learned that Samyaza and Belial were the only two left in Stygia after Alpha had captured everyone else," he replied. "We then went to the Otherworld to find Damian. That boy is crafty. It took us a long time to finally find him, and it was after the loyalists had found him. We watched as he took them down with ease. Then, Alpha's monsters found us."

"Yeah, they found me, too," I shared.

"You should have seen Damian trying to save everyone in the Nightmares and Shadows black market. He didn't want anyone dying for him," Asmodeus declared. "He told us over and over, all the time, that he hated that people were dying for him. He summoned his icy powers and took a lot of the creatures out, but it seemed like if we cut the head from one, two more rose in its place. I finally yelled for him to get out of there, and he listened. Once he was gone, they were too. How did you handle the ones after you?" he asked.

"I burned the Seelie court down to the ground and took them with it," I replied with a smirk.

"Somehow," Asmodeus laughed, "I knew you were going to say that."

"I am in over my head, man," I huffed. "Like, everyone is looking to me for answers as if I know everything. I don't know any more than they do. All of this is new to me, just like it is to them. I am so overwhelmed. Yeah, sure, I have power that's nearly the strength of Alpha, but all of this," I motioned, pointing outside, "I am not ready for this."

"The universe wasn't built in a day, my friend," Asmodeus said, slapping my shoulder. "You will get the hang of everything. I mean, no pressure or anything, but we are all depending on you here. We didn't just pledge allegiance to you and pick a side because you promised us things or because we were afraid of Alpha. We pledged our allegiance because we do believe in you, Brother. We believe you will be a much better leader than our parents. Plus, I happened to have read some prophecies while being a dungeon master."

I laughed. "You read some prophecies?"

He laughed as well. "I did. I stole some books that Damian had been reading to see what he was studying up on. Like you believe, I also believe that Alpha knows more than what we think. Those books… those books helped me pick a side. Sure, I was always on Damian's side. I would follow that kid wherever. He is a helluva warrior. But you," Asmodeus stopped and cleared his throat.

"What about me, Brother?" I asked.

"I was still angry with you for not trying to help me after the darkness took over," he replied sheepishly. "I had a lot of anger and resentment toward you all, including Lilith and Alpha. I was bitter for years until Alpha showed up one day. He came with a promise that if we did what we were asked to do, he would restore us. Years went by, and he never held up his end of the bargain. Then the war happened, and we were told to wait on the sidelines. He told us none of you would fight fairly with us. And then he carried that boy into my life. Just a baby, crying and alone. Damian's cries irritated Alpha to the point where Alpha was just going to kill him. I took Damian and looked after him. I have looked after him for the past seven years as my own kid. He softened my hardened heart and taught me love again. When I learned he was one of the special beings called The Shining Ones, and you were too, I knew then that you were the ones to bring about the change we needed. I decided then I would help you escape from Alpha. The rest is history."

I swallowed hard. "I am sorry, Asmodeus. We had been so busy trying to be the perfect warriors, fighting the fight... I wanted to leave with you, you know?" I asserted, bowing my head. "When Lilith cast you out because you had completely lost your grace, I wanted to go with you. I could feel the darkness trying to overtake me. But she reminded me of Sophie and how I was the key piece to the whole thing. The whole damn game." I wiped my eyes as stray tears formed. "I never forgot about you, though, even though it seemed like everyone forgot about me and how I saved them and returned their light to them. I never forgot about those of you I didn't have the chance to save as well."

Asmodeus smiled. "Well, now you have, Brother," he replied, his silvery blue eyes sparkling. "And I owe you my life for it. I owe all of you my life for it."

"You don't owe me anything, Asmodeus," I said. "I had no idea that when people pledged their allegiance to me, all of this would happen. I don't deserve the praise and thanks for it."

"That right there," he replied, pointing at me. "That is why you are and will be a better god than Alpha. You don't take credit for anything. You are selfless and compassionate. You're not doing this for a power play. You're doing this to set things right again. To right the universe. To right so many wrongs done by Alpha. You are doing this for selfless reasons, whereas Alpha claimed his title of god to hold power over others."

"All I hear is people telling me I need to believe in myself," I sighed. "I don't know how to do that. I have been conditioned to fear my power for so long that I am always afraid of losing it and taking out people I care about."

"I think when you believe in yourself and have the confidence in yourself that all of these people keep telling you to have, all of the pieces will fall into place," he replied.

"I'm supposed to be in charge, and here I am whining to you about all of this," I laughed.

He laughed as well. "It's what makes you a good leader, Brother. You are humble, and you're not afraid to talk to people in confidence about your troubles and hardships. I am sure the others would be just as receptive to your self-doubt as I am and would tell you the same thing."

"Tell him what?" Gabriel asked, walking into the kitchen and snagging an apple from the table. "That he is ugly as all get out?" he asked, laughing and taking a bite from the apple.

"So this is where the party is," Raphael teased, walking in with Samael, Azazel, and Metatron following behind.

"What's going on?" Samael asked.

"Tell them," Asmodeus urged.

I sighed with a groan. "I was talking to Asmodeus about everything."

"Everything is pretty ambiguous," Azazel said, popping a grape in her mouth. "You gotta be more specific than that."

"About my lack of confidence with everything. Like, what the hell am I doing?" I replied.

"You, Brother," Samael began, "are saving us."

"How did I become the savior, though?" I asked. "Do you have confidence in me solely based on my power, or do you really believe in me?"

Samael smiled. "I bowed to you, Brother. I bow to no one."

"Good point," I laughed.

"We follow you because we really do believe in you," Metatron added. "It's not because we are choosing sides in fear of Alpha or fear of you. We aren't picking you because you have all these cool powers or anything like that. We are following you because you are you and always have been. You never bowed down to Alpha. You never listened to anything anyone has ever told you. You have done what you were going to do through choice alone. You saved us so many times when all hope was lost. We believe you will save us again."

"I needed that," I replied. "Good pep talk, everyone. Don't eat all the food," I joked.

I walked outside and sat on the porch of Starfire's cottage as the sound of swords clashing filled the air. All of these people here believed in me and needed me to help change things and restore the natural balance and order of the universe. Training for the final battle against Alpha had commenced, and everyone was preparing. In intervals, the sun would eclipse so the vampires and werewolves could train as well, since the vampires couldn't be out in the sunlight and the moon triggered the werewolves. I sat and watched the Nephilim train beside the angels as equals, and the Seelies and warlocks train in harmony. I couldn't help but smile as I watched them all when Reikal came running up to me.

"Here you go, sir," Reikal stated, holding the flaming sword out for me.

"And it's done?" I asked. "Whoever wields it as my foe cannot activate it?"

"Yep!" Reikal squeaked.

"Thank you," I replied, bowing my head.

"Anything for the savior of the universe," he obliged, bowing and taking off.

I returned my attention to everyone training. My eyes were trained on Damian and Luxina as they went hand-to-hand with one another. I wasn't the only one mesmerized by their lyrical movements. They danced around as if they had been sparring with one another since they were young. A blaze of fire followed them as their powers merged together in perfect balance. Their skin had begun to glow brighter and brighter each day as their powers grew stronger. I watched as Damian drew out his long sword and Luxina handled her two short, dueling swords as a pro. I had never been prouder of her than I was at that moment. I had held her back, keeping her safe instead of letting her flourish.

"You had one helluva trainer," I called out as I watched them.

"I sure did," she replied, smiling at Damian.

"Don't let her fool you," Damian said. "I'm really just hanging by a thread here. She is schooling me."

I laughed heartily. He was a good kid. My instincts were right about him. I wish I had the chance to watch him grow up as I did Luxina. Everything would have been so much simpler had Sophie and I just stayed together. Luxina dropped her dueling swords and pulled out some hand knives I had never seen before.

"That's not fair," Damian said. "Those things amplify your powers."

"Is someone afraid of losing?" she giggled.

If I had just said screw the risk, everything would be better. We could have found Damian together. We could have saved him from Alpha together without risking losing the other two.

"I like a challenge," Damian mused, cocking his mouth with a grin.

He looked like Xavier when he smiled like that. *Speaking of,* I thought to myself, *where is Xavier?*

Luxina pressed her fist into her chest and sank to the ground.

"Luxina," I called out, and I was at her side as quickly as I could get there. "What's wrong?" I demanded.

"I… I don't know," she choked out. "Xavier?"

Damian narrowed his eyes.

"Xavier? Is something wrong with him?" I asked.

She just stared into my eyes.

"Not right now," Damian hissed.

"He needs to know the truth," she shot back. She winced in more pain. "It might be that!"

"It might be what?" Tell me what?" I asked, confused.

"Help me carry her inside," Damian said, lifting her up under one of her arms.

I grabbed her other arm, and we led her into Starfire's cottage. We sat her down in the chair while Damian ran to get her some water.

"What do I need to know?" I demanded.

"There was a prophecy," she began.

"What prophecy?" I asked, shaking my head.

"The one about the birth of the three Shining Ones. Except the third Shining One was never supposed to exist. When I was created, the power between you and Mom split," she explained, clenching her jaw in pain. "I split in half. Part of me staying with you, the other part of me staying with mom."

"This doesn't explain anything about where Xavier is," I replied. *None of this makes any sense.*

"Xavier was me, Dad. Xavier was the dark half of my soul," she said, pressing her hand harder into her chest.

It all tumbled over and over in my head. "So, what happened?"

"I absorbed myself back," she replied quietly. "It happened a lot sooner than what we had hoped it would. But we had to save Damian from Alpha. He had hijacked his mind. It was the only way to save him."

"You sacrificed your brother to save him?" I seethed. *I didn't even get to spend time with Xavier to get to know him. This was exactly what Alpha had warned me about. Damian would destroy Xavier and make Luxina believe he was on our side when he had an agenda of his own. Was Alpha telling the truth for once?*

"Xavier sacrificed himself!" she yelled. "I sacrificed myself. You of all people should understand. Look at what you sacrificed for Mom! For a lie!"

"What do you mean a lie?" I demanded, irritated. *I am starting to get impatient with all of this.*

"Ask your mother," she growled. "It was all a lie. The search for the garden, your darkness leaching mom's light. None of it was true. Your mother played a power trip with both of you."

"Let me guess, he told you?" I asked, glaring at Damian. "It's lies, Luxina."

"He didn't tell me. He didn't have to. I know everything he knows. I can still hear the words echoing from the Dark Queen Mab's lips as she told him in the Otherworld," I snapped.

"Instead of arguing over what is the truth and what is not, how about we focus on what is happening to Luxina?" Damian interrupted. "You can hate me later, but right now, she needs help."

"Indeed, she does," Starfire said, walking into the room. "Something went wrong with the absorption."

"Xavier told me it's Alpha doing it," she cried out, grabbing her chest.

"We know the poison from the injections was removed from Luxina by the Watchers. What about Xavier?" Starfire asked.

"No," I replied. "He wasn't dying from them."

"He had already absorbed them," Damian reaffirmed. "After the first set he received, they no longer affected him."

"So, when she absorbed him, the poisons slowly began to re-enter her system," Starfire stated.

"Why didn't they burn away as mine did?" Damian asked.

"Because she was still transitioning and hadn't fully taken Xavier's soul into hers. The transition is complete now," Starfire explained. "That's why she can hear him now."

"Well, what do we do?" I asked. "We can't just let her writhe in pain."

"I'm afraid that's exactly what we have to do. She has to filter it out of her system," Starfire said, setting the manacles we had tied Damian up with on the table.

"What are those for?!" Damian shouted.

"You know what they are for," Starfire retorted. "Now, put them on her. Alpha will work her the same way he did you."

"No," Damian replied, outright refusing. "We are not chaining her up. I can handle her."

"Damian," Luxina croaked out. "Just do it."

"No," Damian barked. "You are nothing like I was. You won't hurt us."

She rose to her feet as if a machine was controlling her. We all took a step back from her. Her eyes were black, just as Sophie's were in all of my hallucinations.

"Everyone, leave the room," Damian demanded.

Starfire began to back away slowly from her when Luxina's head twisted in her direction.

"No, no, over here," Damian said, jumping into her line of sight. "Get her out, Incaendiel."

"I'm not leaving this room," I replied.

"Just do it!" Damian shouted.

I walked calmly over to Starfire and stood in front of her so she could leave the cottage. We inched slowly to the door until it was safe for her to walk out of it. I closed it behind me and peered through the window to see what was happening.

"Hey," Damian spoke softly. "Right here."

She returned her gaze to Damian, craning her neck like a possessed human, and stared at him. I watched him put his hands up as if to calm her down. She moved forward toward him, but he stood his ground as she walked closer. She reached her hand out slowly to touch his face, and he allowed her to do so.

"Your hair is white now," she mused.

She looked around the room. "Where did Incaendiel go?" she asked.

"He escorted Starfire from the room," Damian replied nervously.

"Why? I wasn't going to hurt her," she declared, walking around the room and touching everything.

"Luxina?" Damian asked. "Luxina, can you hear me?"

"Come with me, Damian," she cooed calmly. "Come with me to where it is safe."

"I'm right where I need to be," Damian responded.

"Safe?" she laughed. "Do you think you are safe here? Safe with Luxina? She killed your brother. She took my Xavier from me, and she will take you from me as well."

"Sophie?" Damian questioned.

"Yes," she breathed. "It's me. It's mother."

"You're not my mother," Damian sneered. "You aren't anyone's mother."

"Don't talk to me like that!" Her voice echoed off the walls with a deafening screech.

I opened the door and walked in. She watched me close the door behind me and advance to Damian's side.

"Incaendiel, you look so different now. Brighter, glowing," she whispered. "Why did you leave me?"

"I didn't leave you, Sophie," I replied. "You refused to go with me. Alpha has brainwashed you."

"Alpha is our one true father, and no one should come before him," she stated. "Why can't you see that?" her voice was pleading.

"No, Sophie. That is one thing that isn't true. We are our own gods and far more superior to him," I declared.

Her skin began to sizzle, and steam rose off as flames burst to the surface.

"She was more important to you than anyone else in the end. Even more important than my precious boy." She lifted her hand, and a flaming fireball formed. "I tried to tell you. I tried to make you see. But you refused to believe that your precious little baby was evil."

"She is not evil!" Damian yelled.

Luxina's head jerked to look at him. "She has you under a spell, son. She will kill you in the end, too. You're nothing but a monster to her."

"I know her better than what you think," Damian spat. "And she would never call me that."

She cackled, throwing her head back. "You are so naive," she muttered. "Alpha was right. You're nothing. You're weak. She has turned you into a mindless drone."

She tossed the fireball in her hand at Damian and struck him in the chest, knocking him to the ground.

Another fireball formed in her hand, and she looked at me while I stood there calmly.

"You're not even going to fight back?" she asked, and then motioned from head to toe. "Too afraid of harming your precious cargo?"

"I don't want to hurt you, Sophie," I replied, walking closer to her.

"Liar!" she screamed. "If you had never wanted to hurt me, you wouldn't have made a choice for me all those years ago. You would have come with me to the Summit, or I would have stayed with you at the Glade."

"Mother is to blame for that," I stammered. "She lied to us, Sophie. She lied to lay claim to power in the little game she played with Alpha. And it just goes around and around, and it always claims us in the end. She wanted to control us. She needed to keep us apart so our power wouldn't overpower her own."

"No," she whimpered.

"Yes," I insisted.

I stood before her with pleading eyes. I wrapped my arms around her and squeezed her tightly.

"I love you so much, Sophie," I breathed. "I never stopped loving you. And when I thought you loved another more than me, my love grew for you in leaps and bounds. Come to me, my love. Come and be with our children."

"Do you love him as your own?" she asked, barely a whisper.

"I was the one who saved him," I assured.

While I kept her distracted, Damian slipped the manacles onto her wrists. She screamed in fury and crumpled to the floor, out cold.

"Quick," I urged. "Get her tied to the chair so she can't hurt anyone or herself. There's no telling who she will wake up as."

We picked her up and sat her in the chair. Damian worked quickly, getting her bound in ropes, and then took a seat across from her. His face was a mess of worry.

"It will be ok, Damian," I assured him. "She will come back."

"Will she?" he whimpered. "When Alpha took over me, I know it lasted forever before I was myself again. He injected Xavier with so many different things; there is no telling what all he put into him, and it didn't even phase him. He was like a golem of her."

"I'm telling you," I repeated. "She will be fine."

Luxina started to slowly come to, and when she had shaken the haze, she stared straight ahead at Damian, who sat with his head bent down and resting in his hands, deep in thought. He looked up, and the kid looked as if he were hundreds of years old, with all the worry and exhaustion settling in.

"Come back to me, Luxina," he whispered.

"I'm here for a while, so get used to it," she snarled instead. "I don't understand why you care so much about her."

"You never will," he replied, annoyed.

"Then, explain it to me," she urged snidely. "I have all the time in the world."

"The only person in this room who would understand is him," Damian said, pointing at me. "He loved you. He loved you more than life itself. He died and came back to life for you. I watched it happen."

"So, you would die for her?" she queried.

"Over and over and over, again and again, and again," Damian affirmed. "She saw me for more than a weapon. She saw me for more than just a chess piece. She loved me without condition. You... you chose Alpha over every person that loved you or that you loved. Luxina, she defied Alpha. You know she did. You were punished for it."

She stared at him, and you could see the thoughts running through her head. Unlike my connection with Sophie, I couldn't read her thoughts at all since she was being channeled through Luxina. There was some sort of block up. And then I heard her voice.

He is nothing like me, Sophie thought within. *How can he be so much like Incaendiel?*

"Because he knows right from wrong right now," I interrupted aloud. "Alpha is injecting you with nothing more than mind-controlling substances. He has gained your trust in him through lies. You weren't strong enough to fight it. You aren't at fault for that. But you can't blame innocents for that. Luxina, she is innocent in all of this. She is your daughter. That should mean something to you."

"There's nothing but cloudiness in my mind. All I can think of is hating her," she replied through gritted teeth.

"That is Alpha thinking through you," Damian declared. "I know more than ever what that feels like."

"Save me," she implored. "Incaendiel, save me!"

I will leave with you this time. I promise!

I went to leave the room.

"No," Damian demanded, halting me in my steps. "This is a trick."

A deep, guttural laugh emerged from Luxina's throat.

"Oh, you were always the smart one," Luxina remarked in a raspy voice. "Did you know that at any moment I could just simply kill her?"

Damian's eyes widened.

"I love these little games we play too much to do that," she laughed.

Damian stood from his chair, kicking it across the room. I stood in shock, unable to move or do anything.

"You give her back," he demanded, yelling into her face.

"Tsk-tsk. Always with that temper," she replied coolly. "I was so sure she would never save you from me that you were mine in finality. But you loved her so much. You came back for her. Do you think she loves you as much as you love her?"

"If she didn't love me, she would have never tried as hard as she did to save me from you," Damian responded quietly.

"That is what you think or what you know? Could it be that she was using you as her own little weapon?" she asked, a smile spreading widely across her face.

"Don't listen to him, Damian," I ordered. "He will manipulate you and will use anything he thinks will make you weak."

"Luxina is already his weakness and has been since he learned who she was. Always fighting how he felt around her. Wanting her and her precious Xavier to stay together. I hold in my hand the only thing that will destroy him," she rasped. "How do you save her when you couldn't even save yourself? Join me, Damian."

"I will die before I join you," Damian sneered.

"Then have fun rescuing your precious Luxina from the darkness," she taunted.

Her head slumped forward, and once again, she was unconscious.

"Luxina?" Damian asked, running to her.

He grabbed her face in his hands, gently shaking it.

"Luxina?" he demanded with growing worry in his voice. "Luxina!" he pleaded. "Luxina, please. I can't do this alone!" he sobbed into his arm. "Incaendiel, what do we do?"

"All we can do is wait for her to wake up," I breathed. "I have no clue what to do from here. She has to find her way back."

"And what if she can't find her way back?" he implored. "What if she is stuck in the darkness forever?"

I was silent. I didn't know how to answer that.

"You know she is afraid of the dark, right?" he asked, stroking her face. "She was so scared of being engulfed in the dark. She didn't know that she was the brightest light in the world."

"She was my light," I choked out. "She saved me when I was left behind by everyone. If it hadn't been for her, I wouldn't be here right now. She was my saving grace."

"Yeah," he cried. "She was mine too."

I wiped a straggling tear rolling down my cheek. "Let's get her up into a bed and untied from this chair," I spoke softly.

"Should we untie her?" Damian asked.

"By the time she wakes up, all of those things should be burned from her system. I think that's why it happened as quickly as it did, because of how her power was growing. It was Alpha's last trick up his sleeve," I replied.

"Ok," he murmured.

He untied her and scooped her up in his arms, and carried her upstairs, still whispering her name, trying to get her to wake up.

I slumped down in a chair and ran my hand through my hair. "What the hell am I supposed to do now?" I whispered. "What am I supposed to believe?"

"There's nothing you can do," Starfire replied, walking through the door. "She has to wake up on her own, like you said."

"Alpha told me this all was going to happen. That Damian would find a way to destroy Xavier and make Luxina think he was on our side when he is just manipulating people for his own gain," I said quietly.

"Do you really think that boy is lying about everything?" Starfire asked, raising an eyebrow.

"That's what it feels like," I huffed. I ran my hands through my hair in frustration. "I don't know what to believe. I don't know what is real and what is manipulation. He told me other things too, you know? Things that actually make sense."

"Like what?" Starfire asked, taking a seat in a chair across from me.

"Like Lilith being the one that kept us away from Alpha to foster a hatred of him and telling us he abandoned us instead," I replied, wringing my hands together.

Starfire was quiet.

"It's true, isn't it?" I asked.

"Yes," Starfire declared. "Not the whole truth, but it's true."

"He sprinkles so many truths in together with lies, and it's so hard to tell which is truth and which is a lie," I sighed.

"I cannot tell you what to believe and what not to believe. That is your cross to bear," Starfire replied. "I know this whole thing isn't something parents should put their children through."

"So do I just keep Damian at arm's length until I know he's really not the mastermind behind the end of the world?" I asked.

"I can't answer that either," Starfire spoke honestly. "But I can tell you that soon, the truth will be revealed about Damian. And it's a bombshell of a truth as well."

"What do I do about Sophie?" I asked. "I know she said she would come with me this time, but with Alpha behind this all, what if it's just another trap for me to be captured again?"

"What does your heart tell you?" she asked in return.

"It tells me that I need to find her and Lilith," I breathed.

"Then that's what you do," she declared. "I will watch over these two. You go save them while you can."

"Let them know if they ask about me, ok?" I asked.

"I will be sure to," she replied. "You going the old-fashioned way, or are you going to use that new power of yours to get there?"

"What do you mean?" I wondered.

"You used a portal to get here," she responded. "Are you going to fly there or portal there?"

"Portal would be faster," I replied.

"Good," she stated. "Now, hurry back!"

Chapter Nine

I WAVED MY hands around like I had done in the Summit and thought of Mother. I pulled up a portal to the Summit. As I looked through the window, I could see Lilith waiting in the throne room. I stepped through the portal, and it vanished behind me.

"Incaendiel?" she whispered, walking over to me. "What are you doing here?"

"I am here to take you to safety," I replied in hushed tones.

"There is nowhere you can take me where I will be safe," she declared.

"Yes, there is," I assured, looking around for Alpha's minions. "But you just have to come with me."

"I was a fool, you know," she remarked. "To think that Alpha still loved me." She began to laugh, and then it turned into a whimpering sob. "He just wants to destroy me."

"I won't let that happen," I replied, extending my hand out to her.

There was a noise in the corridor.

"They're coming," she gasped, wide-eyed. "You have to leave and leave me here. They will kill you."

I smiled devilishly. "They can try, Mother."

"Your eyes," she remarked. "I have never seen them glow like that before…"

The room was filled with Forsaken, who were the loyalists who chose Alpha.

"Well, well. Back so soon?" one of them asked.

"Python? Is that you?" I asked, peering closely at them.

"It is, Brother," he laughed, raising his sword.

"Why are you still loyal to Alpha after everything he has done?" I questioned.

"Why not?" he snickered. "We can be as bad as we want without any repercussions with him. Unlike Mother," he sneered, looking in her direction. "Mother abandoned us when the darkness took over us."

"You were doing hideous things to the humans," she cried, pointing an accusing finger at him.

"Nothing as bad as Alpha will do to you," he replied, stepping toward her.

I stepped in between them.

"You will have to go through me, I'm afraid," I growled. I could see the reflection of myself in his eyes. My eyes blazed like fiery pits.

Python took a step back for a moment, and a look of unease settled on his face.

"When did you get that power?" he asked, taking a step back.

"I have always had it," I glowered. "I just had to find a way to set it free."

Fire blazed to the surface of my skin. For once, I was no longer afraid to use it. I somehow knew I could wield it without it causing damage like before.

"Your eyes," he whispered, visibly shaken.

"Get used to them," I snarled. "I am God now."

They all rushed at me at once, and I lifted my hand. A blinding white light erupted from it, and they were turned to ash mid-step. I heard more footsteps coming down the corridor.

"Are you going to come with me, or are you going to stay to be absorbed by Alpha?" I asked, turning to face Lilith.

"I see Barbelo has been set free within you," Lilith commented.

She reached out her hand, and I grabbed it. I led her through the varying hallways off from the throne room, taking down each person who popped out to try and stop me.

"Lilith!" Alpha bellowed from the throne room.

"Oh no!" she whimpered as I pulled her along.

We made it outside into the Summit, and there were thousands of angels, Watchers, and Forsaken waiting for me who had sided with

Alpha. I pulled the flaming sword from my side, and it leapt to life instantly.

"Where did you get that?" Lilith demanded.

"It's a long story," I replied, as I walked unafraid in front of her.

Those in the forefront of the gathered loyalists who had drawn their swords took a step back. They glanced nervously from me to Lilith and then among themselves.

"Let us through," I growled, staring each of them in the eyes.

"It's our orders," Baraquiel refuted quietly.

"Screw your orders," I hissed, blazing hotter. "Do you really want to challenge me right now?"

"No," Baraquiel cried. "But we must obey Alpha."

"Don't hurt them," Lilith begged, grabbing my shoulder. The fire from my skin singed her hands, but she didn't let go.

I looked at each of them who stood against me and huffed, "Fine!"

I raised the sword in the air, and a blinding light leapt from the tip of the blade. Their swords clattered to the ground, and everyone in front of me grabbed their eyes, screaming.

"It burns!" one shouted.

"I can't see anything!" another yelled.

I took the moment to grab Lilith by the hand and towed her toward the garden's gate.

"Where are we going?" she demanded. "That leads to nowhere! The garden is gone!"

"For you all, maybe," I retorted.

We ran through the gate and entered the garden. Lilith looked around, puzzled.

"How did you do that?" she questioned. "No one has been able to access the garden for a while now."

"That's because it doesn't belong to the Summit anymore," I answered. "We gave it back to the fey as a peace treaty, and they joined our side against Alpha."

As we walked through the garden, sprites and brownies who were lounging in the sun immediately ran for cover.

"Incaendiel!" a sweet voice called out. "Oh, and you have company." Queen Titania walked up to us, smiling at me and then frowning at Lilith. "Why are you here? And with her?" she demanded.

"We were escaping the Summit," I explained. "We needed safe passage or else the war would have started without everyone chipping in."

She giggled. "I see," she replied. "And her?" she mused, glaring at Lilith.

"I am taking her to Lightshade to protect her from Alpha," I replied.

"Why on earth would you need to protect her from Alpha?" she questioned, narrowing her eyes suspiciously at Lilith.

"Because he is reabsorbing his power," I answered. "We can't let him absorb her and become too powerful for us."

Queen Titania laughed. "Oh my child," she cooed. "She still hasn't told you everything yet. But okay. I will allow it."

I looked at Lilith questioningly, and she averted her eyes from mine.

"If you follow this path," Queen Titania explained, "it will lead you to the portal to Lightshade."

I bowed to the queen. "Thank you," I replied.

"Anything for my favorite Shining One," she cooed and disappeared.

We walked the path the queen had instructed us to follow in utter silence. I had questions for Lilith now. What did Queen Titania mean by Lilith not telling me everything yet? We came to the portal quicker than I thought we would. I held my hand out in front of me.

"Go ahead," I urged. "You first."

Lilith hesitated, then stepped through the portal. We were just outside the entrance of Lightshade, where Starfire stood waiting.

"Hello, Lilith," she greeted. "I have been waiting to finally meet you. We have much to discuss, you and I."

She opened the force field around Lightshade and motioned for Lilith to walk through.

"Aren't you coming with me?" Lilith asked, glancing over at me.

"No, I have one more person to rescue," I replied.

"Sophie," she responded with a smile.

"Yes, Sophie."

"Good luck with her, son," she remarked. "Alpha has her in his clutches, and she is far gone."

"I know. I have spoken with her. She is ready this time," I declared. "Now, go."

Lilith walked with Starfire into Lightshade, and the force field went back up. I knew where I had to go to retrieve Sophie. She was at Chernobyl. I opened my wings and took off. It wasn't as quick as using portals, but I honestly didn't have the energy to raise one, so my wings were the only other option. Chernobyl came into view, and I soared overhead. It looked empty enough. I didn't see any of the creatures Alpha had chasing Damian and me, so I landed outside the fortress.

"I should have portaled in," I muttered as I walked through the field.

I entered the building through the giant hole I had made in the sidewall and made my way through the maze of halls. Forsaken popped up everywhere, and I had to obliterate them. There was no conversation to be had with them as made apparent in the Summit. Occasionally, I would run into one of those creatures Alpha had made, just roaming the halls like a guard dog. I began to grow impatient and worried about Sophie. My slow meandering turned into a jog and then a sprint. I stopped long enough to open doors and peer inside just to find them empty. My patience was wearing thin along with my confidence.

"Sophie? Sophie?" I called out as I ran the halls of Chernobyl. "Sophie!"

As I rounded a corner, I heard familiar voices talking, but I couldn't decipher which room they came from.

"You came back after all!"

"Hello, Alpha."

That sounds just like Luxina, I thought. I left Luxina with Damian. How did she get here? Rage built within me. Alpha told me he was using us all. This was their plan. Damian brought her back to Alpha after all. I knew I couldn't trust that little shit. I should have left him for the creatures to eat.

"What is she doing here?" another voice shrieked.

Sophie! I started busting doors one by one, listening to them talk.

"Ah, Sophie. My favorite little angel. Your job is done. I no longer need you. You brought me exactly what I needed. Little Luxina here."

No! I busted another door down. Nothing. *Where in the hell are they?*

"You used me to get my daughter?" she asked, confused. "I thought you needed me."

So it wasn't Damian after all. I sighed in relief. I needed to trust that kid more than I do. I was so conflicted about how I felt about the kid. On one hand, I loved him like he was my own, but then Alpha would sneak into my head and make me feel like I couldn't trust him at all.

"No, Sophie. I no longer need you. It's time for you to go back to sleep and Anniel to come forth," Alpha declared.

I hit the ground with a searing pain shooting through my skull. I could hear Sophie scream out in the same pain. My mind was flooded with memories. Memories that I had never recalled or possibly had been altered. Her name had been Anniel since we were created. My mind seemed to merge with hers, and every single memory she had erased became one with my own. She was Alpha's spy the whole time, unless she was human. She was his first experiment before Damian.

I scrambled to my feet and used her eyes as a guide to where she was. I opened the door just as Alpha snapped his fingers to disappear.

"Daddy!" Luxina shouted and then was gone.

"Sophie?" I yelled as I ran over to her. "Sophie."

She sat with her head in her hands, rocking back and forth. "We both know that's not my real name," she sobbed.

I was silent for a moment. "Anniel," I breathed.

She looked up at me with red-rimmed eyes. "Incaendiel, who am I? What am I? What have I done?" she cried.

I knelt down in front of her and wiped the tears from her face. "You did what you were commanded to do. Just like Damian."

"How do I stop it?" she implored.

"Come with me," I said, holding my hand out. "We can fix this."

"How?" she demanded, torn in two by her emotions.

"Starfire," I replied. "She has what we need to fix you. To fix this."

"I don't deserve to be fixed," she whimpered. "I have done terrible things for Alpha."

"He made you do them!" I insisted, wiping the tears once more that streamed down her face.

She looked up at me with pain written in her eyes. "There's more than what little you have seen."

"What do you mean?" I asked.

"I was never locked in that tower. It was a fake memory," she replied. "I was never with Lucifer."

"I don't understand," I declared, shaking my head. "What?"

"I was never with Lucifer. It was a fake memory," she reiterated. "I never had an affair."

"Then," I began. "Wait." I was the one confused now. "That means…"

"Damian isn't his son," she replied.

"Damian isn't his son," I repeated.

"No," she stated. "Damian was born when the portal opened, and Alpha snatched him. Luxina was born when it closed and was split into two. Damian is your son. Damian is our son."

"Damian is… my son?" I stammered, sinking to the floor.

She nodded. "He is why I have stuck by Alpha. Alpha promised to let him go if I did what I was told. Lucifer promised me he would let him go. Lucifer," she sneered and squeezed her eyes shut. "After we raised the portal, I had my will back. I remember. I willingly came back to Alpha to get Damian back. But he would sleep my memories whenever I was Sophie so that I couldn't tell anyone the truth. And now… I led Luxina right to him, being his little puppet. I'm Alpha's real monster."

I pulled her into my arms. "We are all Alpha's puppets. We just didn't know we were. It's been a game from the beginning," I replied. "But this time, we will win."

"Will we?" she asked. "I know things since he left me awake."

"What do you know?" I inquired.

"I know about Adam," she responded.

"Who the hell is Adam?" I asked, but she didn't answer. I asked another question, "And Lucifer has been a spy for Alpha this whole time?"

She nodded. "Since the fall, Lucifer has been the one who has been in Alpha's ear. He is Alpha's right hand, and I was his left," she cried.

"Who all are really loyalists to him and spying on us?" I urged. "Who else is there?"

"And Mother, Lilith, Omega, whatever you want to call her," she snarled. "She can't be trusted at all. She's been playing this game with Alpha the whole time. The fall was a ruse. He wanted to weed out those who weren't loyal to him. There was an imbalance of power, and it wasn't because there was not enough darkness and too much light. It was because we existed. We had to be separated, but Alpha couldn't just kick you out without a reason and make you an adversary. So he and his mother concocted the fall. They knew one of us would stay, and one of us would fall."

"How do you know all of this?" I asked. "The vision you had?"

"No," she breathed. "That was a lie. I never had a vision. Omega and Alpha told me to tell you that." She buried her face in her hands.

I held her in my arms as I carried her outside of Alpha's fortress. I flew her back to Lightshade as she kept her face buried in my chest the entire time. Starfire stood at the entrance as we arrived.

"I had a feeling I should be here," she said, winking. "Anniel?" she asked.

"You… you know my name? Anniel questioned.

"Of course, I do. I know everything. I'm just not allowed to reveal what's not meant for me to reveal," Starfire replied. "Let's get you in Lightshade and make sure Alpha never hurts you again."

Starfire opened her force field and led us back to her cottage. When we were inside and the door closed for privacy, I sat Anniel down in a nice, soft chair. She looked horrible in the light. She indeed had been tortured by Alpha, much like Damian had been. She saw me looking her over and hid her face in shame.

"I must look terrible," she stuttered, trying to fix her hair and wipe her face.

"What did he do to you?" I asked, kneeling in front of her and examining her closely.

She had bruises and lashes all over her.

"I was punished for allowing you and Damian to escape and not telling Alpha about the plans," she replied softly. She looked me in the eyes. "You two needed to escape him before he turned you into me."

"Should we wait until all of the injections he has used on her are out of her system before we give her the potion?" I asked Starfire.

"There's no need," Anniel replied quietly. "I haven't had injections in a long, long time."

"He did his damage a long time ago to her," Starfire added. "What he was doing to the kids was different than what he did to her. He needed to control her. He wanted to turn them into his own personal creations."

I held her bottle of disenchanting potion. "This potion is agonizing," I told Anniel.

"That's a lot coming from you," Anniel replied nervously, eyeing the bottle.

"We can wait until you feel better," I offered.

She shook her head. "We need to do it and get it over with. We need to be at full power to go up against him. That can be any time now."

"She is right, Incaendiel," Lilith said, walking into the room. "It *can* be at any time."

"Mother..." Anniel gasped. "What are you doing here?" she sneered, standing to her feet.

"Incaendiel rescued me from the Summit," Lilith cooed with a smile.

"Why?" Anniel uttered angrily. "She's just as deceitful as Alpha is. She doesn't deserve to be rescued! She chooses to do what she does. She wasn't forced into it."

"I had to," I defended. "Alpha planned to reabsorb her to be more powerful. Even though she has been mendacious to us throughout the years, we cannot allow Alpha to become more powerful. Without her, he doesn't have nearly half of his powers."

Anniel glared at her in contempt. "Can she go somewhere else? I don't want to be around her."

"As you wish, Sophie," Lilith replied, with tight lips.

"You know that's not my name," Anniel barked. "How long did you go along with Alpha in concealing my real identity?"

Lilith pursed her lips. "Fine. As you wish, Anniel."

Anniel flinched.

"So, you did know?" I exclaimed angrily.

"I'm going to my room," Lilith huffed and left the room, heading upstairs to the many rooms.

My temper began to flare, and I had to reel it in. I inhaled deeply and exhaled the frustration out.

"I see some things have changed," Anniel said with a half-smile. "You can control it now."

I smiled. "I can. The kids know how to control it as well."

"Even Damian?" she asked, cocking an eyebrow. "I know his powers were out of control when he was locked up."

"Yes, even Damian," I answered proudly. "Speaking of, where's Damian?" I inquired, looking at Starfire.

"I'm surprised you didn't run into him at Alpha's lair. He raced as fast as he could there to save Luxina," she replied.

Panic rose in my chest. "You stay here with Starfire," I told Anniel. "I will make sure he is safe."

"There is no need, Incaendiel," Starfire assured. "I believe he just returned."

"Are you sure?" I insisted, pacing the floor. "He could be taken just like her. It could be a trap for him as well! We can't lose them both back to Alpha! We just got him free! I can't lose my-" I stopped myself from finishing the sentence.

Starfire smiled. "Well, I see the truth has been revealed in other topics as well," she murmured, glancing at Anniel.

Anniel smiled and nodded. "Alpha didn't take my memories away when he left me this time. I could tell the truth about everything. He didn't sleep me into being Sophie."

"Well, it's about time Incaendiel knew the truth," Starfire cheered.

"Now we just have to figure out how to tell Damian the truth ourselves," I murmured, frowning.

"Tell me the truth about what?" Damian asked, walking through the door.

I froze, mouth agape. I wasn't expecting him to walk in on the tail end of the conversation.

"About your mother," Starfire replied for me.

Damian glanced around me and scowled when his eyes landed on Anniel. "What about her, other than she is here when less than a day has passed since she took over Luxina's mind for Alpha?" he spat.

"That there is a lot more that we didn't know about her until now," I replied sympathetically. "That even I didn't know about."

"Like what?" he sneered. "Oh! Let me guess. She was tortured by Alpha, and that's why she is such a bi—"

"Watch how you talk about your mother," I ordered, pointing my finger at him.

"You are a completely different person when you aren't around her," Damian snapped, glaring at me. "She makes you weak."

"Now, who sounds like Alpha?" I sneered back.

His glare toward me deepened at the comparison. "Do you even know where Luxina is?" he demanded. "Or were you too busy trying to save your precious Sophie?"

"I didn't get there in time," I replied solemnly. "I found them just as Alpha whisked her way. But we will get her back!"

"What a pathetic excuse," Damian retorted, scrunching his face in disapproval at me.

"Hey!" Anniel interjected, grabbing his arm. "Don't say that about him!"

"You shut up," Damian sneered, shaking off her grasp. "You're the last person who should be speaking right now. You don't have the right to talk to me."

"Don't speak to your mother like that," I commanded, walking closer to him.

Damian began to glow as his anger triggered his powers. "Had you been here instead of running off to save the love of your life, you could have stopped Luxina."

"Boys!" Starfire shouted, but it was already too far into an argument to stop.

"Hey!" I defended, my anger starting to boil beneath the surface. "She's *my* daughter. I care. I cared about her when no one else even knew she existed, including you! I spent a long time trying to make sure she was safe, and as I recall, you were the one who initially helped Alpha take her. So, back off!"

Damian backed up a little but still held his ground. "That's what you see me as still, isn't it?" he demanded. "I'm still Alpha's little monster to you."

"Everyone needs to calm down!" Starfire shouted, raising her hands in a slow, steadying motion. "You're going to both erupt with your powers and burn my cottage to the ground."

Damian and I stared one another down. I glanced up and caught my reflection in the mirror hanging on the adjacent wall. My entire body was a fiery glow, and my eyes were two bottomless pits of fire. I looked like a tyrant who was staring down a child. I returned my attention to him, and I could see that even though he was standing up to me, he was absolutely terrified of me. His eyes were intense and determined, but I could see the fear in them, wondering if I would smite him. I exhaled and felt the energy that had been rising during the argument taper off. Once I had returned to my normal temperament, I could see the glow start to taper from his body, and he returned to normal as well.

I sighed. "You were never a monster, Damian," I replied softly, realizing I must look and sound like Alpha was to him for all of these years. "You were manipulated like we all were. Just a piece in his game of chess with Lilith."

"You hardly know what manipulation feels like," Damian scoffed. "You spent a few months with Alpha in your head in that dungeon. I spent my whole life with him in mine."

"It's been my whole life, too!" I refuted. "It's been both our whole lives," I defended, motioning to Anniel.

"What did he do to her besides lock her in a tower?" he sneered.

"He didn't keep her in the tower," I explained. "Those were fake memories. He has been manipulating her to be his spy, his weapon, and his toy just like you ever since the fall. Hell, he even made us forget what her real name is."

"Whatever," he huffed, shaking his head. "Any excuse to make her seem like a damsel. Any excuse to make a pity party for both of you." He waved me off with a flick of his wrist.

"Do you really think I want a pity party?" I hissed. "Do you really think my one goal in life is for everyone to feel sorry for me? Oh, poor Incaendiel. Useless Incaendiel. Lilith's little pet."

"Then what did he possibly keep from you that was earth-shattering or so enraging? What did he take from you? Memories? Time?" he demanded.

I didn't know what else to say. It just came out. "You, son. He kept you."

Damian narrowed his eyes at me. "You're not my father," he refuted.

"Yes," Anniel interjected, standing up. "He is. The whole Lucifer being your father was a fake memory that Lucifer and Alpha planted in my memory jar."

"I don't believe you!" he screamed, near tears, and looking at Starfire.

Starfire nodded her head. "It's true, Damian," she assured.

"Then why didn't you tell me?" he cried, his eyes glowing ice blue from rage.

"It wasn't my—"

"Oh, don't give me the whole it wasn't your place thing or that you weren't allowed to," he huffed. "That's bullshit. You could have told me."

"Damian," I began, placing my hand on his shoulder.

"No!" he yelled, shrugging my hand off his shoulder. "Just because you just found out I am your son doesn't mean you get to start treating me kinder or differently. It doesn't change anything."

"I have never treated you any other way," I replied. "The few times I did was Alpha in my head, trying to make me believe you are just playing us. I saved you from Alpha! I made sure you got away before he could kill you. It wasn't all Asmodeus. It was me, too! It was me and your mother who made sure you escaped that hell he kept you in."

"This is too much too soon," he huffed and walked toward the staircase.

"Where are you going?" I asked.

"To lie down," he rasped as he climbed the steps. "And don't bother me either."

My heart felt like it was going to tear from my chest. Just like I had been rejected by Xavier when I first met him, Damian was now rejecting me. *Had Luxina not been left with me the way she was, would she even love me the way she does now? Alpha abandoned us and rejected those of us who fell. I had been rejected by Anniel every single incarnation she went through over thousands of years, and then I was rejected by my own children. Maybe I wasn't meant to be accepted in love. Maybe I was supposed to be alone. Maybe I wasn't meant to exist with a family or as part of something as grand as what I had been presented with.*

"None of that is true, and you know it," Anniel cooed.

"No privacy," I replied with a half-smile.

"Just give him time," she urged. "He has been through the ringer with Alpha, trying to attain his love as a parent figure, just to be used. Finding out everything he had ever known was a complete lie is a lot for him to take in, just as it was for us."

I sighed. She was right. But I still felt like a failure as a father for not being there to stop Luxina from doing what she did. How could she have walked right into Alpha's trap like that? She was smarter than that.

"I know you two have a lot to catch up on, and this is all terrible timing for the past few days," Starfire interjected. "But we need to get Anniel full power now," she said, holding the last bottle of elixir.

Anniel shifted uneasily in her seat. *What if this is Alpha's plan?* she wondered in her head.

"Could it be part of his plan?" I asked Starfire for her.

"Could what be part of his plan?" Starfire asked back.

"Her taking this and being all powerful, and then him taking back control of her?" I asked.

"Just trust me," Starfire replied with a wink. "Everything will be fine."

I took the elixir from Starfire and walked it over to Anniel. "Are you ready?" I asked.

"No," she replied with a deep exhale. "But I don't have a choice now, do I?"

I shook my head. "It's the only way to overcome Alpha and to defeat him."

"You said it was agonizing," she stated, taking the bottle from my hand.

"It felt like death," I answered.

"I died once," she mused. "So long ago, but it still feels like yesterday."

"Sadly," I began. "It feels worse than that."

Anniel inhaled a heavy breath and exhaled it slowly. She uncorked the bottle and lifted it in the air. "Cheers," she remarked and drank the bottle down.

Her face pinched from the bitter taste that hit her tongue.

"Bleck!" she groaned. "You didn't tell me it tasted bad, too." She smacked her lips and swallowed harder, trying to get the taste out of her mouth, and waited. "So when—" was all she got out before she doubled over, heaving and screaming. She hit the floor and rolled side to side while holding her stomach and retching. Steam began to rise from her skin, and water droplets dripped from her as she began to crawl in between gasps. "I can't control it," she hissed. "Get out of here!" She erupted into flames like I had.

"It's ok," I reassured her. "This is normal."

"No, it's not!" she screamed as her fire burned hotter and brighter.

Something was wrong. The way she was burning was different with her than it had been with me. The flames grew larger and stronger, setting the floor and furniture on fire.

"Why is it doing that?!" I demanded, looking at Starfire.

"She is the last one to take it," she replied. "The final puzzle piece is sliding into place."

"Incaendiel!" Anniel screamed. "I am going to explode!"

I grabbed Starfire's hand and pulled her close to me while wrapping my wings around her. A ball of white light and fiery flames erupted and knocked us to the ground. The windows shattered, and the walls of the room were blown out. Anniel screamed as her fire raged in her.

"Let me go!" Starfire ordered, trying to push me away. "You are about to finish activating as well!"

Starfire scrambled from my clutches from underneath me and clamored out of the cottage.

202

"What do you mean finish activating?" I shouted.

A searing pain that was worse than the elixir I took tore through my body. I howled in agony as white flames scorched every inch of my skin. The flames began to set the side of the cottage I lay in on fire. Damian came bounding down the stairs as the flames reached the upper floor.

"What the hell is going on!" he demanded before hitting the ground as well in screams.

He began to glow the same white, fiery hue that Anniel was emitting. Tendrils of his flames finished catching the rest of the bottom floor of the cottage on fire, and soon, the whole place was ablaze. The top floor began to cave in.

Are we dying? Damian thought, stricken with panic.

I don't know! I replied.

I heard someone yell my name.

"No!" Starfire yelled, refusing them access to the cottage. "It will kill you! Get back! Reikal! Are you all ready?"

"Yes," the young warlock shouted.

"Now!" she screamed.

Anniel, Damian, and I all released a bellowing yell before we exploded.

Chapter Ten

IT WAS AS if I were holding my eyes shut, but I wasn't. I felt like pure light, pure energy. I had no sense of hearing, no sense of sight, but it was like I could see and hear everything. I didn't have to see anything because I just knew that Anniel and Damian were ok. Everything was dark. There was no light. There was no air. There was no movement. It was as if we were at the beginning of everything.

Incaendiel? Anniel asked. *Are we dead?*

No, I replied.

Then what are we? Damian asked.

I think we are pure energy right now, I replied. *Our former selves have transformed.*

Will we have bodies again? Damian asked.

Of course, I replied. *Alpha and Lilith do.*

When will we return to normal? Anniel asked.

Soon, I replied.

It was like all of the secrets of creation were unleashed in that moment. Light burst forth before us. Knowledge of gods past and present flooded my mind. Everything Sophia had told me about raced through my head as a movie. I saw Maveth just materialize as if Death needed to come before life, which made all the sense now. I saw Azrael spring forth, and like a domino effect, everything leapt into existence. I saw all of the forefathers of gods who were nothing but energy, copulating. The universe Sophi was from crept into my view. Tehom, the deep, intermingled with the Wind. I saw Yahweh, my grandfather, pop into existence, and then he brought Barbelo forth into the light. I saw the entire line of gods of varying universes brought forth in the same fashion. Nanna brought forth Ki and An. Ptah created Atum. I watched as Chaos Gaia, Nyx, Erebus, Eros, and Tartarus leapt into being. I had no idea who the gods over some of the universes were, but they burst into being. Varying gods began to form and create their own universes right before my eyes.

I watched as Sophia created Alpha, and it spilled over, creating our universe. I watched as she hid him away from the other gods so they wouldn't know what she did, but Yahweh knew everything. He knew all, just as we were learning. I felt the compassion he had toward Sophia and the sadness he had when she left before even explaining herself for fear of punishment. I watched as Alpha didn't understand who or what he was and existed in lonely ignorance until Lilith formed as Omega from his energy. I watched as the two spirits acknowledged each other, and the love that was shared between them ignited, bringing forth more creation.

And then I watched the old gods grow old and release their energy into the world to create new and more exciting lineages. Each of the Elder gods imparted their energy onto the next successor in line, like the universe had intended. I watched as Alpha sought counsel with the Council of El. I then watched as Alpha destroyed them one by one, taking their energy just as Beelzebub had said he had after they convened the last time.

"Alpha, it is time to bring forth the creations that are to replace you," Inanna cooed.

"No one will replace me. I am still a young god. I have much power still. I am not old and falling apart, such as my greedy grandfather, who still covets his energy and refuses to bless me," Alpha sneered.

"This is the way of the universe," Drac interjected.

"All of the powers ebb and wane and release to the next ones. It's the law of physics in the universe," Enki agreed. "When our time is up, we pass the torch onto our children. And then our children pass on to their children. So on and so forth."

"It's not *time!*" Alpha bellowed, pounding his fist on the table. "I have so much more to accomplish than the meager humans I have created!"

The room was silent as everyone glanced at one another. "Grandson," Yahweh spoke softly as he entered the Council Room. "Relinquishing your power doesn't mean you fade into nothing. It means you pass on the torch. You still retain energy. You are pure energy. You can't get rid of that. When you are an old man like me, and it's time for you to release to the universe, it is but a drop in the bucket in the grand scheme."

"Ah, he shows!" Alpha laughed maniacally. "Tell me, Yahweh," Alpha spat in sarcasm, bowing lowly, "if it is the way of the grand scheme, then why have I not received my blessing?"

"Because among your ranks exists a power far greater than yours, and they are to receive the blessing of the bloodline. Not you. You are to bless them as well. You are supposed to be compassionate, loving, and doting. You are filled with so much rage. Why?"

Alpha smirked. "You already know why. I was hidden away from you all. Cast aside and abandoned by the lot of you. From the moment I was brought into existence, I have been angry for being alone."

"Why make others suffer along with you?" Yahweh questioned.

"Why not?" Alpha asked.

"You bring great shame upon our lineage," Yahweh replied as he shook his head. "Your mother believed herself to be the one who cast shame upon us, but it's you."

"I bring shame?" Alpha asked as his temper flared. "Then how about I show just how shameful I can be?"

A bright light began to emit from Alpha as he grinned sadistically at all who were there.

"Everyone, get out!" Enlil shouted, and the vision faded into the dark.

Daddy?

Luxina! I gasped as I was brought out of the vision of the past unfolding.

What's going on? What's happening? she pleaded.

We are ascending, I explained. *Your mother took her elixir.*

Where are you? Damian demanded.

I don't know. Some place Alpha created, she whimpered. *There's nothing but darkness where I am. I thought I was dying. I exploded.*

We all did that, sweetie, I said. *We will find you. I promise.*

Hurry, Daddy! There are monsters here. I am pretty sure they are the ones from the vision that Alpha plans to use against us. I can hear them, she whimpered.

We will be there as soon as we learn where you are, Anniel replied.

Mom? Luxina asked.

The darkness faded, and light came into view. Luxina's voice was gone. I squinted, shielding my eyes as they adjusted to my surroundings. I looked around, and we were inside a huge crater. I heard Anniel and Damian moving and rolled over to see where they were. Both sat at the bottom of the crater with me, shielding their eyes in the same manner.

"What the hell?" Damian groaned, rolling over.

He stood up, wobbling on his feet, and my eyes finally adjusted to the blinding light of day. It was as if a soft glow emanated from him. I pushed myself from the ground and walked over to inspect him, brushing the dirt from his shoulders and hair. The scars he had on his face had disappeared. I looked over every visible part of his body, and every trace of the torture Alpha had subjected him to was gone.

"What?" he asked, patting himself down. "Am I part fish or something?"

I laughed. "No," I replied. "You're perfect."

I walked over to Anniel and helped her to her feet. I brushed the dirt from her the same way I had brushed it from Damian. She tousled my hair, and dirt flew in various directions. She looked around the crater.

"Did we do this?" she asked.

"I believe we did," I replied.

Her eyes widened. "What about the others?"

"What others?" Damian asked. "We were the only ones in the cottage."

"Everyone who was in Lightshade," I responded as I began to climb to the top of the crater. "With a hole this big, it would have been like a cataclysmic event."

They trailed behind me, sliding on the dirt. We reached the top, and a hand was thrust in my face.

"Grab my hand, Brother," Samael urged.

I grabbed his hand, and he pulled me from the crater. Asmodeus helped Damian, and Azazel helped Anniel.

"You have seen better days, kid," Asmodeus teased, tousling his hair as dirt flew from it.

"Asmodeus!" Damian shouted as he realized who was helping him. "You look so different!" He threw his arms around Asmodeus and squeezed him tightly.

"Don't break me," Asmodeus squeaked. Damian released his grip, and Asmodeus took in a breath. "Well, you're a helluva lot stronger now."

"What happened?" I asked Samael as I looked around everywhere. Nothing else had been destroyed other than Starfire's cottage.

"You exploded, like, literally," Samael replied. "Nothing but vapors and swirling energy was left in your wake."

"We thought you had died," Azazel added, hugging me tightly. She let go of her embrace of me and stepped back.

"We technically did," I replied, looking at Starfire. "We shed our angelic forms and became our true selves."

"Well, you're just as ugly as you were before," Gabriel joked as he walked over to join us. "What did you see?" he inquired.

"Everything," Anniel replied. "Existence. Gods. Creation. We saw it all."

"Sorry about your house," I told Starfire. "Was anyone hurt in the 'big bang'?"

"We were able to contain it to just this spot," she responded with a wink.

"What about Lilith?" Anniel asked, looking around for her face. "Did she get out of there before it exploded?"

"I... I don't know," Starfire replied, confused. "I can't see her anymore. That's strange."

"Does that mean she was killed?" I asked nervously.

Starfire scrunched her face, her brows knitted together in confusion. "No," Starfire replied. "That's why it's strange. I would see it. But I can't see anything past her walking upstairs to her room. I was distracted by you two, so I didn't see anything regarding her."

"Does that mean Alpha has her now?" I asked, worried.

She peered up at me, her eyes as wide as saucers. "I don't know what it means," she replied, worried. "I have never not been able to see anyone."

Anxiety filled me. "Can you still see Alpha?" I urged.

Her eyes flitted back and forth quickly. "No," she replied with fearful eyes. "I can't see anything at all."

"That doesn't make sense," I replied, chewing my nail.

"I don't see anything at all, either," Gabriel interjected. "I am able to see everything at all times. However, there is nothing about Lilith and Alpha any longer."

"What does that mean?" Anniel asked, turning to Gabriel.

"It must mean we are writing the future," Gabriel replied. "And there aren't any clues as to where it is going either."

"What was your last vision?" I prodded. "You said you couldn't share it with me before. Can you now?"

Gabriel shook his head. "I can't show you, but I can tell you," he replied. "Alpha was surrendering, but it was odd. Like, he knew something we didn't know."

"And now it's just darkness?" I queried.

"Correct," Gabriel replied with a quick nod.

A million thoughts raced through my mind from the events of the last year. The kids were having the visions as dreams. Angels don't dream. That still didn't explain Gabriel because he is the angel of visions… but he isn't an angel either.

"Hmmm," I murmured to myself.

"Hmmm, what?" Anniel asked.

"What if the first vision Gabriel had was a planted vision?" I pondered out loud. "The kids had it as a dream. Starfire saw it. Gabriel saw it. Then it changed, and we all assumed it was because things had changed since Xavier had been absorbed by Luxina and altered that part of the vision. But Alpha knew that was going to happen. He told me it was going to happen to manipulate me into believing that Damian was evil."

"That still doesn't explain why no one else can see that part of the future anymore, though," Damian replied.

"It would, since we are no longer tied to Alpha through his powers. He can't plant the visions anymore," I explained, still mulling over my train of thought. "Everything in this universe and world is Alpha's creation. He held power over it because he was the god of it. But now we exist in the universe as well. Everyone pledged their loyalty to us, including Gabriel and Starfire. Even though Gabriel was not an angel, so to speak, of

Alpha's, he had pledged his loyalty to hide among the ranks. That loyalty and connection were severed. So, Alpha can no longer show us the future he was planning, or that he was faking planning. That last vision was a clue. Alpha was surrendering because he knew something we don't know. And then nothing. Just empty darkness. We changed the future, and he has seen the new future. However, we don't have the connection to see anything fake or not."

"I told you, Brother," a voice called out in the crowd that began to part to make way for the owner of the voice to move forward. "We need my book."

"Raziel," I said with a smile, throwing my arms around him. "I see you found the place."

"I did," Raziel replied.

"What about your book?" Anniel asked.

"Your grandmother's bible," Raziel answered, leaning in to hug her. "It's good to see you, too, Sister."

"My grandmother's bible?" Anniel asked, confused.

"Yes, during your incarnation as Sophie. You had a bible that your grandmother gave you. It was my book. What you seek to learn is in that book. And only one person other than me can read it."

"Eva," Incaendiel replied. "That's right. The prophet."

"Alpha must know about her," Starfire warned. "It can't be a coincidence."

"Well, let's go get it!" Damian exclaimed, bouncing around with newfound energy.

"Oh, sweetie," Anniel began, "I don't know where it is. That was years ago."

"It has to be with your earth family," Damian replied.

Anniel nodded. "Yes, it is," she declared. "But my mother, Lorraine, went into hiding a long time ago. Alpha had already sent me to try to find the book. I couldn't find it or her. I wondered why he wanted it. I thought it was just a family heirloom."

"Even I have been unable to see Lorraine in visions," Starfire replied. "She is heavily cloaked in magic."

"Who possesses magic that strong?" I asked.

"There is magic in the world that is far older than magic taught by the Watchers," Starfire replied. "A magic so ancient, it goes back to where it all began, surprisingly. Adam and Eve learned a few things before they left the Garden, right, Raziel?"

"She is correct. Adam and Eve taught Cain and Seth what they had learned from the Tree of Knowledge of Good and Evil. When they ate the fruit, they became a conduit of knowledge and power. They were so powerful that Alpha was frightened they would find a way to the Summit and rule it themselves. That's why they were forced out of the garden. The fruit of the Tree of Life would grant them immortality in their new state if they were to eat from it first. Once they tasted mortal food, they became mortal," Raziel explained. "And since Lorraine is from the very bloodline of Adam and Eve, her family knows those secrets of magic as well."

"Then, how are we going to find the book?" Damian demanded, annoyed and frustrated.

"I may have a solution for that," Gadreel chimed in, stepping forward. "There is someone who no one knows is still alive, except for me, who can find her."

"Who?" Anniel asked.

"Cain."

Chapter Eleven

"STARFIRE, WHAT DO you know about Adam?" Anniel asked as she set off to the side while everyone filled the hole we had left behind during our ascension.

"Ah… Adam," Starfire mused. "I have been wondering when someone would ask about Adam."

"Who is Adam?" Damian asked, scrunching his face, already not liking where this was going.

"Adam is our new brother," Anniel replied, looking over at Damian. "I know who he is, and I know Alpha and Lilith created him, but that is all I know. Do you know more, Starfire?" she repeated, returning her attention to Starfire.

A riotous commotion started amongst the angels in wait, all asking, "Adam? Who is Adam? Why does she know Adam?" and an array of other comments.

"Do you know more?" Damian reiterated once more to Starfire as I shushed everyone.

"I do," Starfire replied. "But let's rebuild my house first, so I have somewhere comfortable to tell you all about Adam."

The warlocks and angels worked side by side, harvesting wood, turning the wood into planks, and rebuilding the outer shell for Starfire's cottage. It took what would have been half a day, if not for the endless sunshine in the valley, for it to be completed. It was a plain, square cabin, just as she had asked, with four walls. Starfire and Reikal walked inside it, and the magic began before our very eyes. Together, they built a mansion inside just as it had been before, waving their hands around as hallways and rooms appeared. Starfire motioned for us to walk in and led us to a room that was as large as the throne room in the Summit.

"Everyone, please take a seat," Starfire encouraged.

Anniel and I found a seat in the front row, along with Samael, Azazel, Metatron, and Asmodeus. Instead of sitting with us, Damian chose to sit at the far end with Asmodeus. Jealousy and envy swarmed me, and I leveled my composure to focus on what Starfire had to tell us about Adam. *He will never see me as his father*, I thought to myself. *He doesn't need to. He already has one.*

Give him time, love, Anniel replied. *He needs space, and that's all we can do. Alpha did a number on us all mentally and emotionally. Asmodeus was his only father figure. It is going to take time for him to*

218

come to see you as his father. He is angry, and he is a young one.

I know, I sighed. *It doesn't make it any less unbearable, though. He was mine this whole time, and the thoughts I had about him...*

That's all in the past, Anniel cooed. *You know now, and that's all that matters.* She grabbed my hand, and I could feel my mood change instantly.

That's supposed to be my power, I joked.

We are all full of surprises, she replied with a giggle.

I heard a scoff and glanced over to see Damian glaring at us and then returning his attention to the front of the room to wait for Starfire.

"I know you are all eager to know about Adam," Starfire began as she paced in front of us. "It wasn't too long ago that he sparked into being. Right around the time Alpha started keeping Damian locked up was when Alpha and Lilith created him."

Murmurs began to grow in the room when she raised her hands for everyone to settle down so she could continue. I shifted in my seat, waiting for her to continue, nervously glancing around at everyone.

"Adam wasn't created to be an angel," she continued, watching the faces in the crowd. "Much like Anniel and Incaendiel, he was molded to become a god."

"So he has the same powers as them?" a voice asked in the crowd.

"I thought we had the upper hand?" another shouted.

"What does this mean for everyone who took allegiance with Incaendiel?" one more posed.

"I will get to all of your questions. First, you all must know that Adam was in the original vision. He was there alongside Alpha when he was destroying the world. He is the power force that he had hoped our Shining Ones would be for him. He hadn't planned on them not bowing to his requests and resisting him as much as they have. And they have us at a disadvantage right now."

"How?" someone else asked.

"Alpha has Luxina," Starfire replied gravely, staring intently into the crowd of angels. "She finished her transition just as the other three did here. The problem is we don't know where he has hidden her away until he can activate his plans."

"And what are his plans?" Metatron asked, sitting forward in his seat.

"One of two things. He either wants to get Luxina on his side, and he will use Adam to do that," Starfire replied.

"Use Adam how?" Damian asked, piping up.

I watched his hand grip the armrest of his seat as he repressed his rage bubbling to the surface.

Starfire sighed. "By getting him to do what you would not when it was Xavier and her who everyone thought was the bonded pair."

"For what?!" Damian shouted, jumping to his feet.

"To create his own Shining Ones league, of course," Starfire responded.

I watched as the realization settled onto Damian's face. His eyes glowed in fury.

Calm down, I coaxed. *We don't need to hurt anyone here, and we all don't know how to contain this new power.*

I watched him relax and crack his neck in irritation, sitting back down in his seat. *I don't need you in my head telling me what to do,* he shot back.

"What's the other things?" I asked, funneling the direction of information.

"Somehow stripping half of the power from Luxina the way she was split in two with Xavier before," Starfire replied. "He could then either use Adam as is or put him inside Luxina, darkening her. Instead of Xavier being her other half, her true half, it would be evil in his place."

The room fell silent apart from the quiet murmuring around. I breathed heavily, trying to calm and stop myself from leaving the room and trying to find her myself before Alpha could do either of those things to her.

"If Adam succeeds, all is lost. The vision we had prior to everything going dark was of Luxina and Adam in power and Alpha surrendering," Starfire spoke again. "While Adam doesn't necessarily have the same powers as the four of them have, he possesses his own. And Alpha will give him his power to make sure he succeeds in the end."

"Is Adam blind to Alpha's manipulation?" I grunted, tapping my fingertips on my chair arm.

"I have no idea," Starfire replied, looking directly at me. "I saw very little of Adam. Alpha only allowed everyone who could see what he wanted them to see."

"So there's a chance he could be swayed to our side?" Anniel asked, leaning forward.

"It's a very slim chance," Starfire replied. "It was a one-in-a-million variable in the visions. Nearly all timelines had him at Alpha's side."

"But that's a chance!" I exclaimed, pounding the arm of my chair. "I mean, he is our brother."

"He doesn't see you as brothers and sisters. He sees you as disloyalists against Alpha. Alpha made sure to dote extra hard on him. He knew he could never win over Damian, not even with the injections, because his will was strong. He never showered him with affection and treated him as a weapon, which pushed Damian away. He regretted that decision, so when Lilith and he made Adam, he did the opposite with Adam," Starfire explained.

"And he is aging just like Damian and Luxina?" Anniel asked as her interest piqued.

"Faster," Starfire responded. "He is already around the same age as they are, and it has only been a year."

"Why so fast?" I inquired. "For all of them? Why did they age so exponentially?"

"They needed to be old enough to handle the tasks and protect themselves. The universe has a way of protecting its creation," Starfire answered.

"So what exactly is he?" Anniel prodded, trying to understand everything. "How was he made? We know the fey courts had nothing to do with it, and all of the elder gods have vanished. How did they make him into one of us?"

"Me," Damian replied before Starfire had a chance, head hanging low and staring at the ground. "He wasn't just injecting me with his concoctions, but he was also studying my blood after. He used my blood to mold and shape him. Right?" he asked, looking up at Starfire.

Starfire lowered her eyes. "Yes," she declared.

"So it's my fault all of this is happening?" Damian sputtered, looking sheepishly back down at the ground.

"Of course, it's not your fault!" I shouted, and his eyes met mine. "You were kidnapped as a baby, and you fought tooth and nail to stop him from doing the things he did to you."

Damian lowered his eyes, and I couldn't sense what he was thinking.

"So we capture him," Samael interjected. "Show him things from our perspective."

"Yeah, there has to be a way to get that one in a million chance of him not siding with Alpha," Azazel offered, agreeing with Samael.

"But he's not an angel," Michael replied as if withholding information Starfire hadn't told us. "We have no way to contain him. We don't even know if he can freely use his powers. He may not be bound like Anniel and Incaendiel were."

"Have you seen what he can do?" I asked, turning in my seat to look at Michael.

Michael was silent.

"Well, have you?" Anniel prodded further, turning around as well.

"Alpha had another gladiator ring," Michael began, not making eye contact with either of us. "It was set up just like the one Damian fought in, except only certain people were privy to watching Adam fight."

"And?" Metatron asked, turning in his seat to watch him.

"I have only seen Damian fight as an angel, not as a god," Michael remarked, looking off to the side.

"What does that mean?" Damian asked, snidely facing Michael, as a look of contempt plastered his face.

"Adam didn't fight against monsters like you did," Michael continued, eyes to the floor. "He fought against clones of you."

The room fell silent.

"He made clones of me?!" Damian demanded, shooting up attentive in his seat.

"Yes," Michael replied. "And one by one, he fought them until he could beat you."

"How many clones were there?!" Damian asked angrily, pounding his fist onto the arm of his chair.

"Millions," Michael uttered quietly. "Adam has been training since his creation to take you out of the picture. It's his one task. He eliminates you, and Alpha wins."

"Why?" I implored Michael. "Why him and not Anniel or me?"

"It's all part of his game," Lilith answered for him, quietly moving to the front of the room.

"Oh, the prodigal Mother returns," Anniel curtly stated, rolling her eyes in frustration.

"Where were you?" I demanded, narrowing my eyes at her.

"With Alpha," Lilith replied, unblinkingly.

"Of course you were," Anniel huffed and then let out a nervous laugh. "You were divorced and reconciled by having a baby. Don't you know that's how all relationships end? By fixing it with a baby?"

"I admit, I have done things that are… awful," Lilith began, staring at us both. "But he plans to kill me in the end, so I suppose the honeymoon stage is over," she spat as snarky as she could.

"Why are you here, Mother?" Samael asked flatly, unwavering in his poker face of distrust.

"To ask for forgiveness," Lilith cried quietly, tears flowing freely.

"No, you're just here trying to seek asylum is what you are doing," Azazel replied heatedly. "You're not sorry for anything you have done. You're not sorry for anything at all."

"I am here to offer you the upper hand against Alpha," Lilith stated, ignoring Azazel. "Adam isn't going to come to you willingly, but he's going to fight his way in. I can trick him easier than any of you."

"Why?" I asked, interrupting her.

"Why what?" Lilith asked in reply.

"Why do you want to trick him here?" I stood up from my seat and walked over to where she stood. I could see the fear in her eyes as I approached her.

"Because he is my son, like all of you," she replied nervously. Her eyes watched me as I drew closer. "I want to save him from Alpha just as I wanted to save Damian from his clutches."

Her eyes couldn't rest on mine, and she nervously looked around the room.

"Are you afraid of me?" I asked, leaning in to her face.

"Yes," she whispered. "You have always frightened the hell out of me."

"Good," I replied in satisfaction. "Because if you double-cross us one more time, I won't have mercy on you anymore. I will kill you myself." She nodded, acknowledging me, and I took a step back from her. "How do we keep him here without him using his powers?"

"He hasn't been activated yet," she replied. "He is like the children were before they took the elixir."

"I didn't think he needed to be activated?" I prodded. "I thought since he had Damian's blood, he was full-powered."

"Damian wasn't activated when Alpha had him," Lilith replied, cautiously walking around me. "He took the elixir after escaping."

"Can he use Luxina's blood?" Damian interrupted, leaning in closely to listen.

"No," Lilith began. "He has already been brought to life with your blood. It doesn't work the way you're thinking. He was infused with your blood during his shaping."

"I don't understand," I replied, turning around to face her. "If he isn't activated, how do you activate him?"

"One of two ways," she started explaining. "Either with my power or with one of your powers."

"So when he takes out Damian, he immediately absorbs his powers?" I asked furiously.

"Yes, and if Alpha can't get his hands on Damian, then it's me," she replied. "He's not harvesting power for himself, but for him and Adam. Once he defeats what's left of you, he will be the most powerful being in all of the universes. And then he will hand all of that power over to Adam, who will be just as evil as Alpha is."

"He can try to take me out, but I was trained with the best of the best," Damian interrupted, his pride getting the best of him. "Not only the training I acquired myself, but also the training Xavier received, is part of me. I was trained by demons and angels. And now, I am a god."

"Even gods can be slain, Damian," Lilith warned. "You are being too cavalier about this. Or do you not remember Tiamat from your travels to Atlantis?"

"But she is not dead," Damian replied. "She is waiting to return to her home after Alpha's destruction."

"We are not risking your death just for you to have an ego trip with Adam," I ordered, putting an end to the bickering between Lilith and him.

"You don't tell me what to do!" Damian seethed, standing from his seat and walking up to me.

"Damian, enough!" Asmodeus barked, jumping up from his seat as well.

Damian continued his glare at me and turned on his heel to leave the room.

"Where are you going?" I demanded.

"Somewhere you won't be!" he shot back.

Anger tore through me, and I whipped around to face Lilith. "That is your fault there!" I yelled, pointing to the shutting door as Damian left the room. "You and Alpha with your damn mind games and parlor tricks."

Lilith stifled a cry as I stepped closer toward her. "I know, and I am sorry," she pleaded.

"Incaendiel," Anniel spoke up, placing her hand on my shoulder. "Calm down."

"Why should I take pity on her? We aren't going to show Alpha any mercy. Why should we show her mercy? She is just as much to blame as Alpha. She has been right by his side, playing games with him. Separating us and then putting us through the stupid search for the garden that meant absolutely nothing. The garden wasn't gone. It. Was. Just. A. Game. They stood by and watched as we struggled with our identities. Mother being the jealous one, not allowing us around daddy. They watched as Anniel was born, raised, and killed as a human over and over.

It was one sick, twisted game, and we were the chess pieces. Warped our minds so we wouldn't remember certain things. Placed fake memories in us. And for what? Because they were afraid we would steal their power? Afraid we would rebel? Just mad at each other because of a marital spat?" I was fuming and could feel the heat rising to my skin, and I had to snuff out quickly.

"What are you talking about?" Asmodeus interrupted, and the rest of the room mumbled quietly.

"Damian is my son," I croaked, fighting back the rising lump in the back of my throat. "And Alpha kidnapped him when we initially raised the portal to the Summit. The portal in which we were told the only way we could raise was to finally have sex and combine our powers. But it was their sick, perverted game. They wanted us to have offspring because they knew our power, combined for the first time, would result in the kids. Alpha having one of them, and you having the other. Am I right so far, *Mother?*" I thundered angrily.

"Yes," she whispered in reply, taking a step back from me as I advanced toward her.

"And then you could have your own little family after Alpha planted the false memory of Damian being Anniel's and Lucifer's kid. So Anniel would be off with Lucifer, looking for Damian, leaving Xavier behind with you, and

230

Damian with Alpha. But no one knew about Luxina. Not until Alpha started spying in on Damian's dreams, right?" I demanded

"Yes," she cried, once again taking another step back.

"And you could raise them and train them to do your bidding. So you would have their power to defeat Anniel and me when the time came down to it, right?" I raged once more.

A tear slid down her cheek. "Yes," she breathed. "You were getting too strong for me to control, and Alpha wanted to destroy you."

"But Luxina ruined it all, am I right?" I roared, feeling heavier and heavier with her confessions.

"Yes," she replied, wiping away the tears and recomposing herself. "She wasn't supposed to exist, or at least that's what we thought. We thought twins were born like Lucifer and Michael. We had no idea it was Luxina split in half."

"Who all knew the truth?" I ordered.

She glanced at Michael in his seat. "Us two, Lucifer, and Michael," she mumbled.

I glared at Michael in his seat, and he averted his eyes in shame. "You couldn't tell me?" I demanded. He remained silent. I returned my attention back to Lilith, fuming. "Why should I show you mercy?" I cried. "After everything you have put my family and me through, why would I show you compassion and forgiveness?"

"Because it's who you are at the core," Lilith answered softly. "You are not Alpha, and you are not me. You are good."

"Brother," Beelzebub interrupted, standing nervously to his feet. "You were angry when you learned Luxina showed no mercy or compassion when she killed Gwynevere."

"Gwynevere was like us. Just another chess piece with these two." I pointed my finger at Lilith's face. "She's not a pawn. She's a queen to her king," I growled, looking around at all the faces in the room. "But I will put it to a vote. All those in favor of entertaining Lilith raise your hand."

Hands shot up in the air everywhere.

"All opposed?" I asked.

Very few hands were raised.

"Well, you have your mother," I muttered, turning on my heels to leave the room.

"Where are you going?" Metatron asked, jumping to his feet.

"To cool off," I snapped back as I walked to the entrance of the room.

"But we aren't done!" Samael protested, also rising to his feet. "What about Adam?"

"Figure it out and then tell me the game plan," I muttered, dismissing them with a hand.

I continued walking to the entrance.

"We still need you, Brother," Samael declared. "You are still who we choose to side with."

"You all have a funny way of showing it," I snapped, walking out the door.

"Wait, Incaendiel!" Lilith shouted.

As I looked over my shoulder, I collided with another person. I abruptly stopped to look at who I had run into. "Xavier?" I asked, my blood running cold.

"Hello, Brother," he replied. "You don't know me. My name is Adam."

Chapter Twelve

"HOW THE HELL did he get into Lightshade?" I asked Lilith, fuming as I paced the room.

We stood just outside the room of angels who were now arguing whether I had a point or not upon my abrupt departure. I looked over at Adam, who stared around the room as if mesmerized by the whole thing.

"He has learned how to portal just as you all have," Lilith replied, glancing in his direction. "And he has Damian's blood swimming around in his veins, so he is allowed through the force field."

"Why didn't you—" I began to yell and then quieted my voice. "Why didn't you mention before that he looks just like Xavier? And why does he look just like him?"

"I was getting to that before you exited via stage left!" Lilith hissed. "What better way to sway Luxina than to have him look like Xavier?"

"You need to get him out of here *now!*" I shouted in hushed tones.

"Well, now that he is here, why not make the best of it?" Lilith asked, a slight flicker of hope on her face.

"Why? So, Damian can try to kill him?" I replied in a raised whisper, looking around to see if anyone was coming our way.

"Oh, he won't try to kill him," Lilith stated quietly with a wave of her hand, brushing the thought off.

"We just told him Adam was out for his blood, and you don't think he won't act first? That Adam's arena was fighting clones of him over and over," I refuted, flabbergasted. "Do you not remember whose child he really is?" I reminded her, pointing to myself and glancing over at Adam, who was busy staring at the paintings hanging on the wall.

"It will be fine!" Lilith insisted with set eyes.

"What will be fine?" Damian asked, coming through the front door of the cottage and interrupting our private conversation.

"We would like you to—" Lilith began, and I quickly cut her off.

"Train more of the people arriving. They have been coming in by handfuls and are just waiting around for instruction. You have the best militant training track record," I offered with a smile.

Damian glanced from Lilith to me. "You're acting weird," Damian replied, narrowing his eyes and scrunching his face. "But fine. Where are they?"

"Outside with Praeziel," I said, and pushed him off in the direction of the door. "Run along."

He eyed me and shook his head. Once he was out of earshot, my attention returned to Lilith. "I mean it, Lilith. He needs to go."

"But I just got here, Brother," Adam interjected, standing right next to me. "And why do you call Mother by her name, Lilith?"

I scowled at Lilith. "He's like a toddler."

"Of course, he is like a toddler! A toddler with a unique ability to cut your head off, but a toddler nonetheless, mental acuity-wise," she rasped.

"What if this is all part of Alpha's plans?" I queried. "Hmm? Infiltrate the fortress, then help him portal in. Did you think of that?"

"Father doesn't know I am here," Adam interjected while examining a shelf of old talismans. "He doesn't want me around you all because he believes I will become disloyal to him."

"But you're not disloyal to him?" I prodded.

He shook his head. "No, I am very loyal to my father. But that doesn't mean I cannot also be close with my family. It isn't fair that it is a demand of me to choose sides when I just wish to know you all and love you all," he responded, putting an old rabbit's foot down and glancing up at me.

"And if you see Damian?" I pressed.

"I haven't been given his kill order," he replied nonchalantly. "Until then, he won't be harmed."

I glared at Lilith. "That's safe?" I demanded.

I started to walk off when she grabbed me by the hand. "Incaendiel, please!" she begged. "Please let him stay."

"Put. It. To. A. Vote," I hissed heatedly, annunciating each word.

"Put what to a vote?" Samael asked, walking from the conference room.

I pointed at Adam. Samael stared wide-eyed and confused. "He looks just like—"

"Yup," I interjected.

"Anniel will not handle that well at all," Samael replied. "You, Mother, of all people, should know that. And how could you be okay with it? Xavier was your precious boy."

And then it clicked. "Another lie to be caught in," I sneered. "It wasn't only Alpha's idea to make him look like Xavier but yours as well."

She gasped. "You caught me," she responded sarcastically with a glare to match.

"If it is too displeasing how I look, I can cast a glamour," Adam offered as he stared at the antique light fixtures on the wall.

"Oh, see! One problem solved already!" Lilith shrieked in delight.

"If you all are done arguing over whether I can stay or leave, I have news about Luxina for you," Adam interjected.

"News? What news?" I asked, shifting my focus to the murderous little devil spawn.

"I know where she is, but it won't be an easy task getting to her," he replied.

"Why would you let us know where she is?" I demanded, suspicious of his motivation.

"Because she is in danger there," he answered.

"And where is there?" I pushed, annoyed.

"Inside Purgatory, of course," he stated.

"And why do you care?"

"Well, I can't let my twin flame come to any danger," he responded, staring me in the eyes.

"Twin flame?" Samael asked.

"Yes, I can feel her," he replied with a sign. "She is lonely and scared."

"So not only does his blood make him like Damian, but Damian's twin-flame bond courses through his veins? What the actual—" I stopped myself from finishing the sentence and pinched the bridge of my nose in frustration.

I motioned for Samael to follow me to a corner so we could speak quietly without Lilith interrupting me every five minutes.

"What do we do?" I whispered, watching them closely. "We can't keep him here without Alpha looking for him or, worse, Damian finding out who he is. Not to mention, what if Alpha finds out he is here and executes the kill order on Damian?"

"We also can't let him go back to Alpha," Samael refuted.

"I know," I said, agreeing. "So what the hell do we do?"

"Whatever we do, we need to do it fast because the angels just convened, and Anniel will see him. Not to mention, Damian is heading back over this way," Samael replied, looking over my shoulder with his eyes in Damian's direction.

Damian walked with curiosity to the new person standing with Lilith. I rushed over to Adam and told him to glamour. "Your name is Sage, and you are a Nephilim. Got it?" I asked through gritted teeth.

"Yes, sir," he replied with a salute.

"Cute," I groaned.

Samael pulled me aside. "We can't not tell Damian who he is!" he hissed. "That will leave him defenseless."

"He won't ever get close enough to him to even ruffle his hair," I retorted, staring at Adam as Damian walked up. "I will kill him before he ever gets a chance."

"You must be Damian," Adam said, holding his hand out to him. "My name is Sage. I am one of the late-arriving Nephilim ready for training."

Damian took his hand and shook it. "Nice to meet you, Sage. Yes, I am Damian. I will be your trainer."

"Actually," I interjected, "One of us will train him," I stated, pulling Adam away from Damian.

"Why?" Damian pressed.

"Lighten your load," I replied. "We decided we were all going to start training the Nephilim and teaching them their untapped angelic powers."

"I didn't think they had any," Damian declared, narrowing his eyes.

"We didn't either, but apparently they do," I replied, lying. "I mean, at least we believe they should. They are half angel."

Damian shrugged. "Whatever." He began to walk away when Adam piped up.

"It was nice meeting you, Damian. I look forward to getting acquainted with you. I have heard a lot of things about you."

"I'm sure they're all half true," Damian replied, cracking a smile and walking out the front door.

"He is not at all like Alpha described him," Adam said, returning his attention to more relics in Starfire's house.

"And what does Alpha tell you about him?" I asked, watching his face.

"He said he is a monster who wishes to hurt him," he replied.

"Well, that's partly true," I muttered under my breath.

"So, are you going to be the one who pretends to train me?" he inquired.

"Why the hell not?" I replied with a sigh, throwing my hands up.

"Let's go then," he gushed with a grin.

He followed me out the door and to the sparring arena. He pulled out dueling blades as I pulled out my long sword. "Let's see what you got, kid."

Before I knew it, he was on me, and I was parrying his blocks. It was an assault after assault of weapon blows that I could hardly keep up with. I was putting in actual effort to avoid being caught by one of his swords. His movements were methodical and precise.

"Who the hell trained you?" I asked, trying to keep up with his blows.

"Damian," he replied. "You heard what Michael told you about my arena. I learned by watching him and fighting him until I won. It's in my blood to be exactly like him, is it not?"

"Nice moves," Damian remarked as if on cue, walking up to the two of us just outside our designated circle.

Without a moment's hesitation, Adam let loose one of his dueling blades, throwing it as hard as he could at Damian. I tried to jump and grab it, but I couldn't move quickly enough. I watched with a thud to the ground as the sword careened toward Damian's head as if time had slowed down. Damian stepped aside and grabbed the sword by the blade, and the freeze on time disappeared.

"What the hell was that for?" Damian demanded, throwing the knife to the ground. "We don't take kill shots in training here!"

Adam stood there with wide eyes as Damian stalked off. "He moved so fast it was like he slowed down time," he murmured and looked at me. "How did he do that?" he asked.

"Because he is not one of the clones Alpha made of him for you to battle," I replied. "He thinks on his feet, something that can't be replicated. He is always on guard. And he is a god."

"Did Father love him?" he questioned.

"No. He used him in a game with Lilith as a weapon of mass destruction. But when he couldn't get him to bend to his will, he tossed him aside and made you," I answered.

"Why wouldn't he listen to Father obediently?" he pestered.

"He did, for the most part. But it didn't matter to Alpha. He had him tortured anyway," I explained as we both watched Damian training another Nephilim.

"Tortured?" he asked. "How?"

"Whips, chains, monsters. You name it, and it was his torture," I responded.

"Father shows me love, but he also looks at me with disappointment because I am not Damian," Adam stated sadly.

"That's just how he is," I replied, fostering empathy for him a bit more than I should. "Alpha doesn't care about anyone except Alpha."

"I need to go home," he stated, walking away. "I have more training to do."

"Training for what?" I inquired.

"Meeting you and Damian doesn't change my orders. When Alpha gives the order, I am to take him out or die trying," he replied.

"It doesn't have to be that way, though," I said, placing my hand on his shoulder. "You don't have to submit to his will."

"The perfect soldier always submits," he snapped, grabbing my hand and throwing it off his shoulder. "You will not change my mind."

"Will you be back again to visit?" I asked.

"Maybe," he replied with a shrug. "I did enjoy getting to know you, Incaendiel."

He raised his hands, and a portal appeared. He disappeared through the opening, and it closed behind him.

"You let him get away?!" Samael hissed as he ran up beside me.

"Yes. Yes, I did," I declared. "We have a big problem, and we need to be prepared for when he returns."

"How the hell did that Nephilim raise a portal?" Damian demanded, running up beside me.

I looked over at Samael, and he put his hands up in the air. "I told you to tell him."

"Tell me what?" Damian urged, glaring at me.

I sighed. "That was Adam."

"And you let him get away?!" Damian hissed. "He tried to kill me!"

"He didn't try to kill you," I explained. "He was testing you, and he failed."

"You still let him walk out of here without trying to stop him," he replied angrily.

"We *just* learned about him!" I exclaimed. "We don't even know *how* to stop him, and I wasn't going to set a killing machine loose in the valley."

"How did he even get in here?" Damian snapped. "I thought this place was protected."

I stared at him gravely, and the realization washed over his face.

"He got in because he has my blood. So once again, we aren't safe because of me," he insisted, answering his own question.

"It's not your fault," I spoke softly, laying my hand on his shoulder. "None of this will ever be your fault."

He shrugged my hand off just as Adam had. "What if he comes back next time with Alpha?!"

"He won't," I refuted.

"How do you know?" Damian demanded.

"I just do. I can't explain it," I said.

"Well, now that I know what he looks like, I can dispatch him as soon as he steps into Lightshade again," Damian remarked.

"About that," I began. "That's not how he really looks."

"What does he look like?" Damian asked. "A three-headed monster?"

"Alpha and Lilith played a cruel joke on us all," I replied.

"How?" he pestered.

"He looks like Xavier," I responded.

Fury erupted across Damian's face. "Why would they do that?"

"Well, we have the one reason," I began and trailed off.

"What's the other?"

"Now that is the million-dollar question," I started. "It's too easy for it to be because they want to sway Luxina to believing she has a different twin flame. With Alpha, there's always a sinister side to every coin flipped."

"Where is Lilith?" Damian demanded. "I want to speak with her."

"Last I saw her, she was inside Starfire's cottage," Samael chimed in.

Damian stalked off to the cottage, and we followed hot on his trail. He was met by Starfire on the porch.

"Where is Lilith?" he demanded once again.

"She left not too long ago when Incaendiel was sparring with Adam," Starfire replied.

"Where did she go?" he pressed.

Starfire shrugged her shoulders. "I can no longer see her or Alpha."

"Dammit!" he seethed. He glanced over at Samael. "This is your fault. You and your gang of angels, who were all too thrilled to see Mommy Dearest appear. This was a set-up. She brought him here to see if he was ready yet to kill me, and had I not been quick on my feet, he would have succeeded. Lilith isn't to be trusted, just like Alpha. She is a monster, too, and the sooner you and your brothers and sisters get that through your head, the better off we all will be. She will use your love for her against you and manipulate you with love bombs while simultaneously planning your demise. Get over your mommy and daddy issues and get your shit straight or we all die!"

Damian stalked off, leaving Samael and me standing on the porch.

"He is right, and you both know it," Starfire interjected. "Terror has followed Alpha while devastation has followed Lilith. You know, they form a toxic bond with one another and have played games with one another for millennia. Neither of them is to be trusted, nor is Adam to be trusted. I know you want to be a leader who listens to his followers, Incaendiel, but in some cases, you will have to pull rank and follow your gut. And your gut was right about those two. I can feel it. I just can't see it."

"So now what?" I inquired. "How do we prevent either of them from being able to return to Lightshade to harm anyone?"

"Reikal went into stealth mode and collected hair from both of them," she replied. "I will add it to the barrier to keep them out, even from portaling in."

"You good with that?" I asked Samael.

He scowled. "Do I have a choice?" he snapped and stalked off.

"I just have a knack for pissing people off lately," I sighed.

"He will come around," Starfire replied with a wink.

"Have you seen Anniel?" I asked. "I haven't gotten a chance to speak with her alone at all, it seems."

"She is upstairs in your room," she replied with a smile.

"Thanks," I said as I walked past her and inside.

I made my way up the stairs to the room I had had before the fire. I opened the door and found her asleep on the bed. I walked over to the other side of the bed and climbed in beside her, pulling her in close to me. I breathed her scent in deeply and felt more at home and at peace than I had felt in a very long time. She began to stir and rolled over in my arms, placing her head on my shoulder and her hand on my chest.

"Mmmm," she purred. "There's my firefly." Her hand roamed from my chest to my face, and she brushed it along my cheek. "I was wondering when you would come join me."

"I had some things I had to take care of first," I replied, brushing her hair from her face and cupping her chin in it. "And then I thought of you."

She smiled. I hadn't even taken the time to see that her hair had changed colors as I sat there drinking her in. It was the same color as Damian's and Luxina's hair. White tendrils fell around her face, which had highlights of red hues. Her eyes were a beautiful shade of gray with flecks of amber. It felt like millennia had passed since we both had a moment alone together like this. I leaned in and planted my lips on hers as her hands roamed through my hair. I rolled over on top of her as her hands explored my body through my clothes. I kissed her mouth, her chin, her cheek, her neck. My mouth explored every part of her exposed. She pulled my shirt from my back and over my head, running her fingers across every muscle she could see. Her eyes glowed as she looked at me. She was so beautiful.

"You're just as beautiful," she replied as if she had read my mind.

And with that, I gave in and fell into her arms, and after, I slept for the first time in what seemed like an eternity.

Chapter Thirteen

I STIRRED AWAKE and reached over to the side of the bed Anniel had lain on, but found it empty. I had no idea how long I had been out. I rubbed my eyes and stretched my arms before I stood from the bed that beckoned me to stay and sleep my troubles away. I left the room and made my way down the stairs to see where everyone was. A slight panic overcame me when I couldn't find anyone inside, so I walked outside to see what everyone was doing. Once again, there wasn't anyone to be found.

"Where the hell is everyone?" I asked out loud.

"They're all gone, Incaendiel," Starfire replied, popping out from inside her cottage.

"Where did they go?" I inquired, panic-stricken.

"To join Alpha, of course," she answered with a hearty laugh. "Did you really think they were going to stick around when you kicked their mother out? Did you really think Samael would take being bossed around by you? Are you that daft, boy?"

"You're not Starfire," I replied heatedly.

"No, son. I am not," Starfire agreed with a sinister laugh and eyes blacked over.

"Where are Anniel and Damian?" I demanded.

"Right where they belong. Anniel is at my side, and Damian, well, Adam knew what needed to be done with that disobedient brat," he sneered.

"No," I shouted, my flames leaping forward. "No, he isn't dead. You can't trick me this time."

"This isn't a trick or a mind game," Alpha replied. "If I can't have the boy, then no one can! Enjoy your quick death!" he shouted as he blew dust in my face.

I went to tackle Starfire to the ground, but she vanished as well, and I was left all alone in Lightshade. I sank to the ground, breathing in sharp heaves as the emotions welled in my chest. The dust I had inhaled began to choke me, and I couldn't breathe. I crawled across the ground, my flames lighting Lightshade up like a bonfire as I lay in the drifting embers.

"Incaendiel!"

Who is that? I wondered as I tried to suck in breath after breath but was met with only a lungful of ashes.

"Incaendiel, wake up!" the voice insisted.

But I am awake, I insisted, accepting my fate of dying alone.

"Wake up now!"

I sat up from my sleep, drenched in sweat. Fire smoldered around me as I watched Damian put the flames out with his ice. I looked around at the charred and burned room and heaved out in sharp breaths. Damian watched me, and I could see the look of worry in his eyes. I felt my face, and it was wet from stray tears I had let loose while sleeping. I quickly swiped them away.

"I'm fine," I choked out, running my hand through my sweat-drenched hair.

"You sure?" he urged.

"Yes," I replied, sitting up in bed. "It was just a bad dream, is all." Panic tore through me. "Anniel?" I asked, reaching for the empty side of the bed.

"She is fine. She is downstairs. No one was aware of what was happening. I came to wake you up and found you burning in your sleep," he replied quietly, looking around the room. "I've never seen someone use their powers like this in their sleep before."

"Everything is okay," I reaffirmed, shaking off the nightmare.

"Don't let him in your head," Damian warned. "He is a master at making you think you aren't worth anything."

Was it that obvious? Could he see what I was actively dreaming?

"No, I didn't need to see," he replied, reading my mind. "But if you used your powers in your sleep, then it was more than just a bad dream."

Flashes of the dream ran through my mind, and I pushed aside the anxiety that welled in my chest and shoved it deep down. Damian watched me for a little bit longer before he turned to walk out the door.

"No one is going to leave you, Incaendiel," he said as he shut the door behind him.

I quickly wiped the sweat from my face and started to clean up the room. I put everything I had burned into a bag and carried it out without anyone seeing me. I returned to the room to make the bed back up, but it had already been fixed. Even the burned walls had been replaced. I suppose it was the magic Starfire used to create the place.

"There you are," Anniel remarked, walking up behind me and snaking her arms around my waist from behind. "I was wondering if you were ever going to wake up or just sleep the day away."

"Yeah, I slept pretty well," I lied, turning around and picking her up in my arms. "I didn't want to leave the bed."

She smiled and planted a kiss on my lips. "Good. I was worried when I left the bed that you were having a fitful sleep. You were tossing and turning."

"Yeah, because my paperweight left my side," I teased, running my finger lightly down the bridge of her nose.

"I'll have you know I am handier than a paperweight," she retorted with a laugh.

"I don't know. You're pretty lightweight," I taunted.

"Why don't you say that in the sparring arena?" she giggled as she wiggled out of my arms and ran for the door. "Catch me if you can!" she called as she threw the door open and bounded down the stairs.

I smiled and blinked from inside the cottage to the front door just as she opened it and ran out, catching her in my arms.

"No fair!" she yelled, laughing. "You *always* cheat!"

"I thought you were going to show me some moves?" I bantered.

She wiggled from my grip once more and ran over to one of the open arenas and picked up a long sword. "Oh, I have some moves," she goaded.

I walked over to the arena and picked up a long sword as well. "Let's see them then," I baited.

Her sword burst into flames as her powers ran up her hands and into the sword.

"Oh, so we are using powers, are we?" I laughed as I did the same with my sword.

"Don't hold back, love," she murmured before advancing.

254

She brought her sword down hard onto mine, and I parried it. We danced around the circle with our swords clanking and clashing. I caught her sword with mine and tossed it aside. She didn't waste a second, barrel rolling over to a set of dueling knives and blocking my sword as it came down on her.

"Now, that wasn't very nice," she replied with an impish grin.

Her dueling swords sprang to life with her power, and she landed blow for blow against me, just as I had watched Luxina with Damian.

"You fight pretty good for a girl," I taunted and ducked while laughing as she swung out with her sword.

Her eyes began to glow a fiery amber as she began to pelt me with blows from her sword. One after another came down against my sword, and then one nicked my arm. Determination was set in her eyes as she continued blow after blow, coming faster and stronger with each one.

"I don't remember you being this good," I uttered, struggling to counter every move.

Another of her swords nicked my other arm, and she continued on with her fight with determination in her eyes. As I blocked each blow, I could see the hunger in her eyes for more and more of the fight.

"Alright, that's enough," I laughed nervously.

She didn't stop but pushed harder and faster.

"I said that's enough."

It was as if she couldn't hear me anymore and had just one task at hand.

"Anniel, enough!" I bellowed.

She snapped out of whatever trance she had been in and dropped her swords to the ground once she saw the blood dripping from my arms.

"I'm sorry," she whispered and turned to walk away.

"What was that?" I demanded as I picked up a towel and wiped away the blood oozing from the gashes.

"I was conditioned to fight," she replied and walked back inside.

"What the hell did Alpha do to you?" I muttered to myself.

A searing pain tore through my head, and instinctively, my hand went to my forehead as I crouched to the ground.

"Anniel," Alpha called out in the garden as she and I ran around playing our cat-and-mouse game.

"Yes, Father?" she asked, stopping and swiping the hair from her face.

"It's time for training," Alpha replied with a warm smile.

"Coming!" she called back to him as he left. "While this was amusing and fun, Firefly, I have to go do my daily training."

"I want to come," I murmured, pulling her to me by her hand.

256

She giggled. "You know he trains me alone." Her hand slipped from mine, and she went running after Alpha.

The pain stopped, and I stood back up. I don't remember anyone else being trained personally by Alpha. I needed to talk to Metatron. Was she the only one he took aside? Did he train Lucifer? Or Michael? I walked quickly through Lightshade from arena to arena, looking for Metatron. I had no idea who he could be training with or even if he was training until I stumbled across him and Praeziel. Praeziel looked majestic in the arena. I had never seen him fight before, and I couldn't tell if he was or wasn't holding back as he sparred.

"He's definitely holding back," Damian commented, walking up beside me. "I have seen him in action on several occasions. He is the leader and trainer of the Nephilim."

Metatron glanced my way, and I waved him over. He jogged to me and stopped, breathless.

"That little Nephilim gave me a workout," he said through rapid breaths, glancing back at Praeziel and then back to me.

"That's because he's not a Nephilim," I replied with a laugh.

"What the hell is he?" Metatron asked, glancing over his shoulder nervously.

"A demigod," I answered, nodding at Praeziel, who was watching us. "But that discussion is for another day. I have been looking for you."

"What do you need?" Metatron asked, wiping the sweat from his face with a towel.

"In the Summit, who trained you?" I inquired.

"No one, really," he replied, shifting from foot to foot. "We trained ourselves and then honed our skills in sparring with one another. Why?"

"What about Lucifer?" I pressed. "Same thing?"

"Yes," Metatron responded. "Why?" he asked again.

"I just had a memory tear through my head," I replied, instinctively rubbing my forehead. "I suppose a lot of them are repressed from before the fall. Anyway, I was sparring with Anniel when she went into attack mode, and it triggered the memory when she said she was conditioned that way. My memory was of Alpha training her."

"Alpha?" he pondered, a look of confusion spreading across his face. "I thought the whole reason we were warrior angels was because he didn't fight."

"Oh, he fights," Damian added. "There was a time or two when he pulled me off in secret to spar with him. How else do you think he went after the elder gods?"

"So the memory is true," I murmured, running it all through my head. "From day one, he was training her to be a killing machine." I thought quietly for a moment. "I need my memories unlocked. I need to remember everything he warped us into forgetting."

"Starfire would be the only person who could help," Damian replied. "And if you are going to do it, you need it done before Cain arrives."

"I agree," Metatron said.

I nodded and turned around to head back to the cottage.

"Incaendiel, hold up," Damian shouted as he jogged up to me to walk with me. "What more do you think can be hidden?" he asked as we walked.

"I don't know," I replied. "But there's a lot I don't remember, and I need answers."

"Do you want me there with you?" he inquired, rubbing the back of his head nervously. "You know, just in case what happened while you were asleep happens again."

"If you want to be there, I wouldn't mind," I responded.

"Are you ready to talk about it?" he questioned, glancing up at me. "The dream?"

"It was just your usual anxiety about being a leader," I answered. "Nothing more or less."

"I doubt that," Damian scoffed. "You dreamt that everyone abandoned you and teamed up with Alpha. Everyone who pledged their loyalty to you was gone, and you were left all alone."

"Did you lie about spying in on my dream?" I hissed, irritated.

"We can read each other's thoughts, remember?" he replied defensively. "And I couldn't wake you up. So I peeked in."

"There is no privacy in this damn family," I muttered as we reached Starfire's porch.

"That's because you never learned how to put up a block so people wouldn't pry," he retorted with a laugh. "I thought Lilith was the one training you to hone your powers. She didn't teach you?"

I huffed as I climbed the stairs. "The only thing she taught me was to fear them. Push them down and repress them so I don't burn shit down."

"What can I do for you, Incaendiel?" Starfire asked, emerging from one of her rooms as we walked through the door.

"I need my memories unlocked from before the fall," I replied.

"Come in and sit down," she said, motioning with her hand to the sitting room. "What makes you think your memories are locked?

"Because I had one earlier that tore through my brain as if it were unlocked, like when Alpha released his hold on the power around Anniel's name," I replied, taking a seat on the couch with Damian following beside me.

"What was it about?" she asked as she sipped on a cup of tea.

"Alpha coming to get Anniel for her special training with him," I answered. "There has to be more that we all don't remember. Either due to the trauma of the fall or things Alpha kept layering in lies, messing with our memories."

"I see," Starfire remarked. "And Alpha didn't train anyone else?" she asked.

"No, I asked Metatron," I stated, fidgeting with my hands. "He said no one trained us, that we just knew what to do."

"Interesting," she murmured. "I believe you're right. You all have hidden memories."

"Why do you say that?" I urged, staring at her intently.

She didn't reply and instead walked from her seat into her potions room. It took a few minutes, but soon after, she returned with a hot cup of tea.

"Drink this," she said, handing me the cup.

"What is it?" I queried, staring down at it and taking a whiff. "Last time wasn't a pleasant experience."

"Some mugwort and other things," she replied with a smile. "It shouldn't be as unpleasant as the potion before, but I am afraid your skull will feel like it's being hammered open once you take it."

I frowned at the cup and then sighed. What choice did I have? "Bottoms up," I declared as I drank the tea.

"You might want to get comfortable," she offered with a serious face.

I lay back on the couch with Damian switching to another chair, sitting and watching me.

"Will I go to sleep?" I asked as I waited for it to kick in.

"Unfortunately not," Starfire replied, shifting uncomfortably in her seat. "It will be just like when Anniel was receiving her memories."

And without warning, everything went black.

Chapter Fourteen

"WHY THESE TWO?" Alpha asked as he crafted the molding of a body. He was shaping me, and I could feel his hands working every single inch of my body into perfection.

"Don't you want your lineage to be more than warriors fighting for us? Or do you want children who will carry on your legacy and become something grander than this crafted universe?" Omega inquired in reply as she nimbly ran her fingers along the clay figure beside me. "Here, this bottle is for him," Omega dictated as she handed Alpha a bottle and then opened the other bottle she had.

"I believe I am finished with this one," Alpha declared as he placed a few drops of the substance on my forehead. "And you're sure they can't be brought to full power without stripping the enchantment? We put a fair amount of power into both of them. We don't need devil spawn running around and overthrowing us."

"Yes, the fey courts said this would prevent them from coming to full power until we were ready for them to become who they are meant to be," Omega replied, adding the substance from the separate bottle to the other figure's head. "They must never know, though."

"Why not?" Alpha prodded, standing from his kneeling position to marvel at what they had created thus far. "If they are destined for greatness, then they need to know so they can grow properly."

"We don't want the other children thinking we had favorites now, do we?" she ventured, wiping the stardust mud from her hands. "There's enough in numbers where they could easily overpower us since these two are not yet accustomed to their abilities."

"How did you persuade the fey into giving you an enchantment?" Alpha asked, raising an eyebrow.

Omega laughed. "I told them I didn't want you finding out about them, or you would kill them. They think I am creating them all on my own."

"And they believed you?" Alpha teased, chuckling. "Do they not understand you couldn't wield the power we harvested alone? It would take both of us to do it."

"I don't think they know much about us," Omega cooed. "They still think you are ignorant of the fact that there are other gods in the universe."

"I told you our life story would be the best entertaining show ever to hit the cosmos," Alpha joked, nudging Omega with his elbow.

Omega laughed and gently pushed his elbow away. "Stop it."

They both stood silently, unaware that I may have been unconscious, but my spirit was hearing and seeing everything.

"Are you ready to wake them up?" Alpha asked, bending down to inspect us.

"There's one more thing," Omega stated, kneeling beside him while staring at the two of us. "Since it has to remain a secret, and we cannot train them in private without word getting out to the others we are training them, then we need to encrypt their minds before we wake them."

"You mean like a trigger word that will wake and sleep them so they don't remember anything?" Alpha inquired.

Omega nodded.

"Which one do you wish to be the master over?" Alpha asked, eyeing us both.

"I will take Incaendiel," Omega replied, touching my forehead and turning my body from mud into flesh. "You take Anniel."

"Ok," Alpha said, bending down and touching the figure beside me. "I will take Anniel."

Anniel's body began to change like mine had, from mud to flesh.

"Anniel, uwr," Alpha commanded, and a bright light began to glow around her body. "Lishon." Her light snuffed out.

"Incaendiel, uwr," Omega commanded, and the same happened with me. "Lishon." My light was snuffed out.

"All right," Alpha said with a grin. "Let's bring our Shining Ones to life."

Omega leaned down and breathed her breath into me, and my spark lit up in my chest. She repeated the same to Anniel, and her spark lit up as well. "Uwr," Alpha and she spoke. "L'chaim!" We both opened our eyes and rose from the ground, both looking around confused.

"Welcome, my children," Alpha announced, his arms spread wide.

"Where are we?" Anniel asked, glancing around the space we were made in.

"You are in our universe," Omega replied, smiling from ear to ear.

"What happened to our universe?" I demanded. "We were fueling it to prevent its collapse."

"I am afraid your universe supernovaed," Alpha responded grimly. "We harvested your power right before it fell apart."

"Did you save our people?" Anniel implored, looking around at the empty surroundings in which she sat in. "Where are they?"

"They didn't make it, dear," Omega cooed, bending down and rubbing her arm. "You are the only survivors."

"And who are you two?" I snapped, standing up and helping Anniel to her feet.

"We are your creators," Omega replied nervously.

"No, you are not our creators," I stated flatly, hatred brimming beneath the surface. "You stole us from our parents. You brought us here and shoved us into these bodies. That doesn't make you our parents."

My body lit up like the sun on fire. I had total control over it as the flames danced across my skin. Anniel lit up as well, and we stood there prepared to fight.

"What the hell did we create?" Alpha asked, wide-eyed.

"I don't know, but I'm glad we put in that fail-safe," Omega muttered.

"Lishon!" they both shouted.

Our fires were snuffed out, but we were still awake.

"Lamut," they said in unison.

We hit the ground, unconscious.

"I thought you said their power would be suppressed," Alpha seethed, pacing uncomfortably.

"Their power *is* suppressed. This must be the overflow of power," Omega replied nervously.

"How did we make them more powerful than we are?" Alpha demanded, his nostrils flaring in jealousy.

"I don't know!" Omega hissed. "It was your idea to take their power from the sun!"

"No, the sun didn't do this," Alpha replied. "They have to have Barbelo in them."

Omega looked gravely at us while we lay asleep. "How do we fix this?" she asked.

"There's more of the enchantment left in the bottle," Alpha said. "Let's put the rest on them and don't use the trigger word unless we are in private and want to perfect their god powers.

"Ok," Omega agreed as she smeared the rest of the enchantment potion on our foreheads.

A brighter glow lit up our heads and went out.

"This is going to take a while for us to strip their memories from their previous life," Alpha stated, annoyed.

"And never together," Omega replied. "They're too powerful as a unit. We are going to have to handle them on a one-on-one basis."

"Do you think the council will have any advice on how to handle them?" Alpha asked.

"They should, yes," Omega answered. "Let's bring them to life again, and then we will go to the council."

"No, you need to stay here and watch them," Alpha argued. "I will go alone."

"You need to take at least one of them with you so you can demonstrate the issue," Omega retorted.

"Fine," Alpha relented. "I will take the boy since he seems more powerful than the girl."

"Ok," Omega replied with a shrug. "Ready to bring them to life?" Alpha nodded.

"L'chaim," they repeated once again.

"Where are we?" I asked, sitting up from the ground. "And who are you?"

Alpha and Omega exchanged glances. "We are your creators," Alpha replied hesitantly.

"What do we call you?" Anniel asked, her and I standing up.

"I am Father," Alpha replied with a nefarious grin.

"And I am Mother," Omega replied, smiling as well.

***

"I am sure you are wondering why I called you here together today," Alpha spoke to the council members gathered around the table. "We have a problem."

"Is that... Barbelo at your side?" Tiamat asked, peering curiously at me.

"I believe it is," Alpha replied. "She was not part of our plan when we created the two beings we did. I was sure that I had absorbed all of her power released out into the universe, but apparently, she reserved herself for this specific occasion. Now, our twin flame pair are far more powerful than we are, and we cannot control them."

"He doesn't seem like a threat. He is pretty docile," Drac joked.

"Incaendiel, uwr," Alpha spoke, and I awoke.

"Where am I? Who are all of you?" I asked as I looked around the room, resting on Alpha's face. "It's you!" I spat. "You destroyed my universe to harvest my soul from the sun!"

My body erupted into flames, fully controlled. I felt no anxiety or impending doom while in this form. I felt free, something I had never felt. I brought forth a fireball into my hand and was about to destroy Alpha.

"Lishon!" Alpha shouted.

My true self fell back asleep. The room laughed. "You can't even control your own creations. This is amusing," Tiamat remarked.

"This is not a laughing matter. He can burn everything to the ground, including all of you!" Alpha shouted.

Tiamat stood from her seat and walked over to me, looking me over. "Bring him back awake," she ordered.

"Incaendiel, uwr!" Alpha commanded.

I awoke and looked into her eyes as she stood right before me. "Do you remember me?" she asked.

Images started to zoom through my mind of my previous life in another universe, where I was the sun of the universe. "You are the mother of the Na'Thalhûn universe," I replied. "Why were we forsaken?" I cried. "We pleaded with you for help as our universe began to topple."

"You were dying, my child," she cooed. "You were old power. I told Omega about what was left of your power because the multiverses need you, and so you could be renewed again through her, your new mother, and through him," she said, motioning to Alpha, "your new father."

"He will never be my father," I replied bitterly. "I can see into his mind, and it is a wicked thing to witness. He killed—"

"Lishon!" Alpha barked.

"I wasn't done speaking with him!" Tiamat hissed.

"That was enough," Alpha replied, glaring at her.

Tiamat stared intently at Alpha. "There is only one thing that will help your issue. They are too powerful together. Let them grow some more together while their souls are asleep, so they can become acclimated to you being their father, because as of now, he despises you. I am sure his mate does as well. When they come to see you as their father, that is when you separate them and begin their slow transition from being asleep to being fully awake. But you must be careful. You have to keep their memory suppressed of their life before, or else they will destroy you both. Once you are ready to separate them, return to us for counsel so we can see the progress and make sure they are ready as well. You do it too soon, and they will retaliate," Tiamat explained.

"And you are sure this plan will work?" Alpha asked.

"We shall see," Tiamat replied. "That is the best we can do at this point."

***

"I want to come," I replied, pulling her to me by her hand.

She giggled. "You know he trains me alone." Her hand slipped from mine, and she went running after Alpha.

"Incaendiel?" Mother called out.

I turned around, and she was standing behind me, off at a distance.

"You ready for your training?" she asked with a warm smile.

I nodded and walked over to her side. We began making our way to the room she had trained me in.

"Mother?" I began.

"Yes, dear?" she responded to me, looping her arm in mine.

"Does Father not like me?" I asked, looking down at the ground.

She stopped in her tracks. "What in Summit would make you ask that?" she asked, peering up at me.

"He always calls Anniel off but never spends time alone with me," I replied.

She smiled. "We agreed to train you separately. I train you, and he trains her," she explained.

"Why can't we be trained together?" I inquired.

"Because you're special, Incaendiel," she replied. "You know your power requires special attention. It's a one-on-one job for us to do."

"How come my power shows more than Anniel's?" I prodded. "She doesn't even know about her gift over fire because it doesn't burst forth like mine."

"I am not sure why your power overtakes you and hers does not," Mother answered. "But that is why we train both of you, just in case hers does bubble to the top. She will know how to use it properly."

"Why can't I remember when you train me what we talk about?" I pressed. "I don't even remember the private training until you show up and mention it."

"We can't have your brothers and sisters jealous of you, now, can we?" she murmured in reply.

"I am sure they would understand that I need a bit more care than they do, given the fact that I nearly burn down the place all the time," I replied as she opened the door to my training room.

When she closed the door, she spoke, "Uwr."

I felt my whole personality shift. "Where is Anniel?" I demanded.

"She is with your father," Mother replied nervously, making sure to keep distance between us.

"He is not my father," I quipped heatedly.

"You need to calm down, sweetie," she cooed. "Your fire isn't suppressed, remember? We don't want to hurt your brothers and sisters, now do we?"

"I recalled the memories of my split self and sighed. "No, I do not wish to hurt anyone," I responded.

She smiled sweetly. "Thank you, son."

"I am torn at acknowledging you as my mother," I replied. "The part of me who is awake all the time cares deeply for you as his parent. However, I still know who my original creator was."

"Why is it you prefer me to your father, Alpha?" she asked as she took a seat at the table behind the wall I would go behind to train.

274

"I don't know. There's something wicked about his energy," I answered. "I can see thoughts in his head so sinister… he is not like you. Although I cannot read you as I do him."

"That is because I have my thoughts blocked from even him," she stated. "I cannot let him know how your training is progressing."

"Why not?" I asked.

"He would destroy you, my little firefly," she replied with a sigh. "Your powers have grown and grown, no matter how much we try to sleep them away. Even in your sleep state, your powers bubble through the enchantment in waves."

"I'm sorry," I mumbled, looking down at the ground. "I do not wish to harm anyone."

"I know you don't," she cooed sweetly. "And that is why I train you and he does not."

"Would you allow him to destroy me if he needed to?" I asked, bringing my eyes up to meet hers.

"No," she replied intently. "You are my child, even if your soul's power comes from another god who belonged to another pantheon's universe. I made you, and he will not destroy you if I have any say in it."

"Do you truly love me, or do you just see me as an emblem of power, the way he sees Anniel?" I inquired.

"He doesn't see you solely as power," she refuted.

"He might tell you otherwise," I began, "but I can see into his mind. Maybe he only lets you see what he wants you to see."

Mother swallowed hard and then smiled. "Let's begin your training, okay?"

I nodded and walked into the room behind the wall where she sat. I stood in the center of the room and waited for my command.

"Let it loose!" Mother shouted.

A deafening howl escaped my lips as I exploded in fire, like an atomic bomb going off.

"Recall it!" Mother commanded.

As soon as the words left her lips, the fire was sucked back into my body.

"Perfect. Now again!"

***

"We never said we were going to challenge them against one another!" Mother seethed.

"We need to see how their powers are progressing apart from one another and how they are when they are placed together with their powers active!" Alpha hissed. "Or else this will have all been for naught."

Mother looked between Anniel and me. We stood lovingly side by side and hand in hand.

"Fine, but not for long. We don't know how long they can be in the same room together with their powers at the surface."

"Anniel, uwr," Alpha commanded.

"Incaendiel, uwr," Mother commanded.

Immediately, Anniel's persona changed toward me, and she walked over to Alpha's side. One look at Alpha and I was filled with rage. Anniel took a step between Alpha and me and stood, unsheathing her sword and wielding it.

"You trained her to protect you against him?" Mother fumed.

"I did much more than that," Alpha bragged. "Anniel, bring forth your fire."

Anniel's fire climbed to the surface in total control. I unsheathed my sword and looked at Mother.

"Do it," she commanded.

My fire burst forth, hotter and brighter than that of Anniel, and trailed up my sword as I spun it around in my hand.

"How can he do that?" Alpha demanded, pounding his fist down on the table he stood before.

"Training," Mother boasted.

Alpha growled and yelled, "Now, Anniel!"

Anniel advanced against me and brought her sword down on mine. I blocked and parried her blow for blow. Every clank of our swords was like a ricochet effect. Cracks formed in the walls around us as our powers bounced off one another.

"Alpha, they're too powerful!" Mother cried as the room shook. "We need to shut them down before they bring the Summit down!"

"Just a little while longer," Alpha murmured, grinning madly as Anniel and I fought each other.

Splashes of light began to pour through the ceiling, and it was torn from the threshold, and a huge whirlpool formed in the space above us.

"They're creating a black hole!" Mother urged. "It will devour us all without escape. We have to shut it down!"

"A little longer!" Alpha ordered.

"No!" Mother shouted. "Incaendiel, Lishon! Anniel, Lishon!"

My powers deactivated, and I was myself again. However, Anniel was not. She was still fighting me with her sword.

"Why isn't she listening?" Mother demanded.

"She only has one master," Alpha replied.

"Tell her to stop!" Mother urged.

"Let's see how he fares against her without his powers," Alpha retorted.

I fought tooth and nail against her assaults. My fire burst forth on my skin and through my sword. I didn't want to hurt her, but I couldn't be defenseless against her either. Once again, the room began to shake, and the black hole appeared again.

"Why can he do that?" Alpha demanded, pounding his fist down on the table he sat at.

"Because even asleep, his powers still come forth uncontrolled!" Mother hissed. "You know this."

"Why does hers not do the same thing?" Alpha bellowed, enraged.

"Had you focused on controlling her powers instead of controlling her, then maybe hers would!" Mother spat.

Alpha groaned loudly. "Fine! Anniel, Lishon!"

***

"We have a huge problem," Alpha remarked, pacing back and forth in front of the council. "My universe is beginning to fold in on itself."

"Are they ready to be separated?" Tiamat inquired. "Their strong connection and close proximity together are trying to free their sleeping souls."

"I am not sure if they are ready," Alpha stated, sitting and rubbing his forehead.

"This is what happens when baby gods want to play house," Drac sneered. "You decided to create something, and you cannot even control it because you made it from old power you don't even understand. You are an ignorant god."

"I am not ignorant, and I am fully aware of how this all went. But if I recall correctly, Tiamat was the one who aided Omega in collecting the power that rests asleep in them. So are we naïve, or were we fooled by that harlot?" Alpha spat.

"Had you focused more on creating life as opposed to creating power, you wouldn't be in this predicament!" Tiamat hissed. "I helped you as was asked of me. Do not turn this on me as if I deceived you purposefully. I had no idea that Barbelo would bind to them when presented with the chance!"

"They're not ready," Alpha pleaded. "What else can I do?"

"Beg Yahweh for his power," Tiamat replied, shrugging her shoulders. "You have to have more power than they do to control them. It's that simple. If you cannot attain his power, then you have to separate them, whether they are ready or not."

Alpha ran his hands over his face in frustration.

"I am so sorry, Alpha, truly," Tiamat stated. "I know this is a hard decision for you to have to make. But they are indeed your only options."

"What if you were to take one of them?" Alpha asked, motioning to me. "You can have him back, and I keep the girl."

"Is that really fair to either of them?" Tiamat asked, looking at clueless me.

"I don't care what's fair to them!" Alpha shouted. "Not at this point!"

Tiamat glared at Alpha. "No."

"What?" he asked, confused.

"No, I will not take one or the other," she replied. "Fix your problem on your own. We are done trying to counsel you, especially if you won't listen to our suggestions."

"You told me if I separated them too soon, then there would be problems," Alpha refuted. "I did as you suggested. It is not my fault that the universe is pushing me faster when they are not ready."

"That's not our problem," Drac replied.

"You will regret this," Alpha seethed as he grabbed me by my arm and dragged me from the room.

***

"What did the council tell you?" Mother asked.

"It's time," Alpha replied, sitting down in the seat of his throne and rubbing his forehead.

"They're not ready to be separated!" Mother insisted. "Incaendiel's emotions have not been fostered with you at all!"

"I know this!" Alpha spat. "I was hoping for more time to switch them out with one another and I start training with him, but there isn't any time. They can't be together without them tearing the universe apart at the seams. It is time they are separated."

"So, how do we do this?" Mother asked, glancing in my direction.

"I have to cast one of them out," Alpha stated flatly.

"We can't just toss one of them out without a justifiable reason!" Mother refuted. "The others will ask questions."

"Then we lie to them. Tell him the one was disobedient to the point we feared for our safety," Alpha replied.

"That's not going to work!" Mother said, rejecting the idea. "The angels are not stupid."

"I don't know what you want me to do!" Alpha hollered. "They can't stay here together. I tried to get Tiamat to take him for a while, but she refused."

"You tried to give him away?" Mother asked in disbelief.

"I am out of choices," Alpha hollered. "I mean, I am open to suggestions. What do you think we should do?"

"We tell the children that there's a problem with all of our power, and we need one of them to fall," Mother offered.

"And if he doesn't step forward?" Alpha inquired, motioning to me.

"Then I will assume the responsibility of the need for the split of power, and he will choose to go with me," Mother insisted.

"Do you honestly think he loves you more than he loves her?" Alpha asked, motioning over at Anniel.

We both stood quietly as they argued back and forth.

"You can manipulate our thoughts, can you not?" Anniel asked. "Like when you erase the memories of these meetings from our memory so we don't tell the others."

"Yes," Alpha answered. "We can manipulate what we think, see, and do. But we don't like to do it more than necessary. Too many manipulations can backfire on us."

"What if it's a small one?" Anniel offered. "Like you show me something that will tell me to tell Incaendiel to go with Mother?"

"Would that work?" Mother asked.

Alpha sighed. "It's our only chance at this, so it better."

Chapter Fifteen

I SNAPPED UP from my lying position in a cold sweat. I looked around the room to see Starfire and Damian watching me intently.

"I need to go back," I stammered, looking over at Starfire. "I need to see more."

"I think you have seen enough for one day," Starfire urged.

"No!" I demanded. "I need to see what Lilith did to me after the fall."

"Another day!" Starfire insisted. "That was a lot to process, and by the end, your power was starting to grow out of control. You nearly caught on fire."

I moved my body so my legs could hang off the couch, and I rested my head in my hands. "Did you all see what I saw?" I asked, not looking up.

"Yes," Damian replied softly, sitting quiet and still in his spot.

"Are Anniel and I actually at full power, or are we still asleep?" I asked Starfire.

"You are still asleep," Starfire answered quietly.

I rubbed my forehead the same way I had seen Alpha do all those years. "What do I do?" I whimpered with a tear rolling down my face.

"That is a difficult question," Starfire replied.

"Would Anniel attack him?" Damian asked. "That's what she was conditioned to do in her training while awake."

"That is what makes it a difficult question because it's a fifty-fifty chance," Starfire replied.

"Does it have to be Alpha that awakens her still?" Damian pressed. "Because he's not going to activate her without her by his side."

"Yes, it has to be Alpha," Lilith interrupted, walking into the room.

"How are you even here?" Damian demanded, jumping up from his seat.

"Do you really think Starfire's warlocks hold a power greater than that of gods?" Lilith replied smugly. "We can come and go as we please. Alpha just chooses not to while playing this game with us all."

"So he could come here anytime he wishes to?" Damian mumbled in a panic, taking a seat again.

"Yes, but he won't," Lilith replied. "He is afraid of you all together." She looked at me. "Especially you."

"Why me?" I asked.

"Because you never submitted to him as his child. And that shadow part of you that we keep asleep hates him. It bubbled to the surface every so often with your powers. You became so angry with him throughout the millennia. Pair that with your shadow self, and you have pure hatred for him. He doesn't know if I have let that side of you loose yet. So he keeps his distance," Lilith explained.

"And Anniel?" I inquired.

"Her shadow self is bubbling to the surface just as yours does," Lilith replied.

"So every single millennium that passed and he kept her to himself, he taught her to hate me through her shadow self?" I asked, staring in disbelief at Lilith.

A lonely tear fell from Lilith's eye. "I believe so," she whispered.

"So our choices are to keep ourselves asleep and our psyche split apart or awaken and possibly be at each other's throats?" I pressed.

Lilith nodded.

"Why did he hate me?" I implored. "I saw his face while creating me. He was happy. He was enthusiastic. Why does he hate me?"

"He doesn't hate you, son," Lilith replied with a stifled cry. "He fears you. He fears your power. And he is jealous you were chosen by Barbelo to be more powerful than he is."

"I know Yahweh turned him down for power," I stated. "We saw it after we were in the void during our transition."

Lilith nodded her head. "He went to Yahweh first thing because he didn't want to lose his children. But just as you could see into his mind, Yahweh could as well. Yahweh is the all-seeing father, and Barbelo the all-seeing mother. They could see past any blocks put up in our minds. And he saw the future in wait with Alpha with power beyond comprehension, where he used it for greed and not love."

"So that's why Damian could tap into anyone's thoughts?" I pondered. "Because he and Luxina aren't asleep like Anniel and me? Is that why we can only read each other's minds, or the kids when they let us?"

"Yes," Lilith answered.

The room fell silent, and the tension in the air was like waves of sound crashing against one another.

"Do you love us?" I whimpered.

"I divorced Alpha for you," she replied, taking a seat at the table with Starfire. "I would have activated you to take him out if he ever tried to truly hurt you."

"When I was in the dungeon?" I asked.

"He never had one-on-one training with you like he did with Anniel," she answered. "He was trying to break your shadow self. The part of you that has never submitted to him. The part of you that loves Anniel with every fiber in your being and will not hurt her, and he knows it. He was trying to make you despise her and sever that connection."

"Would you abandon me to take his side?" I queried, staring at her intently.

As she fell quiet, I studied her face. She appeared more youthful than she did in the dungeon.

"How have you been regressing your age?" I breathed.

"What do you mean?" she asked, taken aback.

"Every time I see you, you appear younger and younger," I replied.

"We… aged the more we used our power to create this place," she explained.

"So the more the power returns to you, the more youthful you become?" I asked.

"Yes, and the more powerful we become as well," she replied, shifting in her seat. "Alpha only took a small part of the angels back. He took their light but not their grace. Only I can take that back. That is the spark of life I breathed into each of you."

"So, even though they are now in allegiance with Incaendiel and share his power, you can still make them drop dead where they stand if you wish to?" Damian chimed in.

"Yes, but I would never do that," Lilith protested. "I may have been a toxic mother and played games and all while having my spat with Alpha, but I would never hurt my children like that. Even when Anniel was being incarnated as a human, she only died a human death. She was never in any real danger at my hands. Now, Alpha..." she trailed off. "Alpha would if he could."

"I want to awaken," I plainly stated. "I want to be whole again."

"There is no turning back once I awaken you," she warned. "I haven't brought you forth in a long time, and once your sleep self merges with your awake self, it will know all. I cannot control you, and I don't even know if you could control yourself."

"You could put me back to sleep," I protested.

"No, I can't, Incaendiel," she replied, sighing. "You have been stripped of your enchantment. I cannot control anything about you once you are awakened. You will be your own person again. You will be the old soul who awakened when I first created you."

"Can we defeat Alpha without Anniel and me awake?" I asked.

"I don't know," Lilith answered. "And before you ask, I don't know if you being awake is enough as well."

"Starfire?" I asked, glancing at her. "Do you see anything about it?"

"Until you drop your suppressed psyche, I cannot see anything about the end still," she replied.

"Do it," Damian interrupted.

"What if I don't remember the person I am now?" I urged, turning my attention to him. "What if I don't remember you or Luxina? My asleep self has never met either of you."

"You will remember," Damian replied. "Blood remembers blood. It's why your shadow self cannot let go of who you came from. You remember them in your blood, even if your memory won't let you see them. Do it!"

"Will I hurt anyone when I come together?" I questioned, turning to Starfire.

"That I also cannot see," she responded.

"Can you enchant a room to contain me?" I asked.

"Just like when you finished your transition once I stripped your enchantment away, I cannot contain you if you explode," she replied.

"Take me somewhere safe," I told Lilith. "That way, no one can be hurt. Take me to the lake."

"What lake?" Damian asked, scrunching his face.

"The lake he died," Starfire replied.

"I'm going, too," Damian said, standing to his feet.

"No, you're not," I protested.

"You can't tell me what I can and can't do!" Damian shouted.

I stood up, towering over him, and even though he kept the same willful spite, I could see his fear.

"I don't want you to get hurt," I replied softly.

"You won't hurt me," he insisted, fear still creeping through his eyes. "Blood remembers blood."

We were all quiet for what seemed like an eternity.

"So, is it settled?" Lilith asked. "Are we doing this?"

"Yes," I replied, still staring Damian down. "Take us to the lake. Starfire, tell Anniel we will be back."

Starfire nodded, and we all stepped out the door.

"Take my hand," Lilith said, and we each grabbed one of her hands.

"Incaendiel?" Samael said, walking up to us. "What are you doing?"

"Righting a wrong," I breathed as we disappeared from Lightshade and arrived at the lake. I walked around the lake, admiring the foliage and crystal blue water as memories from years ago came rushing forth.

"You burned this place down so many times trying to come to grips with your power that your ego was never supposed to wield alone," Lilith remarked, walking up to my side. "It's fitting that you wanted to be here."

"Do it," I demanded as I turned to face her.

"As you wish, son," she replied. "Damian, go stand over there, please," she ordered, pointing to a spot a reasonable distance from the place I stood in.

Surprisingly, he obeyed and went to stand where she directed. I made eye contact with him, and I saw the worry in his eyes. I gave him a reassuring smile and looked back at Lilith.

I took in a deep breath and then exhaled. "Say it," I spoke softly.

Lilith exhaled nervously and nodded. "Incaendiel, uwr!" she commanded.

My skin blazed to life, and I could feel the power surging through my body. I had never felt power like this before, but at the same time, it felt normal. Out of all the times I had lost control of myself and burned things to a crisp, it didn't compare to the ringlets of fire that coursed through my veins, looking like the day I took my potion. And all at once, my ego and shadow self collided as memories from when I was awake and asleep flooded my mind all at once. I dropped to the ground, howling in pain as my skull felt like it was tearing apart.

"What's happening to him?" I heard Damian demand. "What did you do to him?"

"I freed him," Lilith replied. "His memories are all colliding and fusing together to form the picture he has been searching for. Some of them will fight the others. His split psyche is fighting over which is to become the dominant him."

I burned hotter as every glimpse into the past rolled through my head, and I let out a deafening scream. My power mounted and mounted until I exploded into a huge ball of fire, just like I had seen in the memory. I was an atom bomb going off, and my freed power fed it like gasoline. Unlike before, when I was under the enchantment, I now had nothing holding back the flames as they crawled up the mountainside. Another deafening howl, and the fire burned more intensely. I didn't tire as I used to. There was a constant source of power keeping my rage inside fueled. The face of Alpha appeared in my mind, and all I wanted was him dead. It's all I could focus on, and that he needed to be destroyed.

"Incaendiel!" Lilith shouted, and I whipped my head in her direction, standing from the burning foliage in which I was squatting.

"You," I raged in a hollow voice.

"It's me," she replied, holding her hands up. "It's Mother."

"You are not my mother," I hissed venomously. "You have done things... sinister things."

"I have been the only mother you have known for more than four billion years," she pleaded.

"A mother doesn't do what you did to me," I replied dryly. "A mother doesn't cause the devastation, trauma, and anguish you have inflicted alongside your husband."

"Please, you need me!" she implored, hitting her knees.

"I need no one," I answered, raising my hand and bringing forth my fire into my hand.

Someone jumped in front of her and shouted, "No, Incaendiel!"

"Who are you?" I demanded, shifting my attention to his face.

"It's Damian!" he replied.

"I don't remember a Damian," I growled. "All I can remember is her face and Alpha's face and the torture they subjected me to over and over to try and break me."

"They did it to me, too," he replied, taking a few steps closer to me. "They chained me up, beat me, nearly killed me, threw me in arenas with monstrous beings. And you saved me."

"I have never met you before," I protested.

"But you have!" he insisted. "You know who I am! Please, don't do this!"

"You don't control me," I rasped. "No one controls me anymore. I have been shoved in a box for too long. No one will ever put me back in it."

I focused my hand on him and primed my energy.

"Dad! Please don't!" he cried. *Blood remembers blood...*

It only took one word for my memories to tumble together. Dad. Everything rushed through my mind: The training in secret, Anniel, the fall, her human trials, the fake manipulations of memories, the war against Alpha, Luxina, Xavier, Starfire, and finally, Damian. I howled in pain again as everything crashed around in my brain, and then everything went black.

When I opened my eyes, smoke rose around me. I sat up and looked around at the burning rubble. Once again, I had burned the place down to bare ground. I placed my hand on the earth and recalled the flames back to me. As they retreated, the land healed immediately behind the receding flames as if nothing had happened. And then I was filled with panic. Damian! Where is Damian? My eyes scanned my surroundings, trying to find him through the lingering smoke.

"Damian!" I shouted in panic. "Damian!"

"I'm right here!" he called out through the smoke.

I jumped to my feet and ran in the direction from which I had heard his voice. As the smoke cleared, I saw him standing with Lilith, unharmed. I let out a sigh of relief and walked over to him, pulling him into my chest.

"I almost killed you," I breathed shakily.

He wrapped his arms around me for a brief moment before he pushed me away. I looked at him, puzzled.

"I don't like to be touched," he replied as if answering the question I had yet to form.

Lilith stood behind him, still fearful but trying her best not to show it. I still wanted to destroy her, but I could control the urge now that both halves of myself had melded together.

"I remember everything," I stated curtly.

"I know," she replied, swallowing hard.

"I remember what you put me through," I growled through gritted teeth.

"It was only to get you to learn to control your power," she reminded me.

"There could have been better ways," I snarled.

"No one is perfect," she replied meekly. "Let's get back to Lightshade."

I snapped my fingers, and we were back in front of Starfire's cottage. Samael slowly stood up from his seated position on the steps as he stared at me. Unlike before, when we exploded and activated our powers, he didn't move closer to me and kept his distance.

"What did you do to him?" he demanded, looking at Lilith.

"I took down the wall in his mind that we put up as a fail-safe when he was created," she replied. "He is now at full power."

"He looks…" Samael began.

"Like he grew four feet and has suns for eyes?" Damian asked, amused.

"Yeah, that," Samael replied, swallowing as he nodded.

"Yeah, freaked me out as well," Damian replied.

"How is his power brought forth, but he isn't burning everything down to the ground?" Samael asked, bewildered.

"Because he knows how to control it now," Lilith replied. "The only reason we put up the barrier was because at full power, he was trying to kill us when we first made him."

"Woah," Azazel remarked as she came running up to Samael and slowed. One by one, the angels started making their way over. "What happened to him?" she murmured.

"I am now who I am supposed to be," I replied, my voice deeper than before.

"Even your voice is different," Samael declared in awe.

"Where is Anniel?" I asked.

"No one has seen her since this morning," Azazel answered, not taking her eyes off me.

"Well, we need to find her so we can fill her in on what is going on," I said.

Chapter Sixteen

I SAT ON Starfire's porch, still unsure if I should try to interact with anyone, afraid I could accidentally hurt them. I understood fear and anxiety fuel my powers, so I tried to keep the thoughts from my mind, but having been conditioned for so long to repress my powers, I am lost. I know I have control over them, but there's still that doubt in my head. I looked around at the people gathered in the different arenas, and I could hear them speak even though no words left their lips. Every now and then, they would glance in my direction.

He looks so different now.

He's scary.

Why was he chosen and not one of us?

He could probably kill us all with a snap of his fingers.

Is it safe to even be around him?

Maybe Alpha kept that block up in his head for a reason.

Did we make the right choice siding with him?

They feared me now. And yeah, I probably could kill them with a snap of my fingers. Samael had been actively avoiding me since I returned to Lightshade. I don't know if it was out of fear or jealousy. I couldn't tell with him anymore, and I didn't pry into his thoughts to find out. I didn't want to know. He and I had followed each other to the ends of the earth, and it would be world-shattering to learn he didn't want to have anything to do with me anymore. Damian appeared from inside Starfire's cottage and sat down beside me.

"They had the same thoughts running through their heads when they met me," he stated as he sat down on the step beside me. "They saw me as a monster who couldn't be trusted."

"It's different for me," I replied. "Most of them, I was raised beside them for billions of years. Lilith and Alpha kept my one side hidden so it wouldn't spark fear or jealousy with them, and now, here we are. Lifetimes have gone by with us side by side, and they are doing just as Lilith and Alpha feared they would."

"We still haven't found Anniel," he said, changing the subject. "We have searched all of Lightshade, and she is not here."

"Her memory wall had already been toppled by Alpha," I sighed. "He removed all manipulations of memories from her and me. The only ones that were left for me were the ones Lilith had put up. There's no telling what was triggered when we were sparring earlier."

"You don't think she returned to Alpha, do you?" Damian asked, glancing up at me.

"I don't know," I replied with a heavy sigh. "I don't know anything at this point."

Metatron and the rest of the group rounded the corner of Starfire's cottage and slowed. I glanced over at him. He shook his head.

"We didn't find her," he declared.

I scanned their faces while reading their thoughts.

He's going to kill us for not finding her, Michael thought.

He looks so menacing, Azazel thought. *Are we safe around him now?*

He's the most beautiful and the most terrifying being in the universe, Metatron thought.

My eyes rested on Samael, and I took a deep breath.

We need to keep him calm and rational. This is all new to him, and he had a problem before he was uncaged in keeping his powers in check. I hope none of these idiots say anything to trigger him. There's no telling what he would do. But I will be there. I will keep my brother safe.

Relief washed over me, and Damian nudged my elbow. "Thought you weren't going to do that?" he teased.

"Shut up," I smirked and tousled his hair. "Has Lilith made it back?" I asked the group.

300

They shook their heads. "We haven't seen her since she left to check the Summit and see if Anniel returned there."

I nodded and stood up from the porch step.

"Where are you going?" Damian asked.

"To lie down. I'm exhausted," I answered, yawning and stretching.

"I will let you know if anything changes," he assured as I walked inside.

"Thank you," I replied and headed up the stairs.

I opened the door to my room, hoping someone had forgotten to check in here for her, but I was met with disappointment. The room was empty. I walked over to the bed and flopped down on it, staring up at the ceiling. I knew where she was. We all knew where she was. It was why Lilith hadn't returned. She was there. She returned to her master like she had been conditioned to do. The door opened abruptly, and I sat up as it was closed behind Anniel.

"There you are!" I exclaimed and jumped up from the bed. "We have been looking for you everywhere!"

"I can't stay here, Incaendiel," she whispered. "I have to go."

"What are you talking about?" I asked, confused.

"Every bone in my body is screaming for me to kill you," she replied, turning on her heel and looking me in the eyes. Her eyes were red-rimmed from where she was crying. "And even more so now that you have been woken up," she murmured. "I remember it all. I remember every single time Alpha made us fight, trying to hone our powers in. I remember how he made me his lapdog and how I was to protect him at all costs, even if that meant killing you. Because even then, even in the beginning, you hated him and wanted to make him suffer for what he let happen to our universe. We both did. But for some reason, I grew to care for him."

"Wait, you knew this whole time about it all and didn't say anything?" I snapped.

"At first, it was just bits and pieces," she replied. "Then it started peeling back more and more, and then we sparred..."

"Things will be fine," I proclaimed.

"No, they won't," she insisted, pacing the room.

"You will be fine!" I protested.

"No," she screeched, abruptly stopping in place. "It's just one word, and I awaken, and I do not meld together. Unlike with Lilith and you, it has not been years and years since he has used my powers. He used them every chance he got. I do not meld. I become the machine he made me into. And my only goal is to protect him and to kill you!"

"There is a fifty-fifty chance that this time it will work and you will bond with your other self," I refuted. "It took me a while to bond. I almost killed Lilith and Damian!" I hissed. "You cannot give up on this. The universe needs you. I need you. You're my other half. I cannot do this alone. I cannot do this without you!"

"I'm sorry," she whimpered and turned to grab the doorknob.

"Where are you going to go?" I demanded. "Anywhere you go, Alpha will try and bring you back to him. He knows he can't from here because he will die trying. But out there, without me or everyone else, he will. You have to stay," I pleaded.

"If I stay, I will kill you!" she yelled. "And you are the only hope everyone has of taking down Alpha. I am not. I do not have the same will as you and never have. It's why he was able to manipulate me so easily."

She yanked the door open and was met with the face of Alpha on the other side. He spun her around and held her by her neck as I blazed in loathing and fury.

"I see Lilith has set you free," Alpha remarked with a wicked grin, struggling to hold Anniel in his grasp. "Too bad Anniel didn't fill you in sooner so you could have a better game plan when I came for her."

I looked from him to Anniel, and she looked away from me. "Oh, she didn't tell you," Alpha goaded, mocking me with a sad face. "She knew I would be coming for her this whole time. She was just ordered by her master not to say anything. I needed her enchantment dropped so I could use my best foot soldier."

I went to take a step toward him.

"At, at," he taunted, wagging his finger at me. "I will set her free, and then it will be a showdown between the two of you. You don't want to destroy your precious little façade of a safe haven, now do you? Besides, you have bigger fish to fry. You have to find your precious Luxina still before she comes over to the dark side with her mother."

"What do you want?" I demanded. I conceded, backed down, and then glared at him.

"I've already got it," he snarled and vanished into thin air with Anniel.

"Fuck!" I yelled, pounding the wall and busting a hole through it.

I bounded down the stairs and out the door to make sure everyone was okay outside. Anxiety flooded my body as I looked around. No one was outside. My dream came to my forethoughts, and I began to spiral into a panic attack.

"Where the fuck is everyone!" I screamed in heaves.

"Hidden away," Starfire assured as she appeared from inside. "They are safe and sound. I sensed Alpha's presence and portaled them to a hideaway bunker."

"Damian?" I implored, fighting the tightening of my chest.

"He is with them, too," Starfire affirmed. "We couldn't find Anniel, though."

"He took her," I said, my voice cracking.

Everything was crashing down around me, and I felt like I couldn't breathe. I clawed at my chest, trying to release the tension my shirt had on it, to take in deeper gulps of air, but nothing worked.

"Breathe!" Starfire shouted.

Fire erupted around me as I hit the ground and began crawling. Maybe it was for the best that I died. I am not a leader. I am a selfish person, always putting my needs over everyone else's. First with Luxina, then with Anniel and Damian. I would let the world burn for those three and not even give a shit. As long as they were safe, the world was safe. But now...

"Incaendiel!" Damian shouted, bending down in front of me.

It was like listening through a tunnel. I could see his face and watch his mouth move, but his voice was muffled, and a loud ringing sound echoed in my ears.

"What happened?" I could hear muffled.

"Alpha," was all Starfire said as my vision began to grow dark.

Dad! Damian shouted in his head. *Breathe!*

I snapped out of the dark hole closing around me and back into the light.

"Breathe!" Damian yelled.

I took in a sharp inhale and exhaled slowly, followed by another and another. I looked around to see everything catching on fire. I laid my hand on the ground and recalled the fire back to me as my heart slowed its racing and my breathing started to steady itself. My hearing began to return, and I heard Starfire talking.

"When I found him, he was already going into a panic attack. He thought Alpha had taken you all," she explained, recounting what had happened.

"Or he thought we all left him for Alpha," Damian offered, glancing over at me.

"Why would he think that?" Metatron asked, his eyes on me, and then back to Damian.

"Before he was fully unlocked, he had a dream that was just like this," Damian shared with the group. "He came outside, and everyone was gone, and Alpha told him we all left him to join his side."

"We would never do that, though," Samael insisted.

"He can hear everyone's thoughts now!" Damian hissed, glaring at everyone standing around. "Every single thing that goes through you all's minds, he can hear, and so can I. So I know what you've been thinking about him as well."

"We didn't know he could read everyone's minds now," Azazel murmured, glancing over at me shamefully. "We always knew of the connection between him and Anniel."

"Well, now you know," Damian snapped. "Samael, you're still first in command. Keep them in line," he ordered.

I began to stand when Damian ran to my side to help me up.

"I'm okay," I reassured him.

"Yeah, but you still need some time to rest," he replied, leading me to the steps to go inside.

"Incaendiel!" Samael called out. Damian and I turned around to look at him. "I will follow you to the ends of the earth. I hope you know that, Brother. None of this will ever change our bond. You being who you are now. I am not afraid of that. You have my word, I will not leave your side."

"We pledged to follow you," Michael said, stepping forward. "There's no going back to Alpha. Not after what he did to us all. Not after what he continues to do to everyone."

I nodded. "A discussion for another time because what I have to ask of you is once again selfish," I replied regretfully.

"It's not selfish trying to keep our whole family together," Azazel chimed in. "Anniel and Luxina are both our family, too. And we will tear the universe apart to keep them safe. Asking us to help save them isn't even a question. We are already formulating the plan."

A tear slid down my cheek as Damian pulled me toward the door. I nodded at them all before turning around to go into the cottage. I looked down at Damian, who wasn't much shorter than I was.

"When did you get taller?" I joked.

"Seriously?" he asked, looking up at me. "Now you have jokes?"

I chuckled. "Without humor, what do we have left but self-loathing and dark thoughts?"

"Touché," he smirked.

He helped me into my room and sat me down on the bed. I lay back, exhausted, when it felt like déjà vu all over again from earlier. Another panic attack loomed on the horizon.

"Alpha won't be back," he assured me, reading my thoughts. "He got what he wanted. He pulled the ace he had up his sleeve that we were all thinking he had."

"If only I had thought of the memories sooner," I murmured. "I could have stopped this from happening."

"No, you wouldn't have," Damian replied, sitting in a chair against the wall. "She was going to go back to him to protect us all before he took her. Alpha was just waiting for Lilith to topple your wall and activate you before he let us know his rook was here the whole time."

"How is this our lives?" I asked, placing my hand on my head. "Always running, always hiding, always fighting, and for what? To live? To exist? Sometimes, I don't know what the point is. Not when everything always ends the same damn way every time. We never catch a break, and it's getting so exhausting. Over four billion years of this bullshit."

"It's different this time," Damian refuted.

"Not much so," I fired back. "He has your mother again. He has Luxina again in freaking Purgatory of all places, doing who knows what to her."

"He doesn't have me, and he doesn't have you," Damian replied. "He never has all of us, and this time, you are different. I am different. We aren't defenseless against him anymore."

"If he activates your mother, she doesn't believe she is strong enough to meld her two psyches together like I did," I confessed. "She believes she will just be his mindless lapdog, protecting him from me. You know what that means?" I asked, swallowing the lump in my throat.

"What?" Damian asked in return.

"It means I will have to kill her, or she will kill me," I choked out, tears threatening to spill out.

"Starfire said there is a fifty-fifty chance that won't happen, and she will accept her shadow self and ego as one," he stated confidently. "And if I am betting money on a horse, I am betting on Starfire. Not Alpha."

"I am so tired from this war," I replied, straightening in the bed on my back. "It's been going on for so long, long before you were ever born, back to the very beginning, back to my creation, back before my creation. I can feel it in my bones. Something happened; more than just a sun was dying, and the power was harvested. It feels like I was slain to attain the power. Power that wasn't theirs to have to begin with."

"You need to sleep," Damian ordered, changing the subject. "You will feel better once you rest. You've been through a lot lately. It's wearing you thin. You can't fight when you're battling your own self."

"You don't tell me what to do," I teased with a chuckle.

I was so tired, and the bed was so inviting. But I didn't want to sleep. I was afraid to sleep. Bad things happen when I am not awake. Both mentally and physically not awake.

"This isn't the same sleep Alpha would do," Damian reassured me. "This is the sleep your body needs to rest and reset. Nothing bad is going to happen, and I will stay with you until you wake back up."

"You don't have to do that," I replied. "You don't have to sacrifice your time to make sure I am okay."

"I want to," he assured.

And as his calming vibes hit me, I drifted off into sweet, dreamless nothingness.

Chapter Seventeen

I AWOKE TO silence and sat straight up in bed. Damian was slumped down in his chair, asleep. He looked so at peace when he was asleep. I thought back to the day before. His mannerisms were warming up more and more to me. He was no longer standoffish or belligerent with me. And he had started calling me dad, which secretly made me smile with joy even if it is only to snap me out of shit. He made me feel wanted during a time when I felt like no one wanted me around, which meant so much to me coming from him. I rose out of bed and stood, cracking every muscle in my body as I stretched. I nudged him, and he stirred awake.

"Did you sleep there all night?" I asked, staring at him in the chair.

He rubbed his neck and nodded.

"Climb in the bed and get you a few good hours of good sleep," I ordered, pointing over to my bed.

"What about you?" he asked, looking from the bed and back to me.

"I will be fine," I assured him with a smile. "Sleep did the trick. I will come and get you in a few hours."

He nodded and moved from the chair over to the bed. He snuggled into the pillow and was out within seconds. He had the weight of the world on his shoulders, and the last thing he needed to do was have to babysit me because I couldn't come to terms with things and handle my own shit. I left the room, closing the door quietly behind me, and made my way downstairs. I walked into the kitchen to look for something to eat because, quite frankly, I hadn't eaten in a few days and needed food for energy.

"Well, look what the cat dragged in," Asmodeus teased as he took a bite of an apple.

"Are you ever anywhere except in the kitchen?" I shot back with a laugh.

"You know me," he joked, tipping the chair he sat in back on two legs. "I could eat for days."

"I feel like that now," I said as I picked up some grapes. "I don't even know when the last time it was that I ate some food here."

"Yeah, you gotta watch that figure," he replied, slapping my abs and laughing.

"Where's everyone at?" I asked, popping a grape in my mouth.

"Training, as usual," he answered, taking another bite out of his apple. "Samael is whipping everyone into shape, and everyone is falling in rank."

"Anyone giving him lip?" I wondered, a laugh creeping up through the seriousness.

"You know the same old same old," he declared, laughing. "And then Azazel steps in to bite their heads off."

"Just like old times, eh?" I mused.

"Yep, just like old times, Brother," Asmodeus asserted, patting my shoulder. "The only difference is now you don't get fussed at for burning shit down."

"Hey!" I defended, holding my hands up. "Cheap shot much?"

I grinned, popping another grape in my mouth, and reached for some cheese and bread.

"I'm glad you're better today," Asmodeus said seriously. "We were all worried about you yesterday."

I agreed silently. "Yeah, yesterday was a shit day."

"I can't imagine going through all you have gone through and still waking up the next day to keep going further," he responded in awe. "I admire that about you. It's what I admire about Damian, too."

"That little shit saved me yesterday when I almost lost myself," I said, putting my food down for a second. "He brought me together after Lilith freed me. He brought me out of my panic attack. He's the real hero of the family. Not me."

"No one can blame you for how you reacted yesterday and if they do, I will give them a swift kick in the ass," he replied, tossing his apple core in a bin. "Damian is just like you. It's amazing how he was raised with Alpha, and yet your defiance spoke through his veins."

"I don't know," I insisted, raising an eyebrow. "I do recall it was you who stole Alpha's chariot and horses to joyride around Saturn. I believe he is more like you."

"Hey!" Asmodeus shouted, wide-eyed and grinning from ear to ear. "That was *your* idea!"

I glanced out the window of the kitchen and saw everyone out there training.

"I bet they're all out there waiting for me, aren't they?" I asked, dreading going out there.

"No," Asmodeus assured. "They expect you to sleep like the dead for a few days."

"Has Lilith been back?" I questioned, turning my attention back to him.

He shook his head. "No one has seen her since she left to look for Anniel in the Summit."

"Probably for the best," I replied. "I almost killed her once she set me free."

He nodded. "Damian told me while we were hiding out in the bunker. I couldn't blame you if you did, though. She put you through hell."

"No one understands that if Anniel doesn't meld with her other self and we have to fight, we will tear the universe apart doing it," I declared, looking at Asmodeus. "It's why they separated us."

"What does that mean?" he asked in return.

"It means that if she doesn't find the part of herself where she is split to fix it, I will have to kill her before she ever gets a chance to try and fight me," I explained.

"Can you do that, though?" he inquired, leaning forward. "Can you really kill her? After everything throughout the years. Her human trials and all. Can you really bring yourself to be the one to end her?"

"I don't know," I responded, leaning against the counter I stood at. "But I won't put that on either of the kids' shoulders when it comes down to it. Damian has enough baggage hanging over his head, and Luxina… she had to basically kill her brother for her to be whole again. And I don't think I could let one of you either without feeling some type of way, you know?"

"Our parents really screwed us all the way up," Asmodeus proclaimed, popping a grape in his mouth. "And the generation that followed. All over some stupid games because they were having a marital spat."

"Talk about family drama," I added, rolling my eyes. "We are a freaking soap opera."

I started heading out of the kitchen.

"Where are you going?" Asmodeus asked.

"Outside before Samael breaks out a whip and starts cracking it at everyone," I joked. "You better soon as well before he sends a hunting party after you."

Asmodeus stood to attention and raised his hand in a salute. "Sir, yes, sir!"

"Cute," I smirked.

Asmodeus laughed, and I walked out the front door and into the sunshine.

"Well, aren't you a sight for sore eyes?" Metatron declared, walking up to me and playfully punching my shoulder. "We didn't expect to see you crawl out of bed for at least a week."

"Yeah, I will reserve that kind of sleep for when I am dead," I joked back. "How's the training coming along?"

"A lot better than it had been," Metatron replied. "Even though it was a lie that you were spouting to Damian the other day about the Nephilim and their untouched angelic powers, you turned out to be right."

"Wait, what?" I asked. "They *do* have powers?"

Metatron nodded. "I mean, it makes sense that they do. They're half angel."

"Did they have to do anything special to unlock them?" I asked, watching all of the

Nephilim closely and seeing their powers shine from their skin.

"I think Starfire gave them something," Metatron answered. "Not sure."

"Well, as long as their powers are now active," I said, watching them spar with the angels. "Would that make them our nieces and nephews or cousins?" I asked.

"It makes them a powerful ally," Samyaza replied, walking up to me. "Nice to see you again, Incaendiel. It's been a few days. I heard… things happened and came to see for myself."

"Yeah, it's been a long week," I huffed. "I don't think there's been a longer week since the first week of creation."

"I didn't expect you to be cracking jokes knowing Alpha has taken your mate with him off to the Summit," Samyaza chided.

"If I don't make jokes, I burn shit down and kill people," I remarked in return. "Jokes are safer for everybody."

"Duly noted," Samayaza replied, cocking his head to the side in acknowledgement. "I arrived to tell you that the few remaining Watchers will be arriving in the next few days and wanted to make sure they would be welcomed and not treated indifferently."

"Indifference is a thing of the past among everyone here, Brother," I declared sincerely. "Everyone is family here. And what happened to all of you was by far one of the worst things Alpha did to any of us."

"And when we join your ranks…" he began.

I could hear the thoughts he didn't want to speak freely. "Yes, you will all become your original, angelic selves. No more vampyric blood for you all, and you don't have to hide in shadows anymore, either."

"I want you to know that's not the only reason we are joining the cause," Samyaza replied, lowering his embarrassed eyes.

"I know. You don't have to worry, Brother," I assured him, patting his shoulder. "Don't try to explain yourselves. We wouldn't be whole without you all."

Samael walked over to join the conversation. "Didn't expect to see either of you," he said, looking between Samyaza and me, with his eyes resting on mine. "Are you well rested?"

I nodded. "About yesterday," I began.

He held up his hand. "Don't explain yourself. We know how difficult all of this has been for you, and all at once. I'm surprised it took this long for you to have a nuclear meltdown. I was expecting it much sooner."

"Not sure if that should offend me or not," I laughed.

"Everything makes so much more sense about you now," he offered. "The reason you couldn't control your power was because you weren't whole, and your asleep self was the one who could. If anyone should be apologetic, it should be us. You didn't deserve the treatment you received growing up in the Summit, and you didn't deserve what you heard from everyone's thoughts yesterday. Had Alpha and Lilith not lied to everyone from the spark of creation, we wouldn't have feared your powers either."

"Even though my memories are unlocked from everything post-creation, there are still some suppressed memories from when I was another being," I replied. "I do know that much. I know I came from another place, but everything is hazy now. Lilith and Alpha suppressed them because it fueled my hatred for Alpha. They were able to wipe them, but not the feelings of hatred against him."

"If we find my book, all of those questions will be answered," Raziel remarked as he walked up to us.

"We haven't seen you in a few days," I replied, giving him a short hug. "Did you find Cain?" I asked, looking around for a new face.

"I did and wanted to make sure it was safe for him to come here since Alpha made his grand appearance yesterday," he said.

"Yeah, even Starfire didn't know her force field was useless against gods," I replied. "But honestly, can you really stop gods?"

"Will he be returning?" Raziel asked.

"No, he got what he wanted," I answered, lowering my eyes and thinking about Anniel.

"She knows too much for Alpha," Raziel insisted. "Will she tell him? Were her orders to be a spy and collect information for him?" he prodded.

"I'm not sure," I stammered, shrugging my shoulders. "At this point, who really knows?

"Well, we mustn't waste any time then," Raziel said, lifting his fingers to his mouth and whistling.

We all looked at the portal that formed, and Gadreel and Cain walked through, holding a book.

"Are you all ready to find my descendants?" he asked, holding the book up in the air.

"Yes," I replied, waving my hand. "Follow me to the conference room." I looked around at those who were standing with me. "All of you. And gather the key players."

I led Gadreel, Cain, and Raziel into Starfire's cottage and to the conference room. Samyaza followed along with Samael while Metatron rounded up the others. One by one, they all filled the room. Azazel, Raphael, Michael, Metatron, and Praeziel all took a seat in the front rows of the room. Whispers filled my head from an unknown source, and I couldn't make out what they were saying. I looked around the room at those sitting in front of me, and none of their faces gave away that they were thinking anything I couldn't hear.

"Are any of you thinking something, I don't know, quietly?" I asked, peering at everyone.

"Can you think thoughts quietly?" Michael mused.

I shrugged. "I don't know. Never mind," I said, shaking my head.

We all turned our attention to Cain, who stood beside me, looking up at me with curious but fearful eyes.

"So it's true," he proclaimed, continuing his stare. "You're really a god."

I nodded.

"And you *are* going to take down Alpha, right?" he questioned, watching my eyes intently.

"That's the plan," I answered.

"I need you to say it," he insisted. "I need to hear it said in those specific words."

"I am going to destroy Alpha or die trying," I affirmed.

He studied my face before nodding. "Okay," he said, turning his attention to everyone. "You all probably know bits and pieces of my story."

"It was just a few human years ago we learned what Alpha did to you," Samael replied. "We had no idea that Lucifer possessed your body."

Cain smiled. "I loved my brother, Abel, so very much…" he trailed off. "When Lucifer left me, I stood with the rock still in my hand, staring down at his bleeding corpse. Alpha appeared. It just wasn't his voice like that god awful memoir of his states. He looked from Abel, and then to me...

"Cain, what has happened?" Alpha asked, bending down and touching Abel's body lying in the field. "He is dead."

"I don't know," Cain stuttered. "I wasn't in control of my body, and it was like someone else was doing everything."

"What do you remember being said?" Alpha inquired, standing up and facing Cain.

"Something about the garden," Cain replied. "That's all I can remember, and then Abel was struck down dead."

Alpha sighed. "It is going to be a hard road ahead for you," he began. "People are going to see you as a murderer and blame you for his death, no matter what you say."

"But I didn't do it!" Cain protested.

"I believe you, my child," Alpha responded, placing his hand on Cain's cheek. "So, I will bless you with protection so no one can ever try to retaliate against you for the crime you did not commit. But I am afraid you can no longer live here. You will have to go out into the world and find a new place for you to live. Your parents will not understand what happened here."

"They will if you tell them!" Cain implored, hitting his knees. "Please, my Lord. Show me mercy and explain to them what happened."

"I am showing you mercy," Alpha replied, touching Cain's forehead with the palm of his hand. "You will bear a mark, and everyone who sees the mark will recognize you as Cain and know you are protected by me."

Alpha's palm burned into Cain's forehead, and when he was done marking him, he disappeared, leaving Cain alone in the field to explain what happened to his brother.

We all looked at Cain as he raised his bangs from his forehead to show us the mark Alpha had left behind.

"And that mark made you immortal?" I asked, pointing at his forehead.

He nodded. "Nothing earthly can kill me, and I haven't attempted anything celestial to test."

"What does your mark have to do with your descendants?" Raphael inquired.

"My descendants all bear the mark as a birthmark," he replied.

"How many descendants do you have?" Metatron asked, raising his eyebrows.

"Too many to count," Cain answered. "After the flood, I started my bloodline up again as a means to one day stop Alpha. I know some of them were saved from the flood waters, but not all. I helped them form the first order of protectors over humanity. I gave them my book, and it was passed down through just one single part of my bloodline to where it is now."

"Anniel's human family?" Samael affirmed, leaning forward intently.

"Yes, the people who took her in when she was born," he replied, flipping his book open. "According to my records, they are the Asher family in Tennessee."

"But Anniel didn't live in Tennessee," I interjected, shaking my head in disagreement. "It was New Salem where her mother lived."

"Correct," he declared with a nod. "But she is no longer there. And she is cloaked from me as well. I know you were hoping I could find her, but she has some strong magic protecting her. I don't know what kind of magic it is that could prevent a blood bond search or even Alpha from finding her. But it's old and strong."

"Then how does any of this help?" Raphael interrupted. "If you can't find her, we still won't find the book."

"The Asher family will know how to find her," he replied. "Her brother, Harrison, has kept in contact with her from here and there. Even though she left the Diakonian Order because she married outside of the family rules, he still makes sure to check in on her since their mother died."

"So, who do we send to fetch the book then?" Azazel asked, looking around at everyone. "It can't be just any angel. We would have to be able to trust them inherently."

"Well it can't be any of us because we have all this shit going on here," I answered. "Does anyone have a suggestion?"

"Why not Raziel?" Michael asked. "It *is* his book."

"Alpha will probably expect that," I replied, shaking my head.

"Damian has spent a fair amount of time on Earth," Metatron offered. "He could go."

"Out of the question," I replied. "He's a sitting duck by himself for Alpha to take for himself."

Raphael raised his hand, and I looked over at him. "What about Ariel?" he asked. "She was one of the fallen angels, so she could assimilate pretty easily as a human."

"How do we test her to make sure she is loyal?" Azazel chimed in. "I mean, don't get me wrong. I believe everyone here is loyal, but you can never be too careful."

"Bring her in," I replied and started walking to the door.

"Where are you going?" Samael asked, turning his head around as I walked by.

"I will be right back," I reassured, turning my head to speak to them as I walked. "I just got to grab something."

I walked out of the room and bounded up the stairs to my room. I opened the door quietly so I wouldn't wake up Damian and walked over to one of the dressers. I opened the drawer and pulled out the flaming sword Reikal had adjusted for me.

Damian stirred in the bed. "What's going on?" he asked, sitting up and rubbing his eyes.

"Nothing," I whispered, shutting the drawer back. "You can go back to sleep."

"Nah, I am awake now," he said, sliding his feet off the bed. "What are you doing with that?"

"Testing loyalty," I declared, walking out of the room. "You coming?" I asked.

Damian followed behind me as I made my way back to the conference room. Ariel was already waiting at the front of the room. Terror filled her face when she saw my sword.

"The flaming sword," Samyaza murmured, marveling at the blade.

"I didn't do anything!" Ariel protested, holding her hands up defensively. "Please don't kill me!"

"Incaendiel, what's that for?" Samael demanded, standing from his seat and walking over to her.

I stopped in my tracks and looked around at everyone. Their eyes were all full of fear. I handed the sword over to Damian.

"Take it up to her, unsheath it, and hand it to her," I ordered gently.

Damian nodded and walked it over to her, doing as I instructed. He held it out for her to grab, and everyone in the room relaxed.

"I don't understand," she stammered nervously.

"Pick it up and bring it to life," I instructed, pointing at the hilt.

She hesitated before grabbing it from Damian's hand and willed the sword to life. Flames leapt from the blade.

"She's loyal," I proclaimed, walking up to her and gently taking it from her.

Damian handed me the sheath, and I put it back inside of it and tied it to my side.

"How do you know?" Michael asked, puzzled. "We all can wield the sword."

Metatron snapped his fingers. "That little warlock Reikal put some magic on it to make it unwieldable by anyone who isn't loyal to Incaendiel," Metatron replied, remembering when we had spoken to Reikal.

"We have a task for you to complete, and now that we are sure you are loyal to me, we can tell you what it is," I explained, looking at Ariel and changing the subject. "We need you to go to Tennessee and befriend the Asher family. They are descendants of Cain and have the Book of Raziel. We need the book."

"What if Alpha," she began.

"Alpha doesn't know about them and can't find Anniel's mother to get the book," I replied. "They've tried finding it and have failed. So it is safe for you to attempt."

"And if I fail?" she asked, glancing at the sword at my side.

"If you fail, then it's back to the drawing board," I answered, placing my hand tenderly on her shoulder. "I'm not a mindless murderer like Alpha. I do not punish." Ariel began to walk past me when I gently grabbed her hand. "You do not need to fear me, Ariel. You are still my sister. I wouldn't hurt you."

She nodded and left the room.

I returned my gaze to everyone in the room who was watching me. "I am not Alpha. When will you all trust that I am not going to hurt anyone?" I asked. "It feels like, with every move I make, you all are watching me, waiting for me to be just like him, even though you tell me you trust me and trust in me. Which is it? Because a few minutes ago, you all believed I was going to hurt Ariel. I can't be your leader if you don't put all of your trust in me, which is a big ask, I know. Alpha and Lilith screwed up our heads and we can't put our trust in hardly anyone. But you have been with me since the war. Nothing has changed. I haven't changed. I am still me."

They all lowered their eyes, ashamed.

I closed my eyes and recomposed myself. "Cain, is there anything else we need to know?" I asked, changing the subject.

He laughed. "Where would you like me to start?" he mused.

"The beginning, I guess?" I answered. "I don't know. We need to know as much as we can because we have been spoon-fed lies our entire lives."

He flipped his book to the very first page. "I copied this down from the Book of Raziel before giving it to my grown firstborn," Cain answered and began to read.

Chapter Eighteen

IN THE BEGINNING...

On the sixth day of creation, Alpha and Omega created man. Omega released the waters of creation into the valley of the Garden of Eden to soften the dirt. Alpha gathered the dirt to shape and mold just as he had done with the angels, with the exception of using stardust for them. Alpha and Omega each touched his forehead, and the mud became human flesh. Omega then breathed the spark of life into his mouth, and man was born. Adam opened his eyes. Unlike the idea that Adam was created a full-grown man, Adam was born as a child who aged and grew much slower than what was taught for human years.

Alpha and Omega spent a lot of time fostering Adam's growth and teaching him how his species was meant to flourish. In essence, they were his parents, much like how they were the parents of the angels, except he did not have celestial powers. Adam was alone for a very long time in the garden without another human, but he didn't mind when he was younger. Time moved differently in the garden than it did on the earth

Alpha and Omega had created together. Time in the garden was celestial since it was set gated just outside the realm of the Summit, a gift from Tiamat created by the fey. The years were incomprehensible, differing between celestial time and mortal time. Where everything grew slower in the celestial realm but aged faster on Earth, the years went by quickly in the garden. One celestial day could equal years on Earth, but since it sat outside of space and time, it couldn't be calculated in earthly time.

Adam soon started to become lonely. Yes, Alpha and Omega set aside time to visit him either together or separately, and the angels even came by to play with him or teach him things, but the time periods when he was alone in the garden grew heavy on his mind. And then, the fall happened. Alpha and Lilith had their squabble in front of Adam when Alpha had erased her from his mind. And then they settled on a game to play. They told their children the garden was hidden in a secret location when, in truth, they just hid the entrance to it. Only they could access the garden, and no one else, so that they could keep the charade up, and the children would choose sides on who to love more.

For a brief period, Alpha tried to create humans without Lilith and failed miserably. They convinced everyone that Alpha had to create Eve from the rib of Adam to bring her forth into life.

However, that was also not true. It wasn't Alpha's ability to spark life into creation. When Adam had learned Alpha was trying to make him a mate, the very next time he saw Lilith, he begged her to help Alpha create Eve for him. Lilith couldn't refuse his request and agreed to help bring Eve to life. Adam showed her the body Alpha had made using his blood to wet the earth and his rib to try to bring life into her. Lilith breathed life into Eve, and Eve came to be.

Lilith, still bitter and indifferent to Alpha, picked the fruit of the Tree of Knowledge of Good and Bad and gave it to Adam and Eve to eat. With the power of the Tree of Life flowing through their veins from the fruit they ate every day, they had become little demigods. This enraged Alpha. Once again, he and Lilith fought over what she had done. To punish Lilith for her misdeeds, he banished Adam and Eve from the garden, and once their lips tasted the mortal fruit growing on earth, their bodies became mortal and began to age more rapidly than they were accustomed.

Alpha was always punishing Lilith by using her own compassion and love against her for the creations she coveted so dearly. After every toxic deed he ever committed against her, he would love bomb her and beg her for her forgiveness, and most times, she would concede. Both the angels in the Summit and the fallen ones in the Glade were led to believe that their parents were separated, but it was only partially true. They often met in secret. One of those meetings led to them agreeing that Adam and Eve could have children. They had not been created to be fruitful and multiply like the other men of the earth, as Eve had been created barren. They had been created to remain innocent and pure. However, they agreed that the two needed children since they no longer had the loving embrace of their mother and father. The next greatest love, apart from having parents, is becoming a parent.

But where there is willful ignorance, there is also deceit. Alpha had removed Lilith's memory from Adam's memory long before Eve had been created. So he didn't remember her after she left the Summit. Lilith took this opportunity to foster a relationship that was much more than creator and creation, and she took Adam as a lover. She didn't think that Alpha knew, but Alpha knew everything in his universe, no matter how hard she tried to hide things. She was created from Alpha and, therefore, was always a part of him. Right before the creation of Eve, Lilith and Adam had one more fling, and then it was over.

At least it was over for Adam. After helping Alpha create Eve, Lilith realized she was pregnant with Adam's child. She hid the pregnancy well, too, because none of the fallen ones were ever privy to her visits unless she requested, and for nine months, under the guise of a broken heart from her divorce with their father, she hid away until the baby was born. She ferried the child off to Adam and convinced Eve that her firstborn child had been delivered by the divine, as opposed to her having to have the pangs of childbirth. Lilith believed she had kept the child secret enough that Alpha wouldn't have noticed. But Alpha knows everything, and his punishment to Eve was to make her child with Adam suffer. So he chose Cain and Abel on purpose to be Anniel's first incarnation, so Cain would have the blood of the innocent on his hands while possessed by Lucifer. His final act was to give Cain a mark that would pass through all of his bloodline, so every person would not only recognize who he was but also recognize the bloodline where murder began, ostracizing them until people eventually forgot after they believed the flood had wiped out his family lineage. Alpha didn't know that even though he had been born mortal, once he laid his hand on Cain, he would turn him immortal and therefore soulless, without a soul to return to the Giving Tree and unable to track. Alpha's interest in him dwindled as the millennia passed, and he soon forgot about Lilith's offspring from her act of betrayal. Even though he knows everything in his universe, sometimes he just doesn't care.

Chapter Nineteen

"IS THAT WHAT you heard being plotted in the garden?" I asked Gadreel once Cain closed the book.

"That is a very minute portion of what I had eavesdropped on in the garden," Gadreel replied, shifting in his seat.

"Please, enlighten us," I ordered, extending my hand for him to join me up front.

"Well," he began as he walked to the front. "You already know about Michael and Lucifer. That was revealed before. I don't know how much you remember about prior to the fall, though," he said directly to me.

"I had the wall brought down for the memories of being awakened and put to sleep for training," I replied.

"What about your past life memories? Have any of those surfaced yet?" he prodded.

"No, not yet," I responded, and the whispers began again. I glanced around the room, but everyone's face was solemn as they prepared for Cain to speak.

"Alpha and Lilith needed a couple of guards at the door of the garden whenever they had talks among themselves or talks with you and Anniel," he explained as the whispers grew louder but still unintelligible. "Raziel and I were there when they orchestrated the fall with you in the room and then without you in the room."

The whispers stopped, and my head snapped in his direction. "What do you mean?" I asked.

"The plan they came up with regarding Anniel and you was just the plan for you to hear," he recounted further. "Once you were out of the picture of making the plan, their tune changed quite a bit."

"Show me," I demanded, walking over to him and holding my hand out. "Put your forehead to my hand and think about it."

He did as instructed and leaned into my hand. My head was immediately filled with his memories.

"Are they out of earshot?" Alpha asked, not moving to look to draw attention to himself.

Omega watched us leave. "Yes," she answered, turning toward Alpha.

"We need a better plan," Alpha began, holding a hand up to his chin from his crossed arms. "And it needs to involve more than just us, too. We need others involved."

"We already have Lucifer and Michael in the know of what is happening," Omega replied. "Lucifer is

bitter about Incaendiel being chosen over him. And Michael... well, he has made it known that he will put Incaendiel down if we need him to."

"Those two won't be enough, and we need to make sure they are here alongside Anniel and stay behind for the fall," Alpha mused, tapping his finger against his lips.

"What about Metatron?" Omega asked, serenely rocking back and forth where she stood. "He would be a fine leader to have in on the plan."

"No," Alpha declined, with a shake of his head. "Nearly all of the angels would choose his side if he fell, and we are back to square one."

"What about Samael and Azazel?" Omega offered, raising an eyebrow. "We could let them in on everything like Lucifer and Michael. They are the first and second command and would fall with me anyway."

Alpha smiled widely. "Perfect," he replied. "Gadreel?" he called, looking off to the entrance to the garden.

Gadreel stepped within the gate of the garden. "Yes, Father?" he asked.

"Send for Samael and Azazel to come to the garden," Alpha ordered.

"Yes, Father," Gadreel replied.

I broke contact with his head and dropped my hand. "That's a lie!" I seethed, stepping back from him.

338

"It's not a lie," Gadreel replied calmly. "I have no reason to lie to you, Brother."

I didn't want to make eye contact with them, but I did anyway. I looked at Samael and Azazel.

"Is it true?" I asked, staring keenly at the two.

Samael swallowed hard. Azazel sat wide-eyed, unable to answer.

"It is true?!" I demanded.

"Is what true?" Samael finally answered, more softly than I expected.

"You knew the whole time," I asked, walking over to them. "You knew the whole time and didn't bother telling me?"

"I was following orders, In—"

"Fuck your orders!" I barked, leaning in nose to nose with his face. "I was your brother! You have had this whole time to tell me what was happening that I couldn't remember." I looked at Azazel. "And you!" I looked at Michael. "And you."

I tore the flaming sword from my side and unsheathed it.

"What are you doing?" Damian demanded, rising from his seat.

I swallowed hard. "Take it," I ordered, holding the sword out to Samael.

Samael looked at me and then at the sword, but didn't move.

"Take it!" I yelled, pumping the sword out in front of him.

"Does my word mean nothing to you?" Samael asked, standing and staring me down. "Have I not proven my loyalty to you now? Yes, I fucked up in the past. But it was the past."

"It's not the past when you have been lying this whole entire time to me," I replied, fighting the urge to bring forth my powers and smite him.

"I haven't lied about anything!" Samael hollered, becoming defensive in his posture.

"Omission is betrayal, Brother," I stated, a tear slipping down my face. "Take the god damned sword!"

Samael grabbed the sword, and it flared to life with fire. He handed it over to Azazel, and the flame stayed steady. She handed the sword back to me.

"You asked us to trust in you," Samael snarled, looking me up and down. "We ask the same in return." He patted her arm, and she followed him as he left the room.

"So you're going to gaslight me?" I asked, a laugh slipping out nervously. "This is my fault for not trusting your word when, for millennia, you were sneaking around behind my back with Lilith about me. You knew about everything. And you didn't bother to tell me even after your 'duties' and 'orders' no longer held merit to Lilith or Alpha."

"Do you think you and your little precious family were the only ones whom Alpha and Lilith manipulated?" Samael demanded, spinning around on his heels and walking back toward me while Azazel tugged on his arm to stop.

He walked up to me and stood directly in my face, waiting for me to make a move.

"When they gave us an order, it wasn't out of obedience we saw it through," he hissed. "Free will and the right to choose is bullshit when it comes to those two. We could *not* tell you, even after we joined your ranks. We are still under whatever they did to us, like you were. We weren't even allowed to think about it because they feared you could read our minds. We still can't. We are still their puppets."

"Were there any others?" I asked, not moving and holding my ground.

"If there were, then they were sworn to not say anything about it, just like us," he answered. "We weren't even allowed to talk to Lucifer and Michael about it."

"Did you want to do it?" I questioned, stepping back.

"In the beginning, yes," he revealed, shamefully rubbing the top of his head. "Like Michael and Lucifer, I was jealous of you. I was jealous you were chosen. I was jealous you were so powerful that your powers couldn't be contained. I despised you. And I knew one day, you would outrank me like it was always intended." He stopped for a minute and looked over at Azazel, and she nodded her head. "We watched you fight so hard to win Anniel over through all of those years. And it wasn't really just to make her remember to love you over and over, which was Alpha testing her loyalty, by the way. I can say that. He wanted to see how deep the taproot of his control over her went. And you two beat them at their own game. You fought hard to get us home and to get everyone back together. That's what I admired about you. That's what changed my mind about you and my point of view, and every jealous bone in my body started to buck back at Alpha and Mo—" he stopped briefly and inhaled. *"Lilith.* But I still couldn't tell you the truth. All I could do was pledge my loyalty to you to show you that I would follow you to the ends of the earth if I needed to, because you did love us as your brothers and sisters, while our parents just used us over and over."

He stopped for a moment, and the room was silent. "The reason we weren't trusted to remain silent is because they knew our devotion outweighed our obedience. They knew we would cave and tell you everything because we didn't have a deep-seated hatred of you as Michael and Lucifer did. Their jealousy ran through to their bones because they were created as twins as well, but not like you two. Their obedience was the make it or break it with Alpha and Lilith, and they had to prove to them all the time that they were better than any of us and would follow them to the ends of the earth or be banished."

"It wasn't always solely obedience. At times, Lucifer and I questioned what they had us doing. They threatened to kick us out all the time," Michael added in reply to Samael's confession. "If we didn't follow orders, we lost our light, and we lost our wings. We would be thrown into the abyss and locked away for our crimes against them. And once that happened, if we didn't fight tooth and nail to get back in their good graces and grovel at their feet, they would take our grace as well."

I felt for the nearest chair and took a seat, running my hands over my face.

"You have been the only one of us who was truly free, even if on the inside, you were caged," Azazel chimed in, walking over and kneeling down in front of me. "The way you would speak about Alpha and vehemently stand against him. And we all knew that. We all knew that you couldn't be punished like we were. If he could punish you the same way he threatened us, then he would have done it so long ago. We didn't understand it completely, but we knew you would be the one to save us and set us free, Brother."

"Look, there's more to see," Gadreel interrupted, walking over to me. "And you will understand what they mean." He knelt before me, and I placed my hand on his forehead.

"I have **had** it with these two," Alpha raged, throwing boulders around in the garden.

Omega stood by quietly.

"If we can't bring them forth and they love us as their parents, then what is the point in keeping them around?" Alpha bellowed, kicking the shrubbery beside him. "We wanted a lineage, not children to overthrow us."

Omega swallowed. "What do you wish to do then?"

"What we should have done a long time ago," Alpha muttered, walking over to Anniel and me.

"Lamut!" Alpha shouted.

Nothing happened.

"Aphes!" he uttered, a bit louder.

"Pasu!" he bellowed as Omega gasped.

However, Anniel and I still stood without any harm coming to us.

"Why are they not dying?" Alpha demanded, fuming and muttering.

"Maybe because they are old gods and we cannot destroy the energy we gave them?" Omega offered with a shrug.

"I have slain a few old gods in my time, Omega," Alpha spat, glaring at her. "I am pretty sure I know what I am doing."

"They were the first gods of existence!" Omega hissed. "The first pantheon ever to spring forth. They are not like the others!"

"All gods can die," Alpha muttered. "I will find a way to put an end to them, even if it takes me billions of years!" he hissed.

"Why do you hate them so much when they are your children?" Omega demanded, shaking her head in disbelief.

"Barbelo's power was meant to be mine!" Alpha yelled. "I was deceived!"

"So you are jealous that your grandmother chose your children to bestow a gift upon instead of you?" Omega asked. "Pathetic. If you treated them more like your children and less like a weapon, they would most likely bend to your will and fall in line."

"Not that one," he said, pointing his finger at me. "That one was born with hatred in his heart for me."

"Well, you shouldn't have slain their parents!" she hissed. "They watched you do it before you put them to sleep to take their power from their bodies. Tiamat told us to gather the energy of the dying sun god, but that wasn't enough for you. You wanted more and more and more like you always desire, and instead, you destroyed their universe to gain them."

"It was already dying!" Alpha remarked.

"But they were not!" Omega hissed. "They had plans to fuel another universe until you took these two, and their universe collapsed before they could escape. So many souls, Alpha!"

"And those souls were brought back with me to our Giving Tree," Alpha protested. "They will still have life!"

"Those souls weren't meant for our universe, and you know it!" Omega refuted with angry, wide eyes. "Those souls were meant to recycle in their universe alone. So now, so many of them will incarnate and not feel as if they belong because they don't belong in this universe!"

"Whatever," Alpha muttered. "Mark my words, Omega, I will find a way for those two to die, and I will be the one to put an end to them, and I will take their power for myself."

I removed my hand from Gadreel's forehead and sat quietly.

"What did you see?" Metatron asked.

"Before the fall, Alpha tried to undo his and Anniel's existence," Damian replied, leaning forward in his chair. "He couldn't because of how old their power is."

"And their power is very old," Azrael interrupted, walking into the room.

Everyone turned to watch her walk up to the front and join us.

"How old?" Samael asked.

"They were the first ever born gods along with their parents," she answered, stepping up to the front of the room. "And I do mean born and not created."

"You know where I come from?" I inquired.

"Yes and no," she replied. "Mother has told me the story of your universe. At that time, we didn't govern the life and death cycle of it. We understood death needed to be a part of the life cycle, but your civilization was so grand. Far more advanced than any we have ever witnessed since. Your universe was the epitome of dreamers, of seekers, of knowledge, and of hope. So we left it be in hopes its existence would inspire the rest of the universes to spring forth in life."

"I need to know more," I pleaded. "Will you call your mother here so I can speak with her? So we can learn who we are since they stole away our memories."

"My boy, I thought you would never ask," Maveth chimed in, materializing before us.

"Did you know my real parents?" I urged, looking up at her from my chair.

She nodded. "I did. And they were so wonderful."

Chapter Twenty

"SO MANY CREATION stories begin with in the beginning because it was the beginning of that specific universe. We are starting at the moment of conception of life after death," Maveth began:

There was nothing but darkness, and in that darkness, I existed and brought forth my first reaper, Azrael. And we waited for more than just death to exist for what seemed like aeons before the first shade formed. Her name was Tulu-Ama, the Mother of the Deep. She was the womb of the waters of Zul'Tama, the first universe that sparked to life instead of being forged like many others, such as this one in which Alpha exists. Like many primordial beings, she had no face or form. She was the dark matter that spread like water in the deepest parts of the ocean. She was the whisper of potential, and from her flowed the first currents of energy and the pulse that would become the heartbeat of time itself.

Once aware of her sentience, her voice emerged like echoes of musical notes, whispering in the void with her first breath of life. From this breath emerged Kharuun, the Howling Voice of the Storm. He split the void with a shattering wind of a screaming roar, becoming the howler of the skies. His thunderous cries ripped through the silence as he floated across the inky abyss of nothingness, finding Tulu-Ama. They danced wildly together, and he gave her shape and form with his winds of chaos. As they brushed upon one another, lightning sparked within the thunderous cloud of desire. That flicker created the first creation of heat, and from the steam of meeting the air and water, the first spark of creation came to be as Is'hari, the First Flame and Breath of Fire. Another primordial being who was not created but ignited from the depths of the soulless expanses of nothingness.

Is'hari was the breath of glowing warmth who brought light to the dance with Tulu-Ama and Kharuun, splitting night from day. Together, the three of them awakened life among the inky dark, shaping and molding the galaxies within the void. However, their universe began to grow unstable, wild from the pure energy drifting through the expanse. What was brought forth between the three of them would crumble back into ashen nothingness. But just as the universe knew it needed the three of them to start creation, it knew it needed a fourth. It needed more than just a spark of heat to turn creation into a lasting thought. Vahr-Zhul sprang forth from the deep, born from the ashes of failed sparks and the heat of exploding stars. He was the sacred flame who brought with him a purifying and cleansing flame. He was the destroyer, but also the renewer. He was the judge and the guardian. He did not flicker. Instead, he burned, and wherever he walked, the old was burned away so new could be brought forth. From his flames, the expanses were illuminated, and through their combined fire, they brought forth creation, soon to be followed by more gods and more universes. Together, he and Is'hari formed what would become known as the Guardians of Light with the birth of their twin children, Caelvryn and Valiryen.

The union between Is'hari and Vahr-Zhul was never meant to be. One of them was divine purpose, while the other was pure chaos. However, the magnetic pull between the two, no matter how they fought, caused them to collide in burning stillness and flickering wilderness. Their collision brought forth Valiryen, the Crowned Flame, and Caelvryn, the Silent Ember. Valiryen had the totality of her father and blazed with radiance, bringing judgement, seeing through the smoke and mirrors of lies to the bare truth. Caelvryn was born with the cold fire of stillness. He was the gentle ending to things with a chill that preserved what shouldn't be burned, while Valiryen seared away the rest, he being the Flame of Frost and she being the Flame of Transformation. Falsehood disappeared under her while remembrance remained with him, he wielding sorrowful fire while she wielded sorrowful wisdom. They weaved through the universe, life and death, heat and stillness, what was and could be.

The Tale of the Ashen Sky speaks of the time when their mortal realm was still young and reckless. Much like the tales of the bible, the world was burning itself with its own hunger. But unlike Alpha with his unrelenting judgment and fury, Valiryen knew she would unravel the universe with her fury if she went unchecked. So she asked her twin, Caelvryn, to still the winds, silence the sky, and let the world pause so she could cleanse it properly without bringing destruction beyond their fixing. Caelvryn raised his hand, and through his power of stillness, as that of quiet falling snow, he froze time. Everything fell silent and stopped, including the cries and laments of man, trapping them mid-breath. And she burned, unraveling every misdeed their mortals had made without harming them in wrath. Caelvryn and Valiryen stood in the ashes and, once they realized their task was done, left together. And the world began again, renewed.

.

"So Anniel is Is'hari?" I asked when Maveth was finished.

She nodded. "And you are Vahr-Zhul. Luxina is Valiryen and Damian is Caelvryn."

"How did they gather our power?" I inquired. "Were we really dying?"

Maveth nodded. "You were using every bit of your power to try and sustain the universe as it began to fold in. You would have died trying, as well. Alpha had slain your parents and caused the universe to begin the cycle of renewal and give its energy to other places. Before Alpha learned about Valiryen and Caelvryn, you had already absorbed them back, so they would be safe from him in case he tried to take their power for himself. It was during your memory suppression that he learned about the power overflow and why you were too strong to contain. It's also why you were able to temper yourself better once the children were born. You didn't have all of the extra power swirling around trying to bust forth."

"And then he made the plans for us to create the kids here so he could lay claim to their power," I stated.

"Yes, and the rest is history," she replied.

"And without us?" I asked.

"Light and life of the universe would cease to exist," Maveth explained. "If Alpha destroys you, he destroys everything and everyone, including himself."

"Does he not know he will extinguish himself as well?" Damian chimed in, shifting in his seat. He had been so quiet that I forgot he was even in the room.

"He thinks if he absorbs enough power, he will be able to keep everything going himself," Maveth replied. "His final act would be to absorb the power of you four so he can be the support its needs. However, he doesn't understand the old power you all contain. If he tries, it will rip him to shreds because everything your names stood for is everything he is against. Destruction and renewal, tempered justice and judgment, the order you bring to the cosmos he stands against with his chaos and unadulterated hatred and jealousy."

"How many of us absorbed would rip him to shreds?" I pondered. "One, two, all?"

"At least two," Maveth answered.

"Will it take all four of us to keep the cosmos in order?" I asked tentatively.

"As long as two of you exist, the Guardians of Light will continue on through offspring," she responded.

"The Guardians of Light has a nice ring to it," Samyaza interjected.

"Alpha mentioned taking the souls from Zul'Tama and adding them to the Giving Tree of souls for this universe," Damian began. "What does that mean?"

"I am sure Sophia talked to you about starseeds, correct?" Maveth inquired.

"Briefly. She didn't exactly explain them, just that they were 'extraterrestrial' souls," Damian replied.

"Lilith mentioned them briefly to me as well," I interjected. "She said that once our powers were activated, they would be activated as well."

"Those starseeds she spoke about are all of the souls from your universe. They are the dreamwalkers, the prophets, and many more other things in this world, and you are the power sustaining those souls, not Alpha," Maveth explained.

"So the prophet we are to look for, who is named Eva, she is a starseed, right?" I asked.

"I cannot discuss Eva until we all know she is safe and sound," Maveth replied.

"Why not?" Damian queried, scrunching his face.

"Alpha is always everywhere listening when you least suspect it," Maveth answered.

"Are we sure that Alpha is priming himself to absorb powers, or could he be priming Adam?" Samael asked.

"That is also a possibility," Maveth replied.

"Would the same thing happen to Adam that would happen to Alpha?" Azazel questioned. "Would he rip apart as well?"

"I'm not sure. He might or he might not, considering he was created from the Guardians' blood. It depends on how things unfold for Adam and how his powers are activated," Maveth replied.

"Thank you for speaking with us," I said, standing and bowing.

"I wish you the best of luck. I would hate to exist with only my reaper angels and nothing else once more," Maveth stated as she dematerialized.

We all looked at Azrael with that last remark.

"You can't kill death," she explained.

The low whispers began again as I looked around for the source.

"Ok, who is thinking something that I cannot hear?" I demanded.

"So you hear them too?" Damian asked, sighing in exasperation, but also put to ease. "I thought I was going insane."

Azrael smiled. "So the whispers have begun for you?" she asked.

"Yes, what do they mean?" I questioned in return.

"You hear your mother from Zul'Tama calling for you," she explained, and then turned to Damian. "And you hear your grandmother. She may have been slain by Alpha, but her spirit still lives on through you all."

"What was Zul'Tama like?" I asked, leaning against a chair.

Azrael smiled. "It was so magical and beautiful there. Alpha tried to recreate the beauty of the universe at the Summit. He wanted to find a way to make you more comfortable when you were awake. Finally, he had the Garden of Eden fashioned for you, and while it was the most beautiful and harmonious thing he ever created, it still didn't feel like home for you because it wasn't home," she explained.

"So that's why Anniel and I loved being in the garden and why it was gifted to us by Alpha," I replied, finally understanding.

The whispering began again, and I quickly looked around.

"It's back, right?" Azrael asked, raising an eyebrow.

I nodded.

"Listen to the call," she replied. "Listen with your mind, heart, and soul. She has a message for you."

"How?" I questioned. "I don't know how to decipher the whispers."

"Feel the whispers," she answered.

Feel the whispers, I thought to myself. *Feel the whispers. Feel the whispers.*

I closed my eyes and focused on my breathing. The whispers grew louder but were still inaudible. The sounds of everything else drowned out the words. I could hear the breathing of those in the room, the sounds from outside, but not the words. And then everything went quiet. I opened my eyes, and everyone in the room wasn't moving.

"You needed stillness," Damian said, standing from his seat and walking over to me.

"Did you just freeze time?" I asked, bewildered.

"It made sense when Maveth was telling the story of Caelvryn. She said he had the power to slow down time and freeze it. When Adam threw that sword at me, it felt different when I dodged it. I thought I had moved so fast that it felt like time had slowed down. But I had actually slowed it down to dodge it. So to normal people, it looks like I am moving really fast, but in truth, I have slowed down time around me," he explained.

"It did look as if you slowed down time," I concurred. "And this," I began, looking around the room. "This proves it."

"We needed stillness to hear beyond," he said, with a shrug.

I nodded and closed my eyes. The whispers began again and grew louder, much louder than they had ever been, until I heard a voice.

"My dear, Vahr-Zhul," the voice whispered. "I have been trying for so long to speak with you, my child."

"Mother?" I asked as emotions welled that I didn't know I could feel.

"Yes, my sweet Firefly," she replied. "It's Mother," she cooed.

And all at once, memories rushed forth of Zul'Tama. I could see everything Azrael had described. There weren't enough words to describe the breathtaking marvel our universe had once been. The colors were brighter there, as if I had been looking through painted glass my entire life. I could see my mother, a darkened cloud gathered into stardust and bioluminescence as my father swam around her. A bright light flowed around me as Is'hari brushed my side, our energies in perfect harmony. My fire burned bright and powerful without causing any harm. Valiryen and Caelvryn danced through the sky, leaving trails of fire and ice in their wake. It was peaceful, serene. There wasn't a single feeling of doom or chaos. We all existed as a thriving unanimity. I watched other universes begin to materialize as our power fueled the cosmos, inspiring the birth and rise of gods. There wasn't animosity or hatred, and it was utopic, to say the least.

And then we saw a dark cloud form over the last universe to be brought into existence. I could feel the wicked tendrils of energy weaving their web through the air. We watched the universe unfold and Alpha materialize as nothing but pure light. And then from him another light sprang forth. Omega. But the light was deceitful, for there was nothing illuminating about the two. There was a deep-seated darkness within them, and I could see it.

"We need to purify or extinguish them before they wreak havoc on the cosmos," I said to Mother and Father.

"Give them a chance, Vahr-Zhul," Mother cooed. "They are new and need time to find their place."

"I can feel the wickedness of their hearts, Mother," I protested. "They will bring nothing but the end to all if they are not dealt with."

"Listen to your mother, Vahr-Zhul," Father ordered. "We must give them a chance. It is the law of the universe."

"But as the Guardians—"

"That is an order!" Father demanded.

"And you were right, my Firefly," Mother breathed as the memory faded. "Alpha did just that, and he started at the beginning of life itself."

"I will right the wrongs he has committed," I assured her. "I will fix this."

"I know you will, love," Mother sweetly replied. "I know you all will. And even though you can't see me or feel me or your father, we will be there with you as the ashes of purification and renewal rain down across the universe."

And the whispering stopped.

"So what now?" Samyaza asked, his voice breaking the stillness in the room.

"Holy crap!" Azazel yelled. "How did you get over there so fast?" she asked, looking at Damian.

"He froze time," Azrael replied with a smile. "It's nice to see you again, Caelvryn."

"Damian is still fine for you to call me," Damian insisted.

"Like Samyaza asked, what now?" Metatron asked, redirecting the room.

"Someone needs to go and find Eva," I replied. "Guard her at all costs."

"Who, though?" Azazel asked. "I don't think another one of the angels out in the world is a good idea."

"I can do it," Raphael offered. "It will be like before when we were guarding Anniel."

"No, we need you here," I replied.

"What about me?" Praeziel interjected, standing up. "I can guard her. I have been among the humans before and know their ways, too. It would be easier for me than for another angel.

Everyone looked at me for an answer.

"What about training?" I asked.

"The Nephilim will follow Samael's orders," he reassured. "They respect him, and plus, I may have threatened them just a bit."

I mulled over it for a bit. "I don't see why not," I answered, with a shrug. "But do we know where she is?"

Silence fell over the room.

"We need Lailah. She is the only one who places the souls," Samael stated, breaking the hushed crowd.

"And we can't get to the Book of Life either since it's in the Summit," Michael added.

"Do you have any idea where Alpha could have hidden Lailah?" I asked Azrael.

"I haven't the slightest idea," Azrael replied with a sigh. "She's not in the Summit. That much I can tell you. And the only other thing I know of that could locate her would be Raziel's book, which we don't have either."

"Wait, what about the Watcher's Eye?" Samael asked, glancing over at Samyaza. "Could that find her?"

Samyaza pondered for a minute. "It might. We could possibly see where she is, although it won't take us to her."

"Where is it?" I asked.

"That's the problem," Samyaza replied. "I haven't seen it since before the Watchers were banished to Stygia. I believe one of the last few times I saw it was the last we saw of the flaming sword."

I hmphed. "Gabriel."

Chapter Twenty-One

I WALKED AROUND Lightshade, looking for Gabriel. He wasn't in the millions of rooms in Starfire's cottage, nor in the arenas sparring. My feet began to travel into the forest, and I couldn't help but marvel at the majestic vibe this nature had within the canopy of trees that loomed overhead. I hadn't done any exploring of the place since my arrival, and what better way to explore than looking for Gabriel? I remembered from before the fall how he used to always go off by himself to meditate and commune with those he needed to deliver messages to.

I walked alongside the riverbed, watching the tiny creatures swim through the waters and crawl along the floor where there was shallow water. Birds chirped, and there was something off in the varying types of grasses that made chirping noises, most likely crickets. Butterflies floated in the light breeze, landing on the unique flowers that grew wild within the foliage. It was so peaceful here, and for once, I could feel all of my tension sliding from my shoulders. Lightshade existed outside of time, and I had no idea just how long we had been holed up here, so this brief piece of time I had to myself was calming.

"It's like she made the garden all over, isn't it?" a voice called out, breaking my trance.

"Yes. Yes, just like the garden," I replied, walking over to Gabriel, who was sitting cross-legged in a field of flowers. "I have been looking for you."

"Oh?" he mused, standing up and dusting his pants off. "What do you need?"

"When you stole all the things from the Summit like the flaming sword and Michael's spear," I began, "did you happen to take the Watcher's Eye as well?" I asked.

"Yes, among other things," he answered, walking with me along the river.

"Are they stashed in the Summit or somewhere else?" I pressed, remembering how he went back for his horn.

"They are hidden outside of the Summit," he replied with a laugh. "What do you need it for?" he questioned.

"We were hoping to use it and try and find Lailah," I responded. "We are going to start searching for Eva, and without Lailah or being able to look at Raziel's book or the Book of Life in the Summit, we won't be able to find her."

"Let me go get it," he stated and took off to the sky.

At the sight of his wings, a thought crossed my mind that I hadn't bothered to think of or acknowledge. Do I still have wings? They were usually just always there, and I was aware of them, but since our transformation, I no longer felt the urge to use them. Do I have to will them forth like my power? I shrugged to myself. What better way to take a peek and see while I was alone? I thought about my wings and pushed. Unlike the usual angel wings I had before, wings of fire erupted from my back.

"Holy shit!" Damian squealed, breaking my focus and catching me off guard.

My wings went back into their hiding spot as I turned to face him.

"Do I have wings like that now?" he gushed, glancing over his shoulder.

"I don't know," I answered. "I just now started to think about them. I am sure yours will be like mine. You just have to will them forth."

I watched his face make a strange expression as he focused on his wings. Brilliant, fiery blue wings popped out from behind him.

"Gods have wings?" he ventured as he dropped his wings back into place.

"I don't know," I offered with a shrug. "I have never met one who had them, and let us see them. Alpha or Lilith might have them and just keep them hidden, or just don't know they have them."

"Did you find Gabriel?" he prodded, as he willed his wings in and out, testing out his ability to command them.

"Yes," I replied as I watched him, amused. "He went to go and get the Watcher's Eye."

He fell quiet for a moment.

"Whatcha thinking about?" I asked as we began walking around the forest.

Some deer popped out of the trees to graze, and we quietly watched them while he found the words he was looking for.

"Do you think we can communicate with Luxina the same way we communicated with Tul-Ama?" he asked.

I shook my head. "I don't think so, or else I would have been able to communicate with Anniel by now," I answered. "I think we can hear Tul-Ama because she is in us."

"How is she in us if Alpha took her power?" he inquired, picking up a rock and tossing it at the river water to watch it skip.

"The same reason we have Barbelo in us as well," I responded. "They only gave him what he expected as power since they were old. They reserved the rest for us."

"Do you remember anything else from Zul'Tama?" he asked, skipping another rock across the water as we walked.

"Not really," I replied, rubbing the back of my head. "Just what I saw while talking to Tul-Ama. You?" I asked in return.

He nodded. "I remember everything," he declared.

As I was about to ask him more questions, Gabriel returned, landing in front of us. "Here it is," he said, handing over a purplish stone.

"What else do you have in your stash spot?" I queried with a laugh.

"The answers to that are endless," he replied with a laugh.

"Well, let's get this back to Samyaza," I stated, putting it in my pocket. "Only Watchers can use it."

"Will it work?" Damian asked as we started heading back to the center of Lightshade.

"Maybe, maybe not," Gabriel replied. "It was intended to be used by mortals to help them find us when they needed us."

"But does it find the specific angel they were inquiring about?" Damian pressed, stepping up and over a large fallen tree trunk.

"It did," Gabriel replied, also climbing over the tree.

I jumped over it and landed with a soft thud and asked, "What?" as they just squinted at me with tight-lipped smirks.

"Show off," Gabriel quipped. "So what happens after we find where Lailah is?"

"We go get her and bring her here," I responded.

"And then?" he prodded.

"We find Eva after," I noted. "Praeziel has offered to be her guardian until she activates completely."

"Shouldn't she immediately activate since we have?" Damian inquired.

"I don't know," I answered. "For all we know, she has. I don't know if it's immediate or if it takes time. I just know we need her before Alpha finds her. That's probably who he is looking for instead of Zoe, as he told Beelzebub."

"I didn't think of that," Gabriel remarked. "Everything is always a race against him."

"I know, and it's exhausting," I replied as we stepped through the trees and out into the unsheltered sunlight.

Raphael came running up to us when he saw us emerge from the tree line.

"We have a problem," he stammered, glancing over his shoulder.

"What is it?" I muttered, following his gaze to see if I could make out the problem myself.

"Adam's back," he replied, looking from me to Damian. "He's asking for *him*," he stated, nodding in Damian's direction.

"Did he say what he wanted with him?" I pressed as I scanned the area closely.

Raphael shook his head. "No, he just said he wanted to see Damian," he replied.

"Where is he?" Damian asked, looking around, trying to find him to confront him.

"No," I ordered.

"But—" he began.

"No buts!" I objected, staring at him intently until he got the point.

Damian scowled at me. "Stop bossing me around!" he demanded.

"No," I countered, raising my eyebrows and holding back a laugh. "I know no one has ever told you no or really what to do other than Alpha's demands, but you need to listen to me."

"You've been my father for like ten seconds!" he snapped, throwing his hands up in the air in frustration. "Nothing has changed!"

"Everything has changed!" I growled, my brows knitting together. "You've had new powers since we transitioned, and you haven't even begun to tap into them. You need more experience before you take on Adam."

"I can handle myself!" Damian hissed, stepping up to me and challenging my authority. "I don't need a babysitter."

We stared each other down as Raphael and Gabriel stood there.

"Take this to Samyaza and do whatever he needs you to do," I commanded as I handed Damian the stone from my pocket.

"Whatever," Damian replied, rolling his eyes.

"Thank you," I called out as he stomped off, and he waved me off.

"Would have never imagined that stubborn creature was your kid," Raphael remarked sarcastically.

"Shut it," I drawled. "Where is Adam?" I asked, changing the subject.

"Starfire's cottage," Raphael replied.

I groaned and headed toward her cabin. Just what I needed. The devil spawn returned. As I climbed the steps, Adam emerged from the door. He looked taller than the last time he was here.

"Where is Damian?" he inquired, looking around outside for him.

"Busy," I replied, giving him a deadpan stare. "What do you need, Adam?" I pressed.

"My business is with Damian," he stated, looking down his nose at me.

"Well, I am the best you have right now," I insisted, crossing my arms.

"You don't scare me," he glowered, stepping up to me just as Damian had to challenge my authority.

"And you don't scare me, kid," I shot back, leaning down in his face.

"I wanted to spar with him," he replied nonchalantly.

"Not going to happen," I commanded with dead set eyes.

"Why not?" he refuted, furrowing his brows.

"Because the last time you were here, you threw a sword at his head!" I shrieked.

He huffed. "I cannot fail, Alpha. I need to train with the real thing," he insisted.

I leaned in closer to him. "Not going to happen," I barked, annunciating each word.

"Alpha told me how arrogant you are and how you think no one could hurt you," he spat. "You could hardly keep up with me in the arena."

"I am sure Alpha tells you nothing but the truth and no lies," I quipped, standing back up.

"I've learned a few things since our last time in the arena," he remarked, smirking with arrogant eyes.

"Well, let's see what you have learned, squirt," I bantered, tousling his hair.

He smacked my hand away with a scowl. "You *will* respect me!" he proclaimed.

I got down to eye level with him and leveled with him. "Respect is earned and not given."

He glared at me and pushed past me, bumping me with his shoulder. Why is it that every kid I meet thinks they're the boss of me? Is it because they look the same age? I rolled my eyes and followed him to the arena he chose. No sooner had we entered the arena than his hands began to throw ice at me. I shot back with fire bullets, destroying each ice block as they careened through the air.

"Oh, so we are doing that?" I snapped as he grinned at me wildly.

"Don't hold back," he ordered.

"If I don't hold back, I will burn this place to the ground," I growled.

"Well, I won't be," he beamed as he unleashed a wall of icy fire my way.

I didn't move, and I didn't block it. I let it hit me just to see what it would do. As the ice met my body, steam rose and melted upon impact. When the mist cleared, I stood there, staring Adam down, who stood there bewildered.

"Is that really all you got?" I quipped. "Show me your fury!" I commanded.

His face darkened, and I watched as he reached in deep and brought forth his power. Everything around us began to freeze over. Those who were training in other arenas froze solid in their places, some mid-air. Adam screamed in fury, and the ice thickened. As it licked my feet, it immediately melted, leaving a puddle of water gathered around my feet.

"How are you doing that?!" he whined, stomping his foot in a tantrum.

I walked calmly over to him and leaned down in his face so I could stare him in the eye with my reply. "Because I am *the* god."

I raised my hand, and heat radiated from it, melting the ice that had covered Lightshade. As the ice thinned, those training busted through the sheet that had encased them and turned to stare in our direction.

"Just because you're as powerful as you are doesn't mean Alpha won't stop you, and it doesn't mean Damian is as powerful as you either," Adam seethed. "I will take him down and fully become him in the end."

"You will die trying," I snarled, and he was gone.

"What the *hell* was that?" Samael demanded, emerging from Starfire's cottage.

"Adam," I replied. "We have a problem."

Chapter Twenty-Two

"HIS POWERS ARE advancing," Metatron said as we all stood around the backside of Starfire's cottage.

"I'd say they're more than advancing. He froze you all!" I exclaimed as I paced back and forth. "How are we going to take on Alpha if his little devil can take you all out at once?"

"We have to level the playing field," Samael replied with a shrug. "I don't know how, but we need a game plan because this isn't working out; we are just sparring for training."

"Well, do you have any powers?" I asked, bobbing my head at him.

He shrugged. "I don't know. Alpha only had us train to be warriors."

"You brought out powers in the Nephilim," I argued. "Angels have to have *some* sort of power if they do."

"Look, I have tried to be like you for millennia," Samael remarked. "I have tried willing anything possible forth, and nothing ever happens."

"Then the only thing that can stop Adam is Damian," Asmodeus interjected. "He would have to keep him distracted as we fight whatever Alpha sends our way." He looked at me as I glared at him. "I know you hate the idea, but he is a god just like you. You have to stop babying him. You can't keep sheltering him and putting him in a corner. In the end, it will be him against Adam."

"You don't have to remind me!" I hissed. "I am well aware of what is to transpire. It's still not safe for him!"

"He can't take down Damian without all of Damian in him," Asmodeus countered. "He will be fighting against just another angel with powers, not a god."

"Unless Alpha finds a way to turn him into a god," Azazel chimed in. "And then Incaendiel has a reason to be worried."

"You're not helping the situation, Azazel!" Asmodeus growled, glaring in her direction.

"Stop arguing!" Raphael snapped, and we all fell silent. "It's not doing any good standing around arguing over what might happen and what might not happen. We have to prepare for *all* possibilities, and that includes Damian against Adam, whether you like it or not, Incaendiel."

"Raphael is right," Michael offered, and I scowled at him. "It's not just about you. It's about all of our survival. So we all have a vote in this."

"The answer is no!" I barked firmly. "We do not test Damian against Adam."

"What if he takes him out before Alpha's plan comes to fruition, though?" Metatron added. "We will have the upper hand then."

My frustration took hold of me, and I punched the wall of Starfire's cottage, busting a hole through it. I stood there with my hands placed against the wall, running everything through my head as everyone stood silent.

"Can we just get through one problem at a time, please?" I choked out.

"Incaendiel is right," Samael affirmed. "Let's get through one thing at a time, or else we will all be left frustrated and overwhelmed."

The wood on the wall magically fixed itself, and I sighed.

"What's going on?" Damian asked as he walked up alongside Samyaza.

"Strategizing," Asmodeus grunted and walked off.

I went to walk off after him when Samael grabbed me gently by the shoulder.

"Let him go cool off," he said and patted my shoulder.

I nodded okay and turned my attention to Samyaza. "Did you find her?" I inquired, changing the subject.

"We did," Samyaza replied, grimacing.

"Well, where is she?" I asked, waiting for him to answer.

"She's in Sheol," Damian responded. "She's being guarded there by Aker, Beberos, and a few others."

"We were also able to locate the other Watchers as well," Samyaza chimed in. "They are in Tartarus, the furthest depths of Sheol."

"Seems easy enough," I replied. "Should be a cakewalk."

Damian and Samyaza exchanged glances.

"What?" I asked, looking between the two.

"Alpha has a whole slew of those creatures and more in Tartarus," Samyaza replied. "We would have to fight our way in to get to them."

"What about Sheol?" I asked. "Anything there?"

Damian shook his head. "None that we could see, but you know Alpha. What we could see was just who Alpha has guarding Lailah, but like I said, I was only able to see a handful of them. Plus, there are the human souls there as well. So we have to be careful using our powers or we will destroy the souls before they recycle to the Giving Tree."

"I don't see the problem," I replied. "We can take a handful of Forsaken and angels."

"Sheol has its own monsters from the various voids of the cosmos," Damian replied. "Like Cerberus, Hydra, and all."

"I forgot about them," I replied, chewing on my nail, deep in thought. "We go to Sheol first and bring Lailah back, and then on to Tartarus to release the Watchers."

"We still need to free Luxina from Purgatory as well," Damian piped up.

"We will be better in more numbers going into Purgatory," I replied. "There's no telling what Alpha has stashed in there to keep us from getting to her. I can guarantee you it will be worse than Sheol or Tartarus."

"We will need to bring offerings to Charon so he will let us through the river," Azazel added.

"That, and you need to make peace with Hades, or he won't let you through either," Azrael remarked, walking up to us. "He is still Lord of the Underworld. We need his permission to go through."

We all groaned.

"What?" she asked, looking around at us.

"Hades is so pompous," Samael replied, rolling his eyes.

"I don't even know why Alpha agreed to let him continue to be the Lord over the dead," Metatron agreed.

"Alpha didn't agree to anything," Azrael laughed. "Alpha has no control over the death deities, just like he has no control over the reaper angels or Maveth. *All* souls in the cosmos go through him and the other death deities as we carry them there."

"It doesn't make him more likable," Michael chimed in, scrunching his face in disgust.

"He thinks that he is better than everyone else," Azazel added.

"Well, whether you personally like him or not, he is the only way in, even if you pay Charon the token to take the river," Azrael chirped.

"Well, then, it's settled," I interrupted. "We make peace with Hades. Samael, gather the tokens from Starfire for Charon. I know she has them somewhere among her relics."

Samael nodded and walked around the building to go inside.

"How many of us are going?" Damian asked.

"You're staying here with Samyaza," I replied.

"But—" he began to protest.

I put my hand up. "It's not because you need protection or because I think you won't be safe. Lightshade needs protection in case Adam comes back."

"I thought I wasn't allowed to fight him," he quipped.

"Why not let Damian come with us and you stay behind to protect Lightshade?" Raphael offered. "You handled Adam without breaking a sweat and without hurting him."

I thought it over. "Fine. I will stay behind. Take Asmodeus with you," I urged, looking at

Damian. "And you mind Samael as well. He is first in command."

He nodded and ran off to find Asmodeus.

"I did not expect you to agree as fast as you did," Raphael remarked, surprised and laughing.

"If anything happens to him, it comes down on your head," I replied with a forced, sweet smile.

He stopped laughing and looked around at everyone, who looked off as if they were searching for something in the air.

"You all are asses," Raphael muttered, kicking the dirt.

"While they are off to Sheol," Samyaza began, changing the subject, "You and I can strategize infiltrating Tartarus."

I nodded. "Sounds like a plan."

Samael returned, holding the coins Starfire had given him for Charon. "Are we ready?" he asked, looking around at everyone.

"Yep," Damian replied, walking up with Asmodeus at his side.

Keep him safe, I projected to Asmodeus, and he gave a nod.

You have my word, Brother, he replied in his head.

I can hear you both! Damian interrupted, rolling his eyes.

"Alright, let's go," Samael replied, with Metatron, Azazel, Michael, Raphael, Damian, and Asmodeus falling in behind him as he walked off.

"Is Starfire portalling you in?" I shouted after them.

Samael gave me a thumbs up without turning around and continued back around the cottage. I returned my attention to Samyaza, who stood watching me curiously.

"What?" I asked, feeling like I had three heads.

"You are so different than before the fall," he mused. "You have grown so much as a leader."

"Thank you?" I asked.

We began to walk around the cabin as we caught those remaining of the group walking through the portal, and it closed behind them.

"When you came to Stygia to ask us to join you in your fight against Alpha, we were not thrilled with the idea at all. Sophia pulling rank is why we joined," he explained.

"And now?" I asked.

He stopped and looked me dead in the eye. "I will follow you to Potter's Field, Brother."

I nodded. "That's good to hear," I replied. "Not the Potter's Field bit, but to know I have you on my side and to know it's not because it's just for survival makes me feel a lot better as a leader."

We continued around the cottage and inside.

"Can I ask you something?" I inquired as we walked into Starfire's private collection room full of her books on mythology.

"What?" he asked in return.

"Why haven't you pledged to me yet?" I prodded. "Not that it matters, really. I am just curious."

"I am waiting for all the Watchers to be together so we can all pledge at once," he replied. "I do not wish to overcome my tribulations without them by my side as they have been for millennia."

I inclined my head in agreement. "I understand."

I walked over to a bookcase and scanned the spines. I ran my finger along each shelf of books until I came to the book I was looking for. "Ah, here we go."

"What's that?" Samyaza asked.

"It has every monster listed in it that's in Tartarus," I replied, placing it on a table and opening it.

"Typhon is at the entrance, right?" Samyaza questioned, leaning down to glance through the pages with me.

"Yes, he is the first thing we have to take out," I murmured.

There were tons of monsters listed in the book that Tartarus housed.

"Echidna, I forgot about her," Samyaza said as he turned the page to her portrait.

"The Mother of Monsters," I mumbled. "How are we going to make our way through the maze of monsters to find the others?" I asked. "Did it show you specifically where they were?"

Samyaza shook his head. "No, it didn't. It's going to be a wild hunt getting to them."

"Indeed," I muttered. "How are they being held prisoner?" I asked, looking up at Samyaza.

"Alpha has them bound by their hands and feet," he responded.

"So they're defenseless too?" I asked.

"Yes. From what I saw, they were surrounded by Keres," he replied. "They don't have much time before they grow bored and lead something to them to finish them off so they can start devouring them."

"You need Thanatos to guide you through," Azrael said, popping up.

Adrenaline rushed through me, and I had to control my fire. "I wish you would stop doing that," I muttered.

"How else would you like me to appear?" she smirked, crossing her arms.

"I don't know. Knock, maybe?" I replied, shaking my head in frustration.

She rolled her eyes and continued. "Thanatos can help guide you through there. He travels through Tartarus from time to time and knows his way around."

"Well, why don't you go get him then?" I quipped.

"Because that's not my job," she retorted. "I'm not your messenger."

Messenger!

"Gabriel can find him," I replied, matter-of-factly.

"Now you're using your brain," Azrael quipped.

"You're starting to get on my nerves," I remarked, glaring at her.

"You've been on mine!" she mocked.

I pursed my lips. "I'm going to go find Gabriel."

"We will be right here, going through the book," Samyaza replied, eyeing the two of us.

I left the room, irritation bubbling below the surface. What was the deal with Azrael? I thought we were all supposed to be working together. As I bounded down the steps of the cottage, Adam appeared.

I groaned. I didn't have time for his little games. "What is your deal, kid?" I demanded, walking up to him.

His eyes lit up with a glow, and he held his hand up in the air, focusing his energy to the palm of his hand and fired a shot at me. The blow caught me off guard, and I went careening backward against the steps. All of my anger came gushing forth, and I stood up from the broken porch steps, glaring at Adam.

He stood there, his cockiness apparent in his posture. "You don't scare me," he goaded.

I let a deafening howl loose and burst into flames. He smiled sinisterly and snapped his fingers. A portal popped up behind him, and through the opening, a dark, smoky mass with serpents for legs and wings stepped through.

"I heard you were going to storm Tartarus looking for the rest of the Watchers," Adam began, squinting his eyes at me. "So I brought Tartarus to you."

"Typhon," I growled.

As Typhon finished stepping through the portal, more beings followed. A half-woman, half-serpent slithered through the opening.

"Echidna."

A triple-headed giant followed closely behind her.

"Geryon."

Black ethereal smoke oozed out of the opening as shrieking Keres emerged. More and more monsters poured out into Lightshade as Adam stood in front of them, grinning from ear to ear, looking more and more like Alpha.

"Have fun," he teased and disappeared.

"Samyaza!" I bellowed.

Samyaza came running from inside, slowing as he saw the monsters just outside the cottage.

"What the—"

"Adam," I seethed before he could finish his sentence. "Get everyone to safety who cannot fight while I hold them off."

"What can I do?" Azrael asked, appearing at my side, wide-eyed with fear.

"Get Starfire to safety!" I ordered.

I removed the flaming sword from my side, and it sprang to life. "Here we go!" I yelled, running toward them.

Angels and Nephilim poured in from all sides and began their assault on the monsters as I took on Typhon.

"You call yourself a god," Typhon sneered venomously. "A god could put me back where I came from."

"I'm not putting you back," I replied, walking in a circle around him. "Your head's going on my wall!"

Black fiery smoke snaked its way from his body and wrapped around me, choking me. I hit the ground hacking and coughing, trying to get a breath of fresh air.

"You can die trying," Typhon growled.

I grabbed at the smoke tendrils, trying to free them from around my throat. A horn blew, and I looked over to see Gabriel with his horn, aiming it at Typhon. The sound vibrated in the air, and the force of the sound sent shockwaves of wind toward Typhon. He began to lose mass as the wind carried his smoke away and turned his attention to Gabriel. He loosened the grip he had on me, and I was able to grab him by his serpentine tail. I began to spin him in the air and soon held the end of his tail like a lasso. My arm turned to fire and rushed through my hand and into his smoky, formless body. I summoned thunderbolts from the sky, and they crackled around him like fireworks. The fire began to burn away the oxygen left that kept him in his smoke state until he poofed into nothingness.

I glanced over to my left, and Echidna was tearing through the angels and Nephilim left and right. As they went down one by one, they retreated to safety as I walked up behind her. She whipped around to face me.

"Ah, Vahr-Zul in the flesh," she hissed like a thousand snakes. "I never imagined I would ever meet you. I happily obliged when Alpha asked us to perform this task for him."

I turned toward Gabriel. "Find Samyaza. Tell him it's now or never. He has to go in and get back out quickly!"

Gabriel nodded in acknowledgement and took off to find Samyaza.

"You think you have won when you rescue your Watchers?" Echidna snarled. "I am a dream compared to things Alpha has created for you, and that's saying something, for I am the mother of monsters."

I watched as Samyaza and Belial raced through the portal with Gabriel to retrieve the bound Watchers from inside Tartarus. I returned my attention to Echidna.

"Alpha will win in the end, you know?" she goaded. "He will slay your whole family again just as he did before. And there's nothing you can do to stop him."

"You talk too much," I muttered as I ran toward her, unleashing a ray of fire and burning the ground around her, trapping her inside a circle.

She howled in rage as I jumped through the air. I brought my wings out and began to spin, and soon, she was trapped inside a whirlwind of fire. I hovered just above the fire as she let loose a deafening screech, calling forth her children to save her. I dropped down through the top of the flames and brought the flaming sword down on her neck, severing it clean from her body. I turned my attention to the masses of monsters that had clawed their way out of Tartarus and began hacking and slashing through them alongside everybody else. It seemed the more we killed, the more that poured freely through the portal, including some of the monstrosities Alpha had created as Samyaza and Damian warned about.

"Incaendiel!" Praeziel hollered over the sound of howls and screams of terror. "We have to close the portal!"

"Not until they come back through!" I ordered as I slashed through the monsters with the flaming sword.

"Lightshade will perish if we don't!" he urged as he fought more and more of the monsters popping out.

"I made a promise, and I intend to keep it!" I hissed.

Flames leapt from my feet and burned in precise patterns as I fought my way through the barrage of monsters. It felt like there was no end to the fight as more creatures surrounded me with every burst of flame. They paid closer attention to me than to the angels and Nephilim whom they only attacked when provoked.

"They're here for me!" I yelled. "On my order, I want you all to back down!"

"You can't use your powers here!" Praeziel refuted. "You will kill everyone!"

Samyaza emerged through the portal, with the Watchers following close behind and racing for safety. Once the portal was clear of any stragglers, I yelled the order. "Fall back!"

"We can't do that!" Praeziel insisted.

"Do as I say!" I commanded, my voice echoing through the valley.

They all did as instructed, and the monsters swarmed me. I fought each attacking creature as I slowly made my way over to the portal so I could lure them back through.

"What the hell is going on!" I heard Damian yell as he and the rest of the group stepped out of the portal from Sheol.

I had no time to explain. I stepped through the portal into Tartarus, and the opening filled with all of the monsters.

"Incaendiel, what are you doing?" Damian demanded, rushing toward the portal entrance.

"I have to use my power somewhere, and it can't be Lightshade!" I shouted back.

"Tartarus will cave in and either trap you forever or kill you!" he refuted.

"It's the only way!" I shot back.

"Don't do this!" he pleaded as he began to step through the portal entrance.

"Stand back!" I ordered, waiting for the last monster to surround me inside the portal.

I lifted my hand to snap my fingers.

"Dad! No!" Damian shouted as my fingers clicked against my palm.

The portal shut, and I was trapped inside Tartarus with the ravenous, snapping jaws of evil. It's now or never. I willed every ounce of my power to the brim and exploded just as I had done so many times during my training with Lilith.

Chapter Twenty-Three

IT DIDN'T TAKE me long to get back to Lightshade. Once I unleashed my power, I was able to beam back instantly before Tartarus caved in. Every single monster was now either dead, buried, or forever trapped there. I walked through the field where the bodies of angels and Nephilim killed lay, as well as the carcasses of the monsters that had been slain. Damian ran up to me and pushed me hard. I stumbled back as he began to lay blow after blow against me with his fists.

"You could have been stuck forever!" he hollered. "Why would you do that?"

A blow caught me square in the jaw before I threw my arms around him and wrestled him to the ground.

"Let me go!" he yelled, kicking and screaming as his ice began to wrap up my arms. "Let me go! Let me go! Let me gooooo!"

His powers mounted and went off in my arms. Everything went still as he froze time in its place while ice crept around the valley.

"You have to calm down!" I demanded, holding him as tightly as I could as he wiggled in my arms.

"You don't tell me what to do!" he cried, wrestling free from my arms as my heat melted the ice.

"It was the only choice I had!" I defended. "I would have leveled Lightshade and killed everyone there!"

He stood to his feet and landed another punch to my jaw.

"Stop that!" I barked, my voice echoing and shattering the ice into crumbled shards.

He raised his arms, and the shards rose in the air along with them.

"If you want to die so bad, why don't I just take you out right here and right now!" he cried, his eyes full of pain and fear.

"I wasn't trying to die!" I explained as the shards all pointed toward me. "I was just trying to save everyone!"

"You're always trying to save everyone no matter what the cost is to you!" he shot back, tears falling freely down his face.

"Like father, like son!" I quipped.

"Stop calling me that!" he snarled and let the shards loose.

They each melted into puddles of water before they ever reached me.

"If you don't want me calling you that, then stop acting like it!" I retorted.

He hit the ground on his knees and heaved into his hands. "You're all I have," he cried "If anything happens to you, there is no one left!"

"No, Damian," I replied, walking over to him. "You have everyone. There's Asmodeus, who has been the only father—"

"That doesn't make him my father," he hissed, cutting me off. "I look up to him as a big brother, and I know he took care of me, but that doesn't make him my father. You are my father!"

I knelt before him and watched him intently as he rocked back and forth. I grabbed at him to pull him into my chest. He fought off my arms, and I fought back until I had him pinned to me as he flailed his arms, hitting me in the back. He soon stopped, and I held him. His freeze on time let loose, and everyone who was frozen still stood quietly as I rocked him back and forth.

"I'm sorry," I whispered to him. "I had no idea…"

"Well, now you do," he cried in heaves into my chest.

We sat there for what seemed like an eternity before he peeled himself from my arms. He looked up to see everyone watching us and quickly swiped away the tears from his face. I stood up and held out my hand to help him to his feet.

He smacked it away and stood on his own. "Lailah is inside the cottage," he muttered and walked off.

That boy had me frustrated and sorry all at the same time. I looked around at the carnage lying in the field. So many had died fending off the attack on Lightshade. The angels were waiting to be ferried off by the reapers to Potter's Field as they slowly, one by one, disappeared from the field. I watched the bodies of the Nephilim lie there. I had no idea where they went when they died. Sheol? Potter's Field.

"If they died in the mundane world where they chose to live on as mortals, they will go to Sheol. These will go to Potter's Field since they died in a heroic battle alongside angels," Azrael said, as if reading my mind. She turned to face me, her face stricken with shame. "I apologize for earlier, Incaendiel. I shouldn't have worked you up the way I did. Things may have gone differently had I not riled you up before you met Adam at the steps."

I shook my head. "It didn't matter what happened between Adam and me. This was the plan all along between Alpha and him," I replied. "No fault to anyone." I looked at her and gave a half-smile. "I am sorry too, Azrael."

She looked around at the bodies slowly disappearing. "We don't have enough in numbers willing to come here to ferry them." She looked sad and despondent. "They're afraid Alpha will show up again."

"Samael and Azazel can help if you show them," I offered, and she stared at me, surprised. "You said they were supposed to have been reapers, and Alpha didn't give his lot. Ask them. I am sure they won't mind."

She nodded with a forced smile. "Thank you."

She ran over to the two of them and began talking. I saw them agree, and off they went to help her with their brothers and sisters. I walked inside the cottage, and Starfire sat at her table, with her finger pointing to a room.

"She's in there," Starfire stated.

I walked to the room and began to open the door when Starfire stopped me.

"Incaendiel?" she asked, and I turned to look at her. "Thank you for saving our home."

"No thanks is needed," I replied with a light-hearted smile.

I twisted the doorknob and opened the door to find Lailah sitting at a table. I closed the door behind me and walked over to the table, taking a seat across from her. "You are one hard person to track down," I said as I sat down.

"Do you think this is all fun and games?" Lailah snapped, glaring at me.

"Unlike Alpha, no. No, I do not think this is all fun and games," I answered thoughtfully. I pointed to the door. "Our brothers and sisters are lying in a field out there, dead, because it is all fun and games to him. But instead of having a moment to mourn the losses, I have to move to the next point in strategy to try and defeat him, which I can only do if I had found you. So, forgive me, Sister, for trying to lighten the mood. If you want doom and gloom, that is my specialty."

Her jaw tightened as she fought back the rising anger. "Fine," she stated flatly. "What do you want with me?"

"I need to know the location of a human," I replied.

She laughed and scoffed, "A human? That's all this is about?" she asked with her hand. She leaned forward. "A human, Incaendiel?"

"Yes, a human," I sneered, growing impatient. Why was she being such a pain in the ass? Why does everyone have to be such a pain in the freaking ass?

"I have better things to do with my *free* time than to sit here like another prisoner so you can use me as a geolocator to find a human for you," she huffed and stood from her seat.

"She's not just any human," I said as she walked toward the door. "She's a starseed."

She stopped in her tracks and turned around. "My, you have been a busy boy, haven't you?" she smirked enthralled. "That word doesn't get tossed around that much."

My eyes blazed to life, and fear fell over her face. "A lot of things have changed since we last saw one another, Lailah," I replied.

"When did Lilith let you out of the cage?" she asked, sitting back down and propping her feet up on the table.

"You *knew*?" I demanded.

She waved her hand in the air. "Of course, I knew," she replied. "How else was Alpha going to explain all of the souls from your universe once they started arriving after he took you from them?" she mused.

"How can you be so cavalier about this?" I asked in return. "Why aren't you angry with Alpha?"

She pulled her feet from the table and leaned in close to me. "I don't like you, Incaendiel. I never have. You and your mate ruined it for all of us," she snapped.

"It wasn't our fault," I protested, anger bubbling beneath the surface. "I can't help Alpha meddled with power he had absolutely no business meddling with."

"Had it not been for you two," she continued smugly. "We all would be one big, happy family."

"Do you really think that?" I stammered, standing to my feet. "He and Lilith manipulated all of you."

"I never was," Lailah replied, her uncaring eyes staring up into my eyes. "I had one job and was left to do what I was supposed to do. Meanwhile, Samael and Azazel were pulled from me to babysit you because Mother and Father needed help controlling you more."

"Just give me the location of Eva, and you can be on your way," I ordered, my patience at its last stretching point.

"That's the only reason you rescued me," she declared, standing from her seat and meeting me eye to eye. "You needed something from me. And I was the only person who could give it to you."

"I have rescued so many of you over and over throughout the millennia. Do not patronize me!" I fumed, jumping to my feet and walking over to her. "You were one of the first people asked about, but we couldn't get to the Summit to look for you because Alpha slammed the doors shut!"

"If I give you her location," she began. "Do I *have* to leave, or can I stay if I wish to stay?"

"You can stay, or you can go," I replied, walking to the door. "The choice is yours and yours alone. No one controls you here. No one tells you what to do. No one makes demands of you."

"And if I don't give you the location?" she asked, raising an eyebrow.

I shrugged my shoulders. "The same deal. You can choose to stay or go, and we will just go back to the drawing board to find another way."

She stared at me intently. "She's in Angel Falls, Idaho. Her name is Eva Green. She is a teenager, and she hasn't activated yet."

"Thank you," I replied, uncaring as I opened the door.

"Incaendiel?" Lailah asked.

"Yes?" I turned around to answer.

"Don't get her killed, please," she pleaded, her eyes full of worry. "She's more important than for reading the book."

I nodded and closed the door behind me.

Praeziel sat in the sitting room, waiting for his orders.

I walked over to him and whispered her location in his ear. He nodded and headed out the door. Samyaza appeared, stepping out of the conference room.

"They're in there all waiting to hear," he stated, pointing with his thumb back at the room. "Did Lailah tell you what you needed?" he asked as I began walking over to the conference room.

"Yes, but man, was she a stubborn one about it. I had no idea so many of you hated me throughout all the years," I replied, walking up the aisles to the front of the room. "Is this everyone?" I asked, looking at all the worn faces in the room.

"The last two hundred of us who didn't take Alpha's side," Samyaza answered.

I breathed in deeply, preparing to give my speech. "I know you're tired," I spoke loudly. "And the war has hardly begun. The last time I stood before you, there was derision and fighting over whether to join in the war or to keep to yourselves and remain neutral. Alpha forced your hand over a year ago when he took you all captive."

"Why are you just now rescuing us?" Armaros demanded, and all of them began talking at once.

I motioned with my hands for them to quieten down. "I was taken captive and held in one of Alpha's dungeons," I replied as the room fell quiet. "Believe me when I say, we would have exhausted all resources trying to find you all. Samyaza was able to locate you with the missing Watchers Eye amulet."

"How do we know you won't become power hungry like Alpha?" Sathariel questioned, a look of disdain painted across his face. "How do we know we can trust you?"

"I cannot sway your trust. I will not make you follow me, and if you choose not to and to remain neutral, you are free to stay here where it is safe," I replied, looking intently around the room. "I will not make you do what you don't want to do, and I will also not abandon you. For too long, you have been cast aside like garbage by Alpha and

Lilith. Not with me. I will honor your decisions, whatever they may be."

"And if we decide to join you, then what?" Asbeel asked. "Do we become your mindless drones?"

I laughed. "No. You keep your free will, your free thinking, and everything about you that makes you who you are," I replied.

"But we are restored to our angelic selves, though. Right?" Chazaquiel inquired, leaning forward. "I mean, it's not the determining factor for our loyalty, but it is a key piece in making the decision."

"If you join me and pledge your loyalty to me, then yes. You will be restored," I answered, looking around at them all. "But," I began.

"But what?" Sathariel sneered, shaking his head. "See, there's always a catch. We probably have to bend to his will and do whatever he asks of us."

I shook my head. "No," I replied. "Not at all."

"Then what?" he demanded.

"You can't just say it," I replied. "You have to mean it or it won't work. When you pledge yourselves to my power, the power knows if you are being deceitful or telling the truth. With the angels, I cannot tell because they have nothing to transform out of. They took a knee, and that was it. But when the Forsaken pledged to me, I watched it happen before my very eyes. And those who did not pledge and just sought safe haven did not change."

Chatter filled the room as they all began discussing what I had told them.

Samyaza stepped forward to speak. "Incaendiel is offering us freedom from the curse we have spent millennia trying to fight free from," he spoke loudly.

"The curse that Alpha promised to find a way to life but did not attempt to right," Belial added, stepping up beside Samyaza.

"Why are you two still cursed, then, if you have pledged your loyalty to Incaendiel?" Asbeel asked.

"Because we waited to be reunited with you all before we pledged. We took the curse together and it will be lifted together," Belial insisted.

"What do we have to do?" Armaros asked.

"Yeah, is there some sort of ritual or something?" Chazaquiel added.

"Not really a ritual," I began.

"You take a knee, place your arm across your chest, and you hail the new king," Samael replied, walking into the room. "He is our new King of Kings, and that is how he is heralded."

"Did you?" Sathariel asked. "Did you take a knee to Incaendiel, first in command?"

Samael looked at me. "I did," Samael replied. "And I will follow our brother to the ends of the universe because he speaks nothing but truths while Alpha basks in lies."

"Are you ready, Brothers?" Samyaza asked, stepping forward before them all. "Are you ready to become whole again? To once again be angels instead of the abominations we have become? Are you ready to follow the new cosmic order? Because I am."

"I am! Hail to the King!" Belial shouted, stepping out and taking a knee.

Like with the Forsaken, healing white lights floated around him as my power restored him to his former angelic self.

"It works!" the crowd of Watchers murmured.

"Hail to the King!" Samyaza bellowed, thrusting his hand in the air, drawing it across his chest, and taking a knee.

The entire room echoed Belial and Samyaza's oath, shouting, "Hail to the King!" and taking a knee before me. The lights gathered, and it was like staring at the sun as the healing rays burned away their vampyric blood. When the light died down, the room cheered in happiness and gratitude.

"It was all true!"

"We are healed!"

"Incaendiel saved us!"

"He did what Alpha would not!"

"Incaendiel is the true ruler of the cosmos!"

Samyaza turned toward me, his new icy blue eyes that had replaced the blood red purple ones he once sported, peered at me. "Thank you, Brother," he cried, a tear slipping down his face.

I nodded and walked through the masses of angels there, cheering for the salvation of the Watchers. I made it to the sitting room where Starfire still sat at her table. I flopped down on the couch, tipping my head back for it to rest on the pillow. I sighed heavily and looked over at Starfire.

"Long day?" she mused with a smirk.

"Long lifetime," I groaned.

"Well, it could have gone worse," she offered.

"The day or the lifetime?" I asked with a half-hearted smile.

"Both," she chuckled. "You could have been reborn as a bug."

"I need to find Damian," I began, standing up from my seat, thinking back to earlier when he had his meltdown. "Know where he is?"

"He is with Asmodeus," Starfire replied as I began to walk to the door. "They went back to scour Chernobyl to see if there were any clues left to find Luxina and learn more about what Alpha has planned. They should be fine."

"He shouldn't have gone back to that place. It was questionable the first time, but understandable. It's downright suicide this time. Alpha took Luxina to Purgatory. We know that!"

I started to run out the door.

"Where are you going?" Starfire demanded.

"To Chernobyl," I replied. "There could be a trap set just waiting for him to return, and I will be damned Alpha gets Damian back as well."

I stepped out on the porch and unleashed my wings. Fire tore through the sky as I lifted off and flew. My wings were as fast as lightning compared to my angelic ones, and I was back to Chernobyl in no time to find Damian. As I approached, I felt the static in the air. It was the same static the day that Damian escaped Alpha. Those creatures were here. How many there were was undetermined. I flew faster around the area. I scanned for any sign of him. I finally spotted him and Asmodeus at the edge of the woods there. That's when I saw the creatures barreling right toward them. A new sense of energy I hadn't felt before bubbled to the surface as rage erupted from me. The need to protect him fueled my powers. Fire blasted through the sky like an atomic bomb, turning every one of those abominations to ash, and when the smoke and ash began to clear, some, Damian was nowhere to be seen.

Oh no! I thought to myself. *Did the fire reach them too? Did I destroy them?*

I flew around the area, trying to peer through the smoke and ash still drifting through the sky. Another set of creatures appeared out of thin air, and once more, I used my powers to turn them into floating carcasses of embers and smoke. Their close proximity to Alpha's fortress erupted in a fireball of atomic energy as the radiation met my powers. Flames burned the area in billowing pillars after the pressure of the explosion leveled the forest. I waited for Damian and Asmodeus to appear from somewhere, anywhere, in what was left of the brush, as my heart skipped a beat and anxiety threatened to spill out as fire and brimstone.

Did I kill... was the only thought that floated through my head as I recalled the fires in the fields back to me, and I floated along the wind alone, without a single sign of life to be seen in the burned wasteland.

Kasey Hill has lived in Franklin County, VA, for most of her adult life and is a versatile writer known for her work in several genres, including urban fantasy, horror, thriller, paranormal romance, and metaphysical/New Age topics. She has authored both fiction and non-fiction, with a particular interest in Wicca, specializing in Trinitarian Wicca as the historical archivist with an upcoming historical account of the shift from polytheism to monotheism in Abrahamic religions, where she has published non-fiction works exploring the subject.

Her fiction often dives into the supernatural and the macabre, blending mythological elements with modern storytelling. She has published multiple novels, poetry collections, and short stories. Notable works include her *Guardians of Light* series in the mythology fantasy genre, and her poetry that has received recognition for its depth and emotional resonance. As she grows in the horror genre, she has a particular penchant for Southern Gothic storytelling, such as her Adult Horror novel *Devil's Claw* and her Young Adult horror series, *The Whispering Spirits* featuring *The Haunting at Foxwood Village* and *Dark Coven*. She has several Horror short stories circulating for anthologies and Ezines featuring her unique style of worldbuilding.

In addition to her writing, Kasey Hill has also contributed to the Wiccan and occult community through her non-fiction work, making her a multi-faceted author with a broad range of interests and expertise.